I0548389

ELEMENTAL

THE ELEMENTALS TRILOGY BOOK ONE

DEBBIE KUMP

This is a work of fiction. Names, characters, places, and incidents are products of the author's imagination or are used fictitiously and are not to be construed as real. Any resemblance to actual events, locations, organizations, or persons, living or dead, is entirely coincidental.

World Castle Publishing, LLC
Pensacola, Florida
Copyright © Debbie Kump 2016
Paperback ISBN: 9781629895703
eBook ISBN: 9781629895710
First Edition World Castle Publishing, LLC. November 14, 2016
http://www.worldcastlepublishing.com

Licensing Notes

All rights reserved. No part of this book may be used or reproduced in any manner whatsoever without written permission, except in the case of brief quotations embodied in articles and reviews.
Cover: Karen Fuller
Editor: Lisa Petrocelli

DEDICATION

For Mom and her unwavering support.

PROLOGUE

Chicago, Illinois, October 8, 1871

Some might yearn for immortality. For me, it was a curse I couldn't escape.

Under the cover of darkness, I raced across a field of reaped corn, hiking my filthy, ragged dress up around my knees as I ran faster than my legs liked. Spotting a lone oak poised in the middle of the open land, I paused briefly behind its massive trunk, trying to determine if my pursuers drew near. My wild eyes darted across the open terrain scarcely lit by the sliver of the crescent moon. The field sounded unnervingly silent. I couldn't hear a thing over my heart, hammering, threatening to break free of my chest. Or my pulse thundering in my ears.

An old, weather-beaten barn lay not far ahead. Certain to find it vacant on this unseasonably hot and dry autumn Sabbath eve, I took one last glance over my shoulder and aimed my mad dash for its wide door. My lungs seared with pain as my feet flew over the uneven ground. By the time I reached the rustic barn, I gasped for a decent breath, something I didn't have the luxury to afford. I prayed the hinges wore a fresh lube of oil and cautiously pushed the door ajar to steal inside.

The dank smell of soiled hay and animal dander filled my nostrils. I quietly closed the door and secured the latch behind me then turned, searching for a good hiding place in the thin moonlight that seeped through the lone window high up in the loft.

Tiptoeing across the earthen floor, I passed two dairy cows that lowed, slumbering on all fours. The horses' watering trough looked awfully tempting, but I didn't dare pause to quench my thirst. One second wasted could mean certain doom.

Entering the next stall, I crouched behind a chestnut mare with white socks and a stripe down her muzzle. She whinnied softly when I closed her door with a slow creak.

"Shh, shh. That's a good girl," I cooed, placing a gentle hand on one flank to keep from alarming her. I sank into the shadows of her stall and listened for footfalls outside.

Minutes passed. Too many, in fact.

Though I didn't dare leave my hiding spot, a small part of me rejoiced, almost certain I'd lost them this time. My racing heart gradually calmed and my breath returned, filling my depleted lungs.

Somehow, I managed to elude the three of them. In the morning, I'd head into the city and find passage across Lake Michigan to settle somewhere up north. It didn't matter much to me where I went, so long as they lost my trail.

A small smile played across my face. Safety. Normality.

It wasn't too much to ask for, was it? A chance to be like everyone else? At least for a short time.

Suddenly, a violent gust of wind rushed against the barn, splintering the latch and making the door fly open. A gasp escaped my terrified lips.

Skye found me.

Not the Skye you once knew, I reminded myself. That Skye is dead.

She appeared just a fragment of her former self, but I'd always remember her as my trusted companion those days we spent together...until Gaia and Hydros caught us. They tortured Skye, eventually crushing her soul into submission in their power-hungry quest for total domination.

I vowed I wouldn't let myself suffer the same fate. So I paid for that decision by living in constant fear.

Through the panels of the mare's stall, I saw Skye swagger into the barn. Her long blond hair whipped wildly across her face. She turned toward me, her eyes shining like quicksilver in the scant moonlight as she commanded the air to obey her every whim. Her feet treaded softly upon the earth, the air alone bearing all her weight.

Her powers had grown; she couldn't do that before. No wonder I didn't hear her outside the door.

Skye's voice rang clear and confident through the still night. "I know you're here!" A startled mourning dove fluttered amidst the rafters, filling the barn with its chilling cry.

I shuddered with fear. My legs cramped from holding the same position for so long. Still I said nothing.

"You can't run forever, Pyr," she boomed.

I flinched, despising it when she used my given name

instead of calling me Jordan. It reminded me of a destiny others had selected for me, not the role I wished to play in my future. Ignoring the burn in my legs, I ducked lower beside the mare, praying Skye would abandon her search.

She crossed the floor, quiet like a cat slinking upon its prey. She pushed open one stall door after another with a brush of wind. Only a matter of time remained before she'd spot me. I clenched my teeth together to silence their fearful chattering.

"You know what we want," she called. Her voice resonated through the hot, stagnant air.

I did. But I promised myself I'd never agree to her demands…not for as long as I lived.

"Join us…*or die.*" Her words sent a chill down my spine. Echoing her threat, the wind instantly picked up, stirring the straw into tiny dust devils that swirled across the floor, fanning out in search of me.

I was afraid to breathe.

Next to me, the chestnut mare pawed nervously at the ground. Skye turned, sensing my presence. She lifted one hand toward the stall door and sent a sudden gust that slammed it wide open to expose my hiding place.

I screamed, raising my hands to block Skye's brutal wind. In an instant, my fear and anger fueled a blinding pain that radiated from my chest and down though my arms. I wailed in agony when bursts of flames shot from my palms, right at her face. The pain abruptly ended, ejected from my body with a sudden pulse of heat. My effort didn't stop Skye.

She shielded her head at the last moment, redirecting my fire toward the ground. The straw scattered across the barn floor ignited, spreading out toward the stalls. Within seconds, the blaze grew uncontrollable. Wooden support beams and stall doors caught flame while the tongues danced higher and higher. Stunned by the blazing light, the animals bleated and moaned, panicking in the insufferable heat.

"No!" I screamed through trembling lips. I never meant to harm these innocent creatures. I hated my powers and the hurt they inflicted upon me, so I used my fire strictly for defense.

Desperate to escape the burning barn, the livestock broke free of their stalls, bumping into each other and Skye on their frantic way out the main door. Using this commotion to my advantage, I climbed on the mare and straddled her bareback. With a swift prod of my heels into her sides, we raced out of her stall. A flaming beam dropped from the rafters. I tugged the mare's mane to one side to dodge the falling incendiary, and then sprinted through the barn door in the midst of the other animals.

Knotting my fingers in her mane, I gave another kick of my heels in encouragement to pick up the pace. Not until we crossed half the field did I dare a glance behind me. The barn blazed brightly, a raging inferno against the deep night sky.

Guilt riddled my stomach for stealing the farmer's horse—even worse for torching his barn. But I had no choice. I shuddered, recalling painful episodes from my past…and the horrors that could befall humanity if Skye had actually caught me back there.

I ducked lower, pressing my head close to the mare's bobbing neck. Her breaths came in ragged bursts, like a thoroughbred pushing itself to finish the last leg of its race.

Daring another peek behind me, I spotted a figure moving in the distance. Sure enough, Skye pursued me on horseback.

Her blond hair flailed up and down as she closed the gap.

I turned down a street called DeKoven and headed toward the city, hoping to lose her in one of the alleyways. The mare's horseshoes clomped with each swift step down the dusty street. But she soon tired, strained from exertion. I pushed her too hard too fast, I realized with dismay.

Glancing over my shoulder again, I saw Skye close behind. Ignoring the pain from my last unsuccessful attempt, I raised one hand and aimed another blast of fire at her. The burn resonated from my core and out my arms and my palm exploded with a shocking burst of heat and light. She manipulated it to her will, using the wind to lash the fire against the sides of the buildings lining the street.

Gasping in horror, I watched a building catch flame. *Dear God, what have I done?* Crippled of my one defense, I pressed forward, the fire in close pursuit. It didn't matter that I refused to fight back. Skye had effectively turned my powers against me, driving the fire from one rooftop to the next on the cusp of her superheated wind, generating a raging conflagration that pierced the blackness of night.

I spun down one side street after another, yet the flames persisted, lapping at my heels. The mare panted heavily, her stride continuing to slow as she succumbed to fatigue. Up ahead, I spotted a bridge—my only hope for confining the blaze. We crossed the arc that spanned the Chicago River and turned up its banks.

Pausing briefly, I caught a clear view of Skye on the far side of the river. An intense scowl fixed upon her face. Then, with all her might, she unleashed a powerful wind, catching the embers and rocketing them clear across the bridge. The sparks landed on a church rooftop, quickly igniting it as well.

I swallowed hard. My plan failed. There was nothing left to do but run.

Riding forward with her hand extended, Skye created a swirling gust that enabled the flames to leap from one frame house to the next. I peered over my shoulder once more. The tired mare lost her footing and tripped in a rut on the dry, hard-packed street.

The world around me slowed, my fingers slipping through her mane. I soared over her head and landed flat on my back. Unable to move or breathe, I lay there for a moment, thinking, *Please, God, let this be the end. For me, not the horse.*

Rolling my head to one side, my eyes found the mare. She seemed frightened but uninjured. Exhausted, she staggered to her feet. I shot her a small, grateful smile, hoping she could find her way home. Then I closed my eyes, wishing to find peace at last.

The sound of horse hooves jarred me awake, and Skye ground to a stop by my side. A flood of adrenaline rushed through my veins, forcing me alert once more.

"That was far too easy," she snarled and leapt off her horse's back. Flames of burning buildings danced behind her head, making her whitish hair glow wickedly in the firelight. Her stormy eyes bore into my skull as she neared, relishing in my defeat.

I blinked, surveying the scene to search for a final escape. Cries of panic filled the air. Residents dressed in nightclothes took flight from their homes, their arms laden with whatever meager possessions they could carry.

Off in the distance, I saw Gaia and Hydros, strolling casually down the street, the chaos surrounding seemingly inconsequential. Gaia's iridescent emerald eyes held mine.

Her lips turned up in a malicious grin. Unruly russet hair framed her evil face, accentuating her desire to torture me into submission. Hydros followed a step behind. Her dreadfully deep blue eyes contrasted sharply with her flowing dark brown hair that glinted gold and orange in the light of the blaze.

Skye, Gaia, and Hydros—The Three, I called them—together again. Now with me, the fourth Elemental, they would be unstoppable.

But I couldn't let that happen. My lower lip quivered while I glared at Gaia's iridescent eyes, feeling nothing but hate for the one who robbed me of everyone I loved and everything I owned. If I couldn't battle Skye alone, I wouldn't stand a chance against The Three with their powers combined.

Summoning residual strength I didn't know I possessed, I flew to my feet and dashed toward the nearest flaming home, desperate to escape despite the inevitable pain I would endure once more.

"Stop her. Don't let her jump again!" Gaia cried, sprinting down the street with Hydros close behind.

I slowed, casting Skye a pleading glance. She blinked. For a brief moment, a conflicted expression passed over her face. *There's still hope for her*, I thought, making my heart suddenly grow lighter. Perhaps I might rekindle our friendship and build a new alliance that could destroy Gaia and Hydros. Only then would I redeem myself for losing Skye in the first place and avenge the wrongful deaths of my family and friends.

A small smile flickered across my lips. I reached out my hand, offering her a chance to join me. But Skye's face suddenly hardened. *She's hasn't forgiven me…not yet, at least.* I realized with dismay that my redemption must wait.

Clenching her jaw, she shot a blast of wind, knocking me to my knees. I skinned my palms while bracing my fall, yet didn't relent. Leaping to my feet, I ducked inside the house where fires raged in the windowpanes.

"No!" I heard Gaia shout when I sprang into the middle of the flames. She and Hydros raised their hands toward me, ready to unleash destructive forces to halt my jump, but they were too late.

A golden blaze surrounded me, quickly consuming my arms, my face, and my hair. My scream died in my throat. The intense heat sucked the breath from my lungs and drained the life from my body. The rising temperature permeated my exterior, seeping inward until it licked my core. Though the excruciating pain soon grew unbearable, I persisted, uncertain of any other way to evade their clutches. I remembered how terrified I felt the first time I endured a similar agony. I discovered as an Elemental, not only did I possess the power to create fire, but I also could perish from this time and begin life anew. One catch existed, however…where and when I turned up remained outside my control.

A final cry rose from the depths of my searing throat. I watched a deep darkness engulf the burning city of Chicago, marking the end of my existence in this world. While Gaia's frustrated face shifted to black, my pain dissolved into a deep sense of gratitude for eluding The Three once more. Still, an inevitable dread clouded my joy. Despite my narrow escape, a frightening confidence filled my heart. Just like every other time, it wouldn't be long before they located me again.

CHAPTER ONE

Near Pacifica, California, Present Day

It's hard to know how long I'd lived when I couldn't remember how many times I'd died.

The impenetrable blackness from my former existence soon faded in this new life. At first, the dark gradually softened into a dim, hazy light. I squinted my eyes, trying to focus beyond my tight skin that stung from my fiery exit and my bruised back that screamed in pain from my spill off the mare in the flaming streets of Old Chicago. I wanted to lay still and rest, if only for a moment, but I couldn't allow it. If I stayed in one place for too long, the other Elementals would find me with ease.

Within moments, the light grew brighter and changed into an abrupt display of yellow and orange—all too familiar in color, sound, and heat. I blinked into the crackling light, shocked to see tongues of a developing forest fire dance upon the hilltop and surround my fallen form. A frantic scan of the area revealed no one else's presence...not yet, at least. Still the danger loomed. I forced myself to ignore the aches that plagued my body and scrambled to my knees before the fire threatened to reach my very spot.

The heat from the fire pulsed in waves, leaping from one treetop to another. Flames sputtered and spat around me. I wobbled on unsteady legs, attempting to gauge my surroundings. I noticed a burning evergreen nearby, recently struck by lightning, I guessed. Sweeping branches filled its tall trunk, now completely immersed in flames.

Well, at least I didn't start this fire. I gritted my teeth and started a slow, painful trot downhill. Each agonizing step worked to loosen my sore muscles until my pace grew steady and strong. The dry underbrush behind me crackled loudly, fueling the flames that spread with uncontrollable speed across the hillcrest.

Though I distanced myself from the center of the mounting blaze, I found little relief. Instead, a sudden fear surged through my veins. I dared a glance over my shoulder, searching the fire for the darkened forms of the Elementals: Skye, Hydros, and Gaia. So far, I spotted no one, but I knew I must remain vigilant. The background noise of the fire made it difficult to listen for their approach. I willed my legs to move faster, allowing no time to catch my breath when one thought persisted above all others—*escape.*

My eyes darted madly as I scanned my surroundings, searching for The Three. Aside from the hissing fire far above, I heard nothing. I thought I might have lost them, at least for the moment.

I pressed onward, away from the heat. Racing down

the hillside, the pungent odor of burning brush and dry leaves eventually receded, replaced with the sweet smell of a eucalyptus grove. With streaked paper-thin bark peeling in soft earthen hues and long sickle-shaped leaves dangling from their branches, the eucalyptus trees enveloped the sky in a lush canopy. Far off, I heard the distant crash of the ocean against a rocky shore, much louder than the familiar sound of waves that lapped the pebbled beaches of Lake Michigan.

Where am I? I wondered, though I knew one thing. This definitely wasn't Chicago anymore. But if I could jump to this place so fast, there was a chance they could, too.

Renewed fear gripped my heart. My chest heaved with haggard breaths and I continued my rush downhill, branches whipping my face and arms. I repeatedly reminded myself that this pain seemed minimal compared to the torment I'd endure when they caught me.

And I knew they would, eventually. It was inevitable.

The Ancient Greeks had a name for us: the Classical Elements of Earth (or Gaia), Air (that's Skye), Water (also known as Hydros), and Fire (you guessed it...that would be me). Separate, we Elementals existed as earthly and corruptible entities. But I heard that once united, our powers would swell, making us capable of immeasurable destruction until we plunged the planet into utter annihilation.

Worse, only when the Four Elementals joined forces did we stand a chance against the quintessential Fifth Element that the Greek philosopher Aristotle described as Aether for the heavenly realm. We would wield total control over the whole Earth, and potentially the cosmos as well. But I promised myself I wouldn't let that happen. I'd never join Gaia, not after what she stole from me. So I kept running.

Spanish moss dripped off tree branches while I staggered down the slope covered in dense shrubs and rocky outcroppings. Overhead, turkey vultures soared on the sea breeze. Now that I had distanced myself from the blaze, the air felt less hostile inside my lungs. It seemed moister, with a lingering hint of brine.

But I had little time to guess my current location. Not with the impending threat of their return. I habitually looked over my shoulder for The Three and moved faster. Luckily, I saw no sign of them behind me.

Up ahead, I noticed a smooth ribbon of black winding like a serpent across the verdant hillside. *What is that?* I stared at the manmade surface in puzzlement, amazed by its superior craftsmanship. If it was indeed a road, it appeared the flattest I'd ever seen. I wondered how they made it so perfect and smooth, with a bright, dashed yellow line dividing its surface equally in half. Immediately, I remembered galloping down Chicago's dusty, rutted streets. On a road like this, the mare never would've stumbled and spilled me from its back into Skye's clutches.

But there's something else. I continued my sprint downhill, squinting for a better look. I spied the crushed corpse of a raccoon lying upon one yellow dash, its bushy striped tail distinctly recognizable. A raven—with coal black feathers like my own eyes and hair—tugged at the raccoon's bloody entrails.

Before I had a chance to feel sorry for the raccoon or make sense of how it perished, my foot caught a jagged stone, sending me tumbling head over heels down the steep slope. The world blurred as I struggled to halt my wild descent. Twigs and leaves clung to my hair and scratched my sooty arms and dirt-smeared face. My fingers frantically grasped at saplings and exposed roots, but without success. I rolled off the side of the hill, and then dropped several feet through the air to land with a thud upon the smooth road.

My entire body cried in pain from the fall, my muscles and bones already felt strained and fatigued from my ordeal in Chicago. My brain shouted at my legs to keep running. But when I tried to lift myself back up, my tired limbs collapsed beneath me.

One positive thought crossed my mind when my body sank onto the ground. This road must lead to civilization. Perhaps I could find a place to hide and heal before the Elementals located me again. That thought alone reenergized me. Drawing strength from reserves I didn't know existed, I dragged my battered body to my feet and limped down the road.

I didn't make it far before an alien sound filled the air. It began like a low rumble, growing louder as it neared. I whipped my head around to notice a silver machine on four wheels speed around the hairpin turn. Back in Old Chicago, I'd heard of automated carriages, capable of moving without the power of a horse. But those wheels were narrow and designed for travel at slow speeds unlike the wide tires that now rapidly approached. And those carriages possessed open tops, not sleek, streamlined contours of enclosed glass and metallic paint like the one before me. Behind the images of sky and trees reflected upon the glass, I spotted two shadowed silhouettes sitting comfortably inside.

Rooted to my spot, I stared at the silvery carriage-like machine with surprise and amazement. In an instant, the driver's eyes met mine. A look of utter shock passed over his face. He tightly gripped the circular disc in front of him and spun it with a sudden jerky motion. The tires squealed and slipped into a skid, screeching sideways down the road.

I wanted to dodge out of the way, but had nowhere to move with a rocky wall on one side of the road and a steep cliff dropping off the other. So I stood still, my fearful eyes trained on the machine grinding against the road.

At the last second, I raised my arm to shield my face, suspecting this was the end. After all, no fire existed to hurtle me into another location like in the past. The machine skidded closer until the driver's side door struck my side, knocking me off my feet. On instinct, I stuck out one arm to brace my impact and heard a loud snap when the full force of my body landed on it. Unable to slow my momentum, my body flew backward and slammed my skull against the road.

Then a grisly howl filled the valley floor. It took me a minute to realize I was the one making that ghastly noise.

CHAPTER TWO

I lay on the hard road in silence, unable to move. Though I didn't perish, I almost wished I had to silence the agonizing pain for the last time. A burning bolt shot up my right forearm, threatening to ignite the entire appendage. I moaned, gritted my teeth, and forced my eyes to flutter open and focus on the blurry scene unfolding. White dots clouded my vision as my aching head rolled toward the silver machine, half expecting Gaia or Skye to pop out one door. Instead, I spotted two boys—about my age, I guessed—leap out opposite sides.

One boy ran his fingers through his short dark hair, making it spike up in the front. Thin sideburns trailed down each of his cheeks, accentuating his clenched jaw and drawing my eye toward the diamonds adorning each earlobe. His fingers gripped his head tightly, threatening to explode.

"Oh, God. Oh, God. Oh, God, no," he moaned. His hazel eyes moistened and his face filled with dread. "This is *so* not happening to me."

"Snap out of it, Micah. You think *you're* in bad shape. Look at *her*," the second boy said, pointing an index finger at me. His light brown hair was cut short and concealed under a cap.

Their words made little sense in the muddled state of my hazy mind. I raised my uninjured arm to my head to soothe the swelling lump at the base of my skull. But even that minor motion jostled my body to the point of insufferable hurt. So I lay there instead, letting the twigs and dry leaves embedded in my dull, singed hair form my pillow upon the ground while I listened to the voices and approaching footsteps. It didn't matter that soot and dirt smeared my bare hands and face, or my favorite dress looked burnt and tattered beyond recognition, or that only charred leather remained of my shoes. Nothing mattered anymore except my desire to end the pain.

Micah's friend with the cap knelt down beside me. "Are you okay?" he asked. His pale blue eyes registered shock and mild repulsion at my ragged appearance.

I barely managed to blink my eyes much less verbalize a reply. My gaze left his for a moment as I dared a frightened glance up the hillside. These injuries would prove the least of my concerns if The Three charged down the slope.

"I dunno, man," he said, turning back toward Micah. "She looks pretty freaked out."

"So what're we gonna do, Sully? Call 911?" Micah whipped a small, flat black object from his pocket, tapped its surface three times with one finger, and then held it to his ear.

Sully looked at me, then back at Micah. "No. It'll take them too long to get here. We should just bring her to the ER ourselves."

Though I had no idea what "9-1-1" or "ER" meant, I guessed the "freaked out" part seemed a pretty accurate description of my general state of mind. Besides, I'd learned from my past harrowing experiences with death that I shouldn't ask. Listen more, but talk as little as possible. You see, for me blending didn't just conceal my secrets…

It was a matter of survival.

The boy named Sully surveyed me with concern through pale blue eyes. "It's just down the hill," he told Micah.

"Seriously, Sully?"

"Well, we can't just leave her here, can we?"

Micah frowned and crossed his arms over his chest. "Fine," he said in a tone that sounded anything but fine, and joined Sully by my side. He squatted down alongside of me and said in a low voice, "I'm really sorry. I didn't see you. Honest, I didn't."

Sully shook his head. "What Micah's trying to say is we're gonna get you some help. Can you stand?"

Help, I repeated in my mind. I definitely needed some help to stand a chance against The Three. I glanced back up the hill, grateful to find it vacant.

Nodding slowly, I let them assist me to my feet. Micah took my good arm while Sully attempted to support the other. But as soon as he touched my forearm, I yelped in pain.

"Oh, God," Sully said, biting his lip. "Sorry. I totally didn't mean to do that."

I knew from experience to remain quiet until I had a better understanding of the language patterns used in my new location. Still, his apology warranted a response. So my brain scanned the conversation I'd just heard, searching for the appropriate words to use and pasting them together so I

21

sounded normal enough to blend in and hide.

"It's okay," I replied, masking my grimace of pain with the faintest of smiles.

Sully returned my smile. Fortunately, even in my clouded state of mind, I readily picked up on dialects and accents. If I didn't, I'd be dead by now.

After he helped me into the backseat of his silver machine, Sully strapped a belt across my waist. Then my seat vibrated when Micah turned a key and shifted a lever to make us roll forward. Despite my efforts to support my arm—which now felt puffy and bruised—every slight movement inside the machine sent a jolt of pain shooting up to my shoulder. When we sped off, I couldn't stop my eyes from scanning the hillside, half-expecting Skye or Gaia or Hydros to appear at any moment.

But they didn't. Not yet, at least.

The narrow road wound down the hill and into a town. We soon passed a sign that said Pacifica, Pop. 37,987. Despite the throbbing tenderness in my arm and head, I couldn't help but stare out the window in shock and wonder. Spacious houses nestled against the hillside with sweeping sides of windows facing the bay below. Shops with attractive, bold signage clustered along the sides of the roads, obscuring the view of the beach from my vantage point. Yet most amazing were the vast number of machines like Micah's in a variety of colors and styles that moved back and forth in an orderly fashion down the road, following an unspoken set of rules. Each and every one moved along the right hand side of the road and stopped at red lights that dangled across the intersections—a massive leap from my quiet life in Chicago, though I could never let anyone know.

I closed my eyes for a moment, focusing on Micah and Sully's conversation. I tried to remember every word they said to archive for future reference with the hope of avoiding unnecessary attention upon myself. I understood life would seem dramatically different after a jump through time, only I faced the challenge of making it appear ordinary.

A few red lights later, Micah turned the automated carriage inland and drove up another hill before parking in front of a long white edifice bearing a red cross and bold capital letters that spelled San Mateo County Emergency Room.

Maybe this is the "ER" they were talking about. I hoped I could make sense of other new terms as quickly.

Sully offered me a hand out of my seat and into the back of the hospital. My confused and injured brain shifted into survival mode, trying to formulate a believable plan to explain my general appearance while appearing as if I belonged in this time and place. If only it could be that easy.

Micah and Sully walked through a double set of doors that opened on their own with a loud hiss. Though I leapt backward in surprise, the boys seemed at ease and walked through without breaking their pace. With hesitation, I followed, doubly startled when the doors closed behind me a few steps later. Unable to control myself, I slowed my gait and glanced over my shoulder, watching another person approach the entrance. Again, the doors opened and closed like a pair of sentries waiting at attention, ready to admit the individual inside the facility. *Amazing,* I thought and paused mid-stride, eager to see the doors automatically open once more.

"Let's go," Sully called, interrupting my thoughts. He waved me to follow them into a chilled room where calming piano music filled the air. A few people sat in plush chairs along the windowsills, flipping through flimsy paper books decorated in flashy pictures and colorful text. Others whispered into black and silver devices similar to the one Micah had whipped from his pocket when he intended to call 911.

We looked for an available seat when a voice asked, "May I help you?" The woman behind the welcome desk stared at me, her face pale with repulsion. She crinkled her nose at my tattered clothing, sooty face, unkempt hair, and cradled, injured right arm.

I turned away, letting them do the talking.

"We found her on the road," Micah began, conveniently omitting the part about striking me with his carriage-like machine. "Her arm's hurt. Maybe broken."

A strained smile crossed the woman's lips as she scanned me from head to toe. Then her expression softened until her initial aversion transformed into sympathy. "Take a seat and fill out these forms," she said, handing Micah a brown board with a shiny metal clip and a pen with a pink carnation wrapped along its side.

Great. I hadn't even come up with a believable storyline yet and she expected me to answer a bunch of questions already.

I followed the boys to a set of plush teal green chairs, cringing with pain when I settled into one. I blinked, trying to clear my mind and focus on the little amount I had learned so far. But my brain ached, making it difficult to concentrate. How did I ever end up in this mess? Wistfully, I thought of the home and family I lost so very long ago when this entire disaster began, changing my life forever. I sighed and closed my eyes in defeat, sinking deeper into the chair.

"Okay. Since you don't look like you can complete this stuff, I guess I'll have to. Lucky me," Micah muttered. He rolled his eyes and released a weighty sigh. Glancing at the sheet, the flower pen in his hand stood poised to record my response. "Name?"

That's it? I thought and sat a little taller in my chair. Maybe I could answer these questions easier than I thought and get the help I definitely needed for my arm. I quickly replied, "It's Jordan."

Micah scrawled my name in all upper case letters on the first line, then asked, "Last name?"

"Um." I bit my lip. I'd had so many different last names over the course of my life, depending on my location at the time. Was I supposed to choose one of those or make something up? Plus, how did I even know what surnames sounded typical for this region? My black eyes flitted across the room, searching for a commonplace word, until they landed on the nameplate beside the receptionist's desk. It read Leslie K. Smith, Receptionist.

"Smith," I answered, thinking quickly.

"Age?"

Hmm, another tough one. I was almost fifteen when this whole nightmare began. And if I added up at the months I spent in different times and places, it would probably equal about two years on the run. So I guessed that made me around...

"Seventeen," I told Micah with more confidence than I felt.

"Hey! So are we," Sully chimed in. But the look on Micah's face led me to think he couldn't care less that we shared anything.

"Birthday?" Micah asked, eager to move on.

Was he kidding? No one kept track of actual birthdays back when my mother brought me into this world, thousands of years ago. Back then, parents felt lucky enough to have the child survive and provide another set of hands to help on the farm. Infant mortality seemed so common an occurrence that I couldn't even recall how many babies my own mother lost between my little sister, Sarah, and me. But at least a birthday I could make up easily enough.

"April first," I said, choosing a random date.

"You were actually born on April Fool's Day?" Sully asked in disbelief. "That's pretty cool."

Again, Micah's face registered little interest. He proceeded to the next question. "Permanent address?"

I blinked. *This is getting ridiculous.* I hadn't had a permanent address since my family died. My eyes darted from side to side, searching for an acceptable answer to this question. Sweat beaded across my brow and I knew I couldn't keep up this charade much longer, even to fix my injured arm. Maybe I should just admit the truth about my identity. At this rate, they'd find out sooner than later.

"I don't know," I conceded in defeat. Another painful twinge jolted up my arm when my shoulders slumped forward, heavy and tired. A discouraged sigh left my lips. I'd never given up this easily before.

"What do you mean you don't know?" Micah asked in disbelief.

I frowned, mumbling, "I just don't know." I squeezed my eyes shut and sank lower in my chair. My burning, swollen arm no longer mattered. At this rate, I'd be dead in no time. In my mind, I saw the faces of my family backlit in a bright light welcoming me to my final resting place. I would never avenge their wrongful deaths, but maybe that no longer mattered. Maybe joining them in the afterlife was reward enough.

Sully shot Micah a concerned look. "You don't think she has amnesia, do you?"

"Oh, please, Sully. You can't be serious."

"It's possible," Sully replied with a shrug. "She hit her head pretty hard when you came around the turn and —"

Micah's eyes narrowed. "Thanks for reminding me."

"I'm just saying —"

"Well, you can stop right there," Micah said as he jammed the flowery pen into the metal clip on the board. "I didn't hit her that bad."

"Except for messing up her arm," Sully retorted under his breath.

"And maybe I wouldn't have messed up her arm if I didn't have to stop you from messing around with my iTunes."

"Well maybe I wouldn't have had to mess around with them," Sully snipped back, "if you didn't listen to such crappy music."

Despite my current predicament, I couldn't help but chuckle. As Micah and Sully bickered, a glorious idea formed in my head. Without realizing it, Sully had presented a valid cover for me, guaranteeing my survival just when I thought my future held none.

Amnesia. It was perfect.

But before they escalated into a heated squabble, a nurse arrived to take the papers from Micah and guide us into the examining room. Though she asked me a heap of additional questions, I felt no fear in replying, "I don't know," to them all. Even better, Sully piped in, "I think she might have amnesia," justifying my responses.

I felt my shoulders relax. At this rate, I'd be out of here in no time and ready to find a new place to hide until my arm properly heals. Then I could end things with Gaia.

This will be so easy. The nurse deftly conducted a series of tests and informed me of the results. I glanced over at Micah and Sully, wondering if my results sounded as normal as she professed. But they both stared at the tiny screens of their similar black devices, completely oblivious to my presence. I couldn't understand what they found so interesting in such a small object.

A minute ended up seeming more like ten before I heard a polite knock on the door. Without waiting for a response, a balding, bespectacled man in a white lab coat entered the room. Micah and Sully peeked up from their screens for a fraction of a second to mumble a greeting. The lab coat man showed little surprise by their reaction, though his eyebrows quickly found their way to the top of his head when he took one look at me. "I'm Doctor Atkins," he said. He stuck out one hand to shake mine, but reconsidered at my ragged appearance. He tried to mask his initial impression by asking, "Now, Jordan, what seems to be the problem?"

Out of habit, I prepared to reply, "I don't know," when I realized I *did* know the answer to that particular question. With a grimace, I gestured toward my swollen arm that throbbed in pain.

"Right. Let's take a look at that." He placed his fingers upon my forearm, rotating it slightly.

Gritting my teeth, I closed my eyes and squealed.

"It may be broken," he predicted. "We'll have to take some X-rays to be sure."

The nurse brought in a chair on wheels and took me down the hall. After the X-ray woman revolved my arm in several painful positions, the nurse wheeled me back to the examining room. The doctor fastened each picture to a special board and turned on the light to illuminate the images from behind. My mouth fell open as several pictures of my arm appeared...if viewed from the *inside*! I glanced down at my arm whose skin remained intact and then back at the pictures, astonished by the ghostly glow of each bone against the black background. I peeked at Sully and Micah — whose gazes hadn't left the screens of their black devices since we entered the room — puzzled that they didn't find this as intriguing as I did. As the doctor studied the X-rays, his mouth slid into a frown. He declared that I suffered from a displaced fracture on my right radius (whatever that meant), as well as smoke inhalation, bruising, mild abrasions, and possibly a concussion.

The nurse wheeled in a cart of supplies, ready to assist the doctor in setting a waterproof cast on my arm. Wrapping a liner around my arm, he asked what color I'd like. Uncertain of how to respond, I merely shrugged my shoulders. So the nurse grabbed the closest material, soaked it in water, and quickly wound bright pink layers around my forearm that bubbled and fizzed while hardening. I looked at my highly visible arm with alarm. I didn't mean to sound ungrateful, but perhaps I should have been a bit proactive and selected a more subdued color.

Satisfied with their work, the doctor reminded me to rest and avoid contact sports for the next four weeks while it healed. I almost told him I didn't play any sports — unless you considered running for your life a "sport" — when a woman with a worried face and dark glasses wedged into her short

29

brown hair rushed in to the room, towing behind her a little boy with big brown eyes.

"I got your message," she blurted breathlessly to Micah. "Are you okay?"

"I'm fine, Mom," he said, barely looking up from his screen.

Her eyes darted to Sully. "And how about you? Are you hurt?"

Sully also glanced up for half a second to shake his head. "No, Mrs. T. I'm fine, too."

Then Micah's mom looked at me, puzzled.

Micah nodded in my direction. "This is Jordan."

"Jordan? Is she one of your friends from school?" she asked.

"Nope. We just met her," Micah replied.

While she studied Micah and Sully with skepticism, I looked at the little boy, unable to take my eyes off him. He seemed about the same age as my sister Sarah—at the time of her death. He caught my gaze and ducked behind his mom in fear. But when he peeked out, I flashed him a wide smile. When he smiled back a toothless grin, my heart leapt up in my throat. Sarah was also missing her front teeth.

"All right. Tell me everything," Micah's mother said.

"We were coming back from Half Moon Bay…" Micah trailed off with a sigh.

"And…?" She narrowed her eyes.

Sully continued, "She was in the middle of the road. We didn't see her right away."

Micah's mom crossed her arms over her chest. "*And…?*"

"I wasn't going that fast. And she wasn't on the shoulder."

"*And…!*"

Micah and Sully caught each other's eye, but refused to speak.

"Oh, you did not," she gasped. "God, Micah, tell me you didn't."

Micah's eyes found the floor. He stuffed his hands deep into his pockets.

Aghast, his mom turned to me. "Did Micah actually *hit* you?"

I glanced from Micah to Sully and back again, unsure of what to say. Then I remember what he told Sully in the waiting room. That he didn't hit me that bad.

"Not that bad," I managed, though the words stuck inside my throat.

Micah's eyes immediately found mine. He glared at me with unexpected hostility. I swallowed hard, my back knotted with sudden fear.

His mother's jaw hit the floor. "I don't believe it. After all we've been through since the..." She couldn't complete her sentence before tears brimmed in her eyes. It took her a few minutes to regain her composure. Then her voice came out firm and strict. She pointed her index finger at Micah's face. "No driving the car for a month."

Car? So that's their name for the automated carriage.

Micah's face fell. "But, Mom, I didn't see —"

"Want to make it two?" she challenged.

Shutting his mouth, Micah shifted his glare to me again. "I can't believe it," he muttered, too low for her to hear. "Grounded from the car...for a *month*." His venomous hazel eyes sent a chill down my spine.

Why did I ever open my stupid mouth?

"So, Jordan," she continued, her tone softer and more

compassionate now, "do you live around here?"

I shook my head, afraid to speak. It didn't seem to take much to set her off.

"Do you have family in this area?" she asked.

I shook my head again, still silent.

"Relatives?"

I shrugged. Only this time I felt compelled to explain, "My family died a long time ago."

"Your whole family?" she said in disbelief.

I nodded silently.

"Oh, my God!" she exclaimed, clamping her hand over her mouth. "I had no idea. I'm *so* sorry." And she sounded like she truly was. "So you're telling me you're the only one left?" she asked incredulously.

"Yes," I said. Perhaps I should stick with shorter responses. Maybe those would generate less emotion from this woman.

"But what will you do? Where will you go? Who will you stay with once you leave the hospital?"

"Can she stay with us?" her little son chirped in a sweet, high-pitched voice. His big brown eyes looked at her with brightness and sincerity. "She can have my room and I can stay with Micah."

"Oh, please. You're not inviting one of Lady Gaga's Little Monsters to live in our house," Micah protested. "Plus Cam snores in his sleep. And hogs the covers."

Though I'm not sure what swine and covers had in common, I found his description most puzzling. "Lady Gaga's Little Monsters?" I repeated softly, my eyebrows knitting together.

Sully leaned over. "Well, yeah. I mean, look at your hair. How you're dressed."

I glanced down at my clothes, still confused, when Micah's mom asked, "So how about it?"

"I'm sorry?" I raised my head in confusion.

"How about you stay with us?" she repeated.

I politely declined, "Thank you, but I couldn't possibly—"

"Nonsense. I insist. Micah can keep his room. I'll pull out the futon in the basement. We've got a storage room down there that no one uses. It may not be much, but you'll have your own space."

"I really can't. I have to go—"

"Go where? You've already said your family's all..."— she swallowed hard—"gone."

"Um," I trailed off. How could I get out of this situation without revealing too much? That I must rest so I can fight the other Elementals...and hopefully eliminate Gaia.

"It's final. What happened today is bad enough," she said, shooting Micah a pointed look. "I won't have the guilt of leaving you alone on the streets weighing on my conscience, too."

"Yay!" Cam cheered, his arms raised in the air as he jumped in jubilation.

I bit my lip. "But I—"

"It's settled. I'll speak with the nurse and see if they're ready to release you." She moved to leave but only made it halfway to the door before she turned around and marched back to my bedside.

As an afterthought, she stuck out one hand toward me. When I lifted my cast to take her hand, a jolt of pain shot from my wrist to my shoulder. Seeing my grimace, she awkwardly shook my good hand instead. "I almost forgot. I'm Celia Trudeau. And this is Cameron," she said, nodding her head toward the bouncing boy. She placed her hands on his shoulders to keep him still for a moment while he flashed me a broad, toothless grin. "And you've already met my other son, Micah. And obviously Sully who's over at our house so much it's like he's adopted."

Sully gave a small wave, but Micah simply turned away, crossed his arms over his chest, and sulked in silence.

"Now about that release." Celia exited the room with the same flurry of activity in which she entered.

I glanced over at Micah. Unlike Cam who started dancing in a circle again, Micah didn't look the least bit thrilled. In fact, he looked almost irate, as if I completely ruined his life.

What had I just agreed to? I always lived on my own. *Always*.

CHAPTER THREE

After the slip of my tongue left Micah grounded from driving for a month, I learned to keep my mouth shut. Things were better this way, I convinced myself. If I focused on listening and remembering, then I'd be ready to mimic others' speech when needed.

So the longer I remained hidden, the better. Especially with my injury.

Only I wished I had decided to keep my mouth shut earlier. Celia asked Sully to drive Micah's silver car that said Nissan Sentra across the tail end...and Micah did *not* look happy about her demand.

Micah heaved a deep breath when Sully situated himself behind the wheel. Wringing his hands together, he kept his eyes glued to the road, refusing to look at me even once the whole way to his house. After Sully returned the keys, Micah dropped them safely inside his pocket, then barged through the front door and slammed it shut for effect.

But before I could apologize, Celia directed me to the bathroom and closed the door behind her, leaving me alone in a room full of unfamiliar contraptions. I stripped off my ruined dress and tossed it in the garbage can next to the sink, then stepped into what she had called a shower, slid the door shut…and wondered what to do next.

It took me a couple of trials to figure out how to turn on the water and then a couple more to figure out how to make it hot, but I finally succeeded. I spun a small circle on the floor as a shower of water ran off my body and washed away some of the pain from landing in this time. At that very moment, I felt glad the doctor had the foresight to give me a waterproof cast, even though it was bright pink. After scrubbing off the layers of soot and grime with my good arm and rinsing clean, I shut off the water and stepped out of the shower. Celia had left a fluffy white towel and a pile of clean clothes on the tiled floor. I wrapped the towel around me when I heard a soft knock.

"Did you find the towel?" Celia called through the bathroom door.

"Yes, thank you."

"I also set out a T-shirt, a pair of Micah's old jeans, and a hoodie that might fit you. But I'll have to take you underwear shopping tomorrow. All I could find were Micah's old boxer shorts."

My face blushed, wondering who else could hear this conversation. I sifted through the clothes pile to find items that matched her description. Too preoccupied to respond right away, Celia added, "Don't worry. The boxers are clean."

Better than nothing. I found something that looked like short silk pants with a polka-dotted print and a cinched waist and slid them up my legs. In fact, this seemed a huge improvement over those whalebone corsets I squeezed myself into when I lived in sixteenth century France. I threw on the shirt with short sleeves that actually resembled the letter T in shape. Well, at least I should be able to recall this new term with ease.

I finished jamming my cast through the sleeve of the only article with a hood that I guessed was the "hoodie." I pulled up the faded blue pants, which I suspected by process of elimination must be the "jeans" and opened the bathroom door. Celia helped drag a comb through my gnarled tangles, which definitely seemed a two-handed job. She held a strand of hair up to the light, frowning at its crisp, burnt ends. "You need a trim," she stated and pulled a pair of scissors from a drawer under the sink.

After Celia finished cutting my hair to an even length, the thick black strands that previously fell halfway down my back now bobbed lightly about my shoulders. Surprised by its short length, I didn't know how to respond. Except her intentions were good, so I managed a small, "Thanks."

But Celia appeared far from done. Next, she scrubbed the soot from my nails and filed each smooth. "Is Primrose Passion okay?" she asked, grabbing a bottle from the counter. I shrugged, uncertain of what she meant. I caught a glimpse of the label that said Nail Polish in small letters before she twisted off its top to reveal a tiny brush suspending a thick drop that glistened pink in the bright bathroom lights. Then she painted each of my nails in two coats to match my cast and masked the dirt and chips.

No one had ever taken such good care of me. Speechless, I grinned back at Celia, my tired eyes reflecting gratitude.

Satisfied with her work, Celia smiled. "Much better... though you should probably get some rest. You look exhausted. I've already pulled out the futon for your bed, downstairs in the basement. The boys are on the couch but they're too wrapped up in their video games to bother you. Get some sleep, and let me know if you need anything else."

I nodded. "Thank you," I said, though the words didn't adequately describe my true appreciation. Then I walked downstairs to my futon bed, wanting nothing but to stretch out and rest as she'd suggested.

When I reached the bottom of the stairs, I found Micah and Sully on the couch, staring at a flurry of vibrant movement on a giant screen with resonating sound effects...probably the *video games* Celia had mentioned. I felt too weary to make sense of the game, so I glanced at the boys instead. Still bitter from his punishment, Micah didn't look up. But Sully did.

"You clean up nice," Sully said, his blue eyes lighting up. One side of his mouth turned into a cute, crooked grin.

An unexpected smile spread across my face.

What do you care, Jordan? Remember, you're here only to absorb, assimilate, and heal. You don't have time for distractions.

Right. No distractions.

But despite my fatigue, it couldn't hurt to sit down and listen in on their conversation for a bit. I was still in the basement...still hiding, after all. Plus, maybe I could actually learn something in the process.

I found a spot on the edge of the cushiony leather couch, as far from Micah as possible. Not that it mattered; he didn't seem to notice my presence. For several minutes, I watched their fingers manipulate controllers to move small, ugly green figures on the giant screen. I'd never seen anything like it.

Almost as if they wielded the power to determine the fate of those *things*.

"What are you playing?" I asked, assuming they used this game for personal enjoyment. Though with how red Micah's face grew, I doubted "enjoyment" accurately described his feelings, either.

Without answering my question, Micah swore under his breath when his creature withered away and disappeared in a cloud of smoke. "Not again," he moaned, slamming his controller down on a low table resting on short legs.

Sully laughed. His fingers adeptly moved his controller, quickly scooting his figure out of harm's way.

With his tongue stuck out one side of his mouth in concentration, Sully leaned one way then the next on the couch, quickly evading the attackers, until the battle swallowed his figure in another cloud of smoke.

"Crap. I thought I had them that time."

"You should have used your plasma cannon," Micah offered.

"Easy for you to say. You're already dead."

I felt extremely confused. Plasma cannons? Already dead? Why did this sound more like a scene from *my* life?

"What are you playing?" I asked again, thinking maybe they hadn't heard me the first time.

"Zombie Dominion," Micah grunted without looking at me, as if those two little words explained everything. He picked up his controller and aimed it at the screen again.

"Zombie Dominion?" I repeated, more bewildered than ever.

"It just came out last week," Sully added, leaning forward to get closer to the screen. He aimed his controller, pushing buttons at a frantic pace. "You've got legions of the undead that you have to—"

Undead? Well, that explained the ugly, green creatures in various states of decay that rose out of the ground and limped toward the incoming attackers.

"Have to what?" I wondered aloud.

"Prepare for battling the boss...oh, crap!" He stabbed the buttons harder now. "Get that one, Micah."

"I'm trying," Micah snipped.

"Well, try harder."

"I *am*, Sullivan," he muttered through clenched teeth.

Hang on. I thought Micah called him "Sully."

"*Sully* Sullivan?" I asked, a puzzled look crossing my face.

Sully's mouth turned up in half a smirk. "My real name's Shayne but everyone calls me by my nickname, Sully. Even my teach—".

I blinked, waiting for Sully to continue, but he focused all his attention on the screen instead. His tongue wedged out one corner of his mouth.

"Sweet!" he exclaimed. "Five hundred points for that one, baby. Beat that!"

I rolled my eyes. With Micah and Sully so absorbed in their game, I probably wouldn't get much of a response out of either of them. Nor would I get much sleep, even with the door closed. So I settled into the couch, watching them farm more zombies up from the graveyard to send off into battle against the incoming gang of pirates—while their bantering continued.

"Aw, c'mon," Micah groaned after losing another life. "Why can't you pull your own weight?"

"Puh-lease," Sully replied. "Like *you* could do better."

Micah's fingers frantically pushed a series of buttons on the controller. "I *can* do better. Maybe that's why you're like making me do everything here."

"Okay, you want some help? How's this?" Sully touched a button that shot a laser from his zombie's eyes, effectively destroying two pirates at the same time.

"Really, Sully?" Micah said. Then I heard a buzzing noise. Micah whipped the flat black object from his pocket—the same one he used in the emergency room. A smile filled his face when he read its lighted screen.

Sully glanced over at Micah, clearly irritated. "A little help?"

"Gimme a sec. I'm just texting Tessa back."

Sully groaned. "Well, put down your phone and hurry up. I'm getting destroyed here."

Micah didn't look at the game. His thumbs flew across the object Sully called a phone, its surface covered with tiny letters and numbers.

"Oh, *come on*," Sully grumbled. "Are you texting a novel?"

"Fine," Micah consented and placed it on the table to pick up his controller again. A few seconds later, the phone buzzed again.

Despite Micah's phone repeatedly humming when another half dozen texts arrived in a matter of minutes, he and Sully soon defeated the pirates, celebrating with whoops of glee and congratulatory hand slaps as their points racked up on the screen. I assumed their game had finished so I could finally get some rest when the screen announced *Level 2*. Micah and Sully readied themselves and prepared to launch troops against the tougher Viking clan.

I rolled my eyes again and settled deeper into the soft

leather of the couch.

After about an hour of listening to them bemoan each other's failures, I felt confident I had mastered the skills needed to carry on a believable conversation—at least for antagonizing another teenage boy. But if I'd only see Micah and Sully down here in the basement waging zombie war, then I figured I knew enough for now.

Their army slowly dwindled, making Micah increasingly agitated. Sully let a few expletives slip off his tongue as one zombie after another succumbed to the powerful Viking horde. Eventually they lost their entire army.

"That really sucked," Sully muttered as he removed his hat to wipe his brow on the sleeve of his charcoal gray shirt.

"You said it," Micah agreed. He folded his arms over his chest with a sigh of annoyance.

"Well," Sully said, placing his controller on the table and letting out a big yawn. "Guess I should probably get home now. Mom'll be pissed I haven't finished my math homework yet."

"Yeah. Mine, too."

Sully rose off the couch and stretched again. His arms reached so high I could see his belly button and striped boxer shorts sticking out of his jeans. "See ya, Micah," he said and grabbed a set of keys off the table.

"Yup."

"Hey, Jordan," he paused, catching my eye. "I guess I'll see you tomorrow, too." He jammed his keys in his jeans pocket and then flashed me a quick smile.

I couldn't help but smile back. "Okay," I agreed from my spot on the couch.

Sully headed upstairs and Micah glanced over at my side

of the couch, as if he noticed me for the first time. He blinked, his face turning a fast shade of pink. But the color quickly drained from his cheeks.

He said coolly, "Like Sully said, I've gotta go finish my math." Reaching for a different controller on the table, he pushed a button to turn off the light on the large screen. "You didn't want to watch TV, did you?" he asked gruffly.

I shook my head, afraid to irritate him more than I had already.

Without another word, he stuffed his hands into the front pocket of his hoodie and plodded up the stairs, his feet heavy on each step.

I wrapped my arms over my chest and released a deep sigh. I knew I'd figure out all these new words and inventions soon enough. But how would I ever manage to survive the six weeks until my cast comes off with someone who despised me? Maybe I should scope out a new place in the morning. Somewhere safe.

And far away from Micah.

With another sigh, I climbed off the couch and headed to my room. I changed into Micah's old flannel pajama pants and T-shirt that Celia had arranged on the futon, crawled under the sheets, and pulled the covers tight around my chin. Rolling over on one side, I squirmed until I found a comfortable position to rest my cast. The light of the full moon filtered through the small basement window, casting an eerie glow around the room. Shadows lurked in every corner. I shivered beneath the covers, partially from the cold and partially out of fear.

Though exhausted from the strain of my escape, it took forever for sleep to find me. And when it finally did, it was anything but restful.

Halfway through the night, I woke to an unusual sound of scratching and clawing at the grassy yard outside. Suddenly, my eyes fluttered open with newfound terror.

Where's that noise coming from? I wondered, sliding from under the covers. Hesitantly, I stood on the futon and peered out the window.

In the light of the full moon, a partially decaying hand broke up through the lawn. It emerged from the ground like a grotesque blossom that unfurled its petals under the chilling moonlit sky. A shiver of fright raced down my spine. I watched the hole widen enough for a spindly arm encrusted with dirt and rotten flesh to follow.

I gasped, cupping both hands over my mouth to stifle my scream. Memories instantly flooded my mind. I remembered the howling winds that whisked my flames from one rooftop to another while the fire raged down the cobbled street.

I recognized that arm. It belonged to Skye.

Soon, another hand clawed free of the confining earth, dragging the rest of its decomposing body behind. I watched in horror as zombified versions of Skye, Gaia, and Hydros crawled from the ground, shaking their gruesome heads to rid their hair of mud and filth.

I scooted down on the mattress away from the window and bit my nails, wondering how to escape this time. Outside, I heard the shuffle of legs dragging limply behind as they traversed the driveway and neared my room.

It's now or never.

I rose, intending to flee up the stairs, when the windowpane shattered. Shards of glass flew across the room. Screaming, I shielded myself from the rain of debris. But before I could leap off the bed, bony hands grasped my shoulder.

"Aaaaahhhhhh!" I wailed, struggling against their grip. One hand after another grabbed at anything they could reach. Their rotting fingers clenched my shirt, my arms, and my hair. Skeletal fingers wrapped around my naked throat. I yelped in pain, gasping for a decent breath, when they yanked me up through the window. The jagged windowsill of broken glass lacerated my back and thighs. Then they dragged me away from the protection of my new, temporary room. My legs flailed wildly and I tried to wiggle free of their clutches, but I could not escape from their inhumanly strong grasps.

Leaving a trail of blood across the freshly cut lawn, I kicked and screamed, constantly battling my monstrous captors. I raised my good arm toward Gaia's head and gritted my teeth. Bolts of pain shot down my forearm until a glowing ball of fire rested in my palm. I aimed the fireball at her torso, but it missed, hitting one of Celia's cedars instead and transforming the tree into an instant tower of flames. Focusing my energy, I launched a second fireball at her skull. It hit directly and ignited her moldy hair, but could not slow her progress. I screamed again, louder this time and aimed painful jets of fire at all their decomposing bodies with little effect.

How could Celia and Micah not hear me? And why hadn't anyone come to my aid yet?

Before I could raise my hand again to unleash a more powerful plasma blast, the zombies halted. Bony fingers encircled my wrists and ankles to lift me clear off the ground. My back and thighs stung from the dirt ground into my open wounds. I howled and thrashed, unable to loosen their grip before they tossed me into a deep, fresh grave.

Far above, Hydros laughed wickedly. Gaia raised one

hand toward the hillside, commanding a shower of rocks and debris to tumble upon me.

"*No!*" I screamed and cowered in my pit. My arms futilely shielded my head.

Hydros's unnerving cackle drowned when the rocks piled higher and smothered my screams.

Suddenly I flew up in bed. Sweat poured down my brow. My pajamas clung to my cold, damp skin. Struggling for a breath of air, I glanced around the room, wondering how I managed to get out of that grave and end up here in the house. Early morning sunlight streamed in through the pane, illuminating the room with its cheery glow. Surprisingly, the window still appeared intact, with no signs of blood, broken glass, or moldy earth anywhere.

I took a deep breath to settle my racing heart.

Why did I need to have such graphic nightmares? Wasn't there already enough horror in my life without inventing more?

That settled it. No more video games for me.

Dragging the fingers of my good hand through my hair, I took another calming breath. *Relax, Jordan. You're safe. No one can find you here.*

That's right. I remained safe, nestled deep within this house. And while I stayed here, protected and unseen, they couldn't trace my location. As the sun rose higher, my stomach released an unhappy gurgle. So I headed upstairs to scrounge up something for breakfast, my hair a tangled mess from disrupted sleep.

"Why aren't you dressed?" Celia asked the second she saw me. Her voice rose an octave with exasperation.

"Huh?" I said, studying the boxes with pictures of huge

bowls containing flakes of corn and wheat doused in milk. In all that had happened since yesterday, I never realized the extent of my hunger until now. *But which to try first?* I wondered when I noticed Celia staring at me with an open mouth.

"I thought I asked Micah to wake you up to get ready," she exclaimed.

"Get ready?" My brow knitted. "For what?"

"School," she said. "You have to leave in ten minutes!"

"School?" I repeated. My face paled. What about my plan of staying safely concealed in the basement? Or finding a new spot to hide, far away from Micah?

"Micah," Celia snapped. "I thought you said you'd wake her up for me?"

"Oops," he replied in a flat tone. "Guess I forgot." His gaze never left his half-eaten bowl.

I rolled my eyes, wondering what I ever did to deserve this attitude from him. Wasn't *he* the one who injured *me*? Shouldn't I be mad at him instead?

"Well, go on," Celia said, shuffling me back down the stairs. "Get dressed and I'll toast you a bagel to eat on the way."

I struggled into the same set of Micah's old clothes I wore yesterday, still not used to the bulky cast weighing down my arm. After dragging a comb through my hair, brushing my teeth, and splashing water over my face, I headed back upstairs to find Micah and Cam already waiting in the car. "And don't forget your backpack," Celia said. She passed me a bag and breakfast and then dashed out the door.

She started the car, adding, "I normally don't drive Micah to school, but since it's your first day and he's grounded from car privileges for a while, I figured, why not?"

Yeah. *Why not?* I frowned. So much for my plans of hiding out.

CHAPTER FOUR

I swallowed hard when we pulled up in front of a long brick building set up on the hill, exponentially larger than any one-room schoolhouse I'd ever seen. I climbed out of the car with the backpack full of supplies Celia had assembled sometime last night. Shutting the door behind me, my gaze automatically fell on the ocean where gentle waves rolled toward the shore and lapped at the sandy beach. I turned toward the school, flooded with conversing teens checking their phones as they headed through the bottlenecking double-wide doors.

My stomach churned. Even with the threat of Hydros pinpointing my location the moment I stepped in the water, I'd choose the beach over this school in a heartbeat.

"Jordan, first stop in the office to pick up your schedule. And I hope you both have a great day!" Celia warbled. She gave a friendly wave and drove off.

I turned to Micah, "Where's the office?"

He glared back at me in stony silence, and then headed toward the front doors. But he only made it a few paces before a girl excitedly shuffled up to him, wearing white leather sandals, tight jeans rolled up to her knees, and a short jacket. She pulled her long blond hair back in a ponytail accentuating her widow's peak and painted her fingernails and toenails in bright blue polish. And like everyone else I saw, she had a phone poking out of the back pocket of her pants.

"Hey, Tessa." Micah's grimace instantly faded. She laced her fingers through his and animatedly talked the rest of the way into the building.

I looked down at Micah's old baggy jeans, hoodie, and sneakers (according to Celia who'd dug an old pair out of the closet this morning). I noticed my painted nails sticking out from my conspicuous pink cast and ran my fingers through my short, black hair.

Heaving a heavy sigh, I glanced back at the beach wistfully, then slung my backpack over one shoulder and followed Micah up to the building. Suddenly, an unfamiliar rumble pierced the sky. I peeked up, startled to see a metallic winged object soaring above the clouds. Watching with bewilderment, I tripped over my feet and stumbled across the road. I picked myself up before anyone noticed, then closed my eyes and took a deep breath to regain composure. *You must blend in,* I scolded myself, hoping I could do a better job of masking my surprise in the future.

When I stepped through the double doors to enter the school, the conversations around me amplified. I saw no sign of Micah or Tessa, though I doubted I'd spot them in the massive sea of passing bodies. Still, I restrained the urge to swivel my head and soak in the new surroundings, navigating the crowded hallway. Instead, I concentrated on catching bits and pieces of student dialogues. My brain acted like a sponge to absorb patterns of speech and mannerisms with astonishing speed, ready to mimic and repeat, digest and regurgitate.

Assimilate or perish. There were no other options.

After picking up my schedule from someone called my "guidance counselor" in the office and following her directions to my first period Environmental Studies class with Mr. Horowitz, I settled into my seat, watching the other kids around me pull out paper and pens from their bags. I reached inside my backpack, looking for similar supplies.

The girl sitting in front of me was dressed much like Tessa but with shorter, curlier blond hair. She turned around to gawk at me with sudden interest. When I caught her eye, she whispered in disbelief, "Is it true?"

I glanced over my shoulder, assuming she meant someone in the row behind me. But no one else responded.

Pointing at my chest, I raised my eyebrows and mouthed, "Me?"

She rolled her eyes and nodded. "So is it?"

"Is it…?"

"True?" she finished for me. "That you live with *Micah Trudeau*?" Her voice ended her question about two octaves higher than where it began.

I shrugged. "Yeah." For some bizarre reason, I felt like she put me on the defensive. Did Micah have issues that I didn't know about, aside from the fact that he couldn't stand to see me in the same room as him? "Is that a problem?"

A smile played across her face. "Only if you want to be on the hate list of Tessa Bradshaw and every girl at school."

"Hate list?" I thought, *what's that?* But I said, "Why's that?"

"Oh, I dunno…" She tucked a curly lock of hair behind her ear. "Except for the fact he's got half the girls in the junior class in love with him."

Including you, I guessed. A deep frown crept across my face. *Just great.* And here I was, trying to lay low. Now I'd unwittingly drawn more unwanted attention upon myself. And to think after all those narrow escapes from The Three, I found myself suddenly intimidated by a bunch of gossiping high school girls.

"You are *so* lucky," she added, the blush rising in her cheeks. "He's like *the* nicest guy."

Micah? Nice? Then why did I seem to bring out the worst in him?

"What I wouldn't give to trade places with you," she finished. She turned away to wait for Mr. Horowitz to start class.

Okay, I felt officially confused. She said I made the hate list. Why would she wish that fate upon herself, too?

Then she spun around in her chair once more, her blond curls bouncing around her cherub face. "Oh, I forgot. My name's Bethany." She gave a small wave. "Bethany Donovan."

And now she wanted to be my friend? An unexpected smile crossed my lips. All those times I'd hidden in solitude, hoping to avoid The Three, I'd forgotten how much I missed having friends…especially Skye.

"I'm Jordan," I said. My grin widened. "Jordan Smith."

She smiled back before returning her attention to the teacher who propped on the edge of his comfy rolling chair, his hands stuffed deep within the pockets of his khaki pants.

Wearing a cotton floral print shirt more befitting of someone who resided on a tropical island, Mr. Horowitz dragged his fingers across his full brown beard, discussing something called commensalism: a form of symbiotic relationship between two organisms where one benefits and the other neither benefits nor endures harm.

For a brief moment, I wondered if this term accurately described my relationship with Micah, or if in reality I seemed more of a parasite. I clearly used his home for a place to heal my wounds. As long as Gaia, Hydros, and Skye never found out, Micah and his family should be okay. But if The Three discovered me there…

I shuddered at the thought, a chill racing down my spine. *Best that never happens.* Without a second thought to Mr. Horowitz's lecture, I glanced around the room, intent on memorizing and mimicking the girls' mannerisms — how they slouched in their chairs, played with their hair, and secretly checked their phones under their desks.

Then I frowned. Unlike everyone else, I didn't have a phone. Hopefully it wouldn't be enough to make me stand out from the others.

Behind me, two girls whispered across the aisle. I strained to hear their discussion about someone named Jake liking someone named Isa, intently focusing on remembering every word and intonation of the conversation.

Listen and blend in. Because not only did I place *my* future at stake but unfortunately Micah's, Celia's, and Cam's, too.

Occasionally throughout the class, Mr. Horowitz paused to ask a question. When no one volunteered an answer, he'd randomly call on a student. Each time, I hoped to God he wouldn't choose me. But by the end of the class period, the students' conversations had grown louder than Mr. Horowitz himself.

And apparently, I wasn't the only one who noticed. The apathy of his class sent Mr. Horowitz into a tirade. He rose from his chair and slammed a book on his desk to silence the students' buzzing. "Perhaps you've forgotten that you'll have a test on this next week."

One boy raised his hand.

Exasperated, Mr. Horowitz sighed, "Yes, Mark?"

"A test on what?" Mark asked with false innocence.

Mr. Horowitz looked hot under the collar of his floral shirt. His voice rose a few notches but he didn't answer Mark's question. Instead, he turned toward the whole class and ranted, "If in twenty years I find you have a slab of arid land on a knobby hill with a sign that says Mr. Horowitz's Garden…and if in that so-called 'garden,' the only seeds that survive bear scraggly, thorny shrubs that grow low to the ground and are coarse to the touch while all the smart seeds don't even bother to land…then I'll know I've done my job. But until then—"

I had no idea what he meant by that analogy when a dissonant bell interrupted his speech and sent me flying out of my seat. Though a few classmates behind me laughed, they all seemed unalarmed by the noise and stood up, robotically shuffling toward the door.

Mr. Horowitz's face turned red. "Remember, people, the bell does not dismiss you. *I* do."

Though the few kids closest to the door bolted for their freedom, the rest of the class sulked back to their seats and sank into their chairs. Under their desks, they pulled out their phones, quickly texting a message like Micah had to Tessa during his video game the night before.

I snuck a glance around the room. Though I found Mr. Horowitz's tone harsh, no one else seemed fazed by it. Which led me to think this wasn't the first time he'd lectured them and made them late to their next class.

Nor would it be the last.

After Mr. Horowitz reluctantly allowed us to leave with what he called a "generous" minute of passing time, I squeezed out the door jammed with students eager to catch their friends in the hall before their next class began. Lucky for me, my next class lay just a few doors down so I managed to make it there in time, without asking for directions.

Unlucky for me, I had Algebra II. And I didn't even know what topics they taught in Algebra I.

Even unluckier for me, I walked in and immediately saw Micah. I supposed the guidance counselor thought it might help ease my adjustment by having a familiar face in my classes.

And her plan probably would've worked...if that familiar face didn't despise me.

After showing the teacher, Mr. Pulanski, my admit slip, I passed by Micah's desk and took the last empty seat in his row.

Micah's phone hummed, vibrating on his desktop. He picked it up, and then rolled his eyes. "It's for you," he said with annoyance. He reached over the kid sitting between us to hand me his phone.

I grabbed it, looking at him in confusion.

"Well, hurry up," he prodded. "Class'll start any second." He made a sign with his thumb and pinky, placing them up to his ear as if he talked on his phone.

So I mimicked Micah's behavior and placed the phone by my head. "Yes?"

"Hey, Jordan. S'up?"

When I heard Sully's voice mysteriously transmitted to my ear, I immediately released my grip, assuming the thing was possessed. Micah looked at me, more agitated than usual for dropping his phone. I scrambled to pick his phone off the floor, finally understanding why Micah and every other student except me checked them with eagerness and regularity. Instant contact with any friend, day or night. What more could you ask for?

"How's your first day going so far?" Sully's voice asked.

"Um. Okay, I guess."

"Cool. Gotta go."

"Oh. All right." Before I had a chance to say good-bye, Sully ended the call. I blinked, staring at Micah's phone for a second before passing it back to him. He stuffed it in his pocket just as the bell rang again.

Instantly, I felt lost in a world of what Mr. Pulanski called coefficients and variables while he explained how to solve systems of equations by substitution and elimination. After struggling to process his examples for a quarter of an hour, I gave up. Unlike my last class, here I found no muffled conversations for me to listen in on, either. So with nothing better to do, I put my head down on the desk like a few other students.

The grueling morning dragged on for what seemed like forever. By the time I finished my math, art, and British Lit classes, my brain entered shutdown mode. Exhausted, I wanted nothing better than to find a quiet space to myself where I could eat my lunch in peace.

But when I entered the crowded lunchroom that buzzed with chattering teens, I realized my request seemed impossible to meet, unless I sat by the windows.

I headed in that direction when Sully waved me over. "Hey, Jordan," he called. "I saved you a seat." He tapped the bench next to him.

I sighed, spotting Micah also at that table, sandwiched between Tessa and another girl whose name I'd already forgotten. And looking the happiest I'd seen him yet.

Figures. I plopped down next to Sully and opened my bag lunch, wondering what Celia had thrown inside during our morning rush out the door.

"Jordan, do you know everyone already?" Sully asked, gesturing around the table.

I shook my head. Though I'd seen most of these people at one time or another throughout the morning, I couldn't recall a single name, except for Tessa Bradshaw's.

"Okay, guys, this's Jordan. And Jordan, this's everyone: Isa, Jake, Liz. And you know Micah."

But Micah didn't hear him. Either that or he deliberately chose to ignore me.

"And Tessa, Justin, Karli, and me, of course."

By Karli's frown, I could tell she didn't look pleased with him devoting this much attention to me, even on my first day.

Just then, Bethany Donovan skittered across the floor and dropped her lunch tray between me and Sully so fast I could barely move my bag out of the way.

"Oh, and hey, Bethany," Sully finished, looking awfully surprised to see her joining their table for lunch.

Bethany squeezed her tiny frame into the even tinier space left on the bench, effectively bumping my cast into Isa—who shot me a nasty look. I offered a small, "Sorry," but it didn't erase her irritation.

"Hi, Jordan. Hi, Sully," Bethany said, curt and businesslike. She swooshed her curly blond hair to one side. Then she turned to Micah, batted her eyelashes once, and gushed, "Hi, *Micah.*"

Micah looked up as if noticing her for the first time. Giving Bethany a withering look, he nodded slightly in recognition before returning to his conversation with Karli and Liz.

Still, it seemed like more recognition than he'd given me.

Sully leaned forward to grab my attention again. "Think you know everyone, Jor — ?"

But Bethany interrupted, "I can't believe Mr. Horowitz kept us after class. *Again.* Can you?" Without waiting for a response, she continued, "And then you should've seen what happened in choir. It was ridiculous! Mrs. Watkins actually made us stand on the risers singing the same song for the whole period. Now the stupid thing's stuck in my head and — "

I blinked, my head hurting from trying to keep up with her incessant chatter. I leaned forward and whispered to Sully across Bethany's tray, "Is she always like this?"

With a shrug, he rolled his eyes, and then took another bite of his sandwich.

Talking nonstop, Bethany ate little of her lunch. Her gaze remained fixed on Micah the entire time. I wondered if she seemed as interested in being my friend as I'd thought. Or if I provided a convenient excuse to get closer to Micah.

In the middle of chewing my first bite, I noticed Karli sitting across the table. She glared at me through narrowed eyes and then shot Sully a possessive look before returning to her meal. I got the feeling she hated having me and the chattering Bethany sitting next to her guy.

Squeezed into my narrow space on the bench, I didn't look up from my apple again, eager for the lunch period to end.

CHAPTER FIVE

I walked with Micah and Sully to our next class.

Okay, scratch that. Actually, it was more like Micah walked five paces in front of me and Sully, even though we all headed to the same American History class.

Unlike Mr. Horowitz's casual beachcomber style, this teacher appeared bookish, wearing a tweed jacket and small round bifocal glasses that perpetually slid down his nose. With thinning hair combed over the shiny bald spot on top of his head, he introduced himself as Mr. Tabor, gave me a weak handshake, and then directed me to an empty desk in the back of the room.

While he spoke to the class, I soon battled imminent sleep, listening to his dull, monotonic voice delve into length about one of our past presidents and naturalists, Teddy Roosevelt. I found it confusing that society would regard someone who hunted a bunch of rare, large mammals a "naturalist."

The room seemed so warm. My desk so inviting. I hadn't realized before how tired I was after the zombie nightmare. Shaking my head to refocus, I pressed my Primrose Passion fingernails into my skin, hoping to make myself more alert as the lecture continued in anguishing detail. Only nothing worked. Sneaking a glance around the room, I searched for a nearby conversation to preoccupy me instead, but I had no such luck. Mr. Tabor droned on about Roosevelt's "Speak softly and carry a big stick" policy, and one student after another drifted away.

In the row next to me, Micah struggled to take notes, his eyes glazing over. Across the room, I saw Sully's head bob, fighting impending slumber. A few moments later, he succumbed and laid his head upon his folded arms across the desktop.

In a last resort to combat my sleep-induced trance, I cracked open my book and flipped through the pages, wondering if I'd missed anything more interesting than this class during my last jump to the present time.

I passed a bunch of pictures of presumably famous people I didn't recognize and stopped on a picture, pausing to read the caption beneath.

"Oh, my God!" I gasped, cupping both hands over my mouth. I stared in disbelief at a photograph of a mushroom cloud that ended the Second World War. *There were* two *of them?*

"Jordan?" Mr. Tabor asked. He pushed his bifocals up his nose. "Do you have something to share with the class?"

"Oh, I...um," I stammered. My face flushed hot and I sank lower in my seat. "No. I'm sorry."

Mr. Tabor released an irritated sigh. "Okay, then, class.

Who can remember why President Roosevelt pushed to complete the Panama Canal?"

No one raised a hand.

After waiting for Mr. Tabor to return to his notes, I quickly glanced next to me, noticing Micah perked up, but not because of the lecture. When I caught his eye, he shot me a quizzical look.

"Oops," I mouthed to him with a sheepish smile before returning my attention to the book, eager to discover what else I had missed in my fiery jump through time.

I thumbed through to the next chapter, pausing on a color photograph of someone dressed in a protective white suit. His mirrored face shield depicted another similarly clad figure and the American flag on a vast cratered surface, devoid of other life. The caption below read, *Apollo 11 Eagle Moon Landing*.

"I don't believe it," I whispered, too low for Mr. Tabor to hear. But not too low for Micah. I peeked over my shoulder to see him craning his neck across the aisle.

Be more discreet! Only I never imagined I had missed so much. World Wars, a moon landing…what else could've happened? Going back a few chapters, I found a nationwide Depression. And when I leapt ahead, I saw more titles about wars in Korea, Vietnam, and Iraq. Soon Micah started flipping through the pages of his book, too, trying to keep pace with me.

Presidential assassinations, civil rights movements, terrorist attacks, school shootings, revolutions in the Middle East—every page I encountered held another unbelievable headline. My head reeled, attempting to comprehend them all.

Start with baby steps, Jordan. I closed my eyes, thinking back to the last place and time I remembered: Chicago in October 1871.

I skipped ahead to the index in the back of the book and looked up *Chicago*. Suddenly, my face paled. A wave of nausea passed over me when I read the subheading, Great Chicago Fire, 347.

Coincidence, I convinced myself. Not a chance I started it. It couldn't be the same one.

I turned to page 347, my throat growing excruciatingly dry. I read the first sentence:

The Great Chicago Fire raged from late Sunday, October 8 to early Tuesday, October 10, 1871.

October of 1871.

"Oh. My. God." I clasped my hand over my mouth, my eyes widening. "It can't be." Despite the pain of ascertaining the truth, I forced myself to keep reading.

The conflagration began around 9 P.M. in or near a small barn that bordered the alley of DeKoven Street. Aided by the city's abundant supply of wood buildings, a recent drought, and strong winds –

"No way." I breathed.

Skye.

I really hadn't meant to start a fire in that old barn. She just startled me and the flames came out unexpectedly. It was my only way to stop her. And just as unexpectedly, the entire scene abruptly played back in vivid detail.

I fled on horseback with Skye in close pursuit. Startled, I screamed, "Leave me alone!" Before I knew it, another agonizing burst of fire erupted from my trembling hand. Then she manipulated the flames to her will, driving them from building to building on the backs of her violent winds.

I read on...

The blaze quickly spread, eventually destroying approximately 4 square miles, killing more than 300 people, and leaving 100,000 others homeless.

I couldn't bear to look at another word as I imagined all those people, homeless — or worse — because of *me*.

I felt awful. Terribly, dreadfully, awful.

Leaning back in my chair, beads of guilt-ridden sweat broke across my brow. It seemed like a vice gripped my heart and squeezed it to oblivion. I buried my face in my hands, wishing I could alter the course of history to erase my unintentional mistakes. All of a sudden, I remembered that everything would be repeated — perhaps worse this time — if I blew my cover now. In fear, my eyes darted around the room, trying to see if anyone else had noticed my unexpected change in behavior.

Apparently, they had.

Micah wore one eyebrow perched high on his forehead, studying me with a mixture of curiosity and embarrassment. The look on his face begged, *Why do I have to live with such a dork?* Karli, Liz, Jake, and a couple of others sitting near me whose names I couldn't recall woke up and stared at me with utter shock and disbelief.

In fact, only Sully remained fast asleep, and Mr. Tabor, who stood with his back toward the class and wrote a set of dates on the board, seemed oblivious to my reactions.

What was I thinking? I closed the textbook and pulled out my notebook. My hand frantically scribbled across the page, hopefully to give the impression of taking copious notes. In reality, I scrawled nothing but dribble as my mind raced through the events in Chicago again. Did Skye even know what she did? Did she even care?

I guessed a "no" to the latter question. And if she had lost all feeling for humanity, that only meant one thing — our next encounter would prove far more destructive.

I glanced down at my cast, knowing I must do everything in my power to remain inconspicuous until my arm healed. Only then would I be ready to take her on again.

The rest of the period lasted an eternity while I struggled to devise a new plan in preparation for their return.

Almost a minute before the bell rang, Sully woke in a puddle of drool on his desktop. While a couple of kids laughed, I collected my books and prepared to make a fast exit. Out of the corner of my eye, I spotted Micah edging toward the aisle, undoubtedly anxious to question me about my repeated outbursts in class. I stared back at the clock, waiting for the second hand to make its last click before the bell rang, then darted out of the room, praying Micah couldn't catch up.

My heart thudding loudly inside my chest, I raced down the hall through the throngs of students milling around their lockers. What happened if they found me before the cast came off? I swallowed hard, certain of the truth. Everyone here would die.

It seemed bad enough to learn about the fire in Chicago in a book. I could not, would not, let that happen again.

Stay hidden. Stay smart. If only for six weeks until my arm healed. How hard could that be?

CHAPTER SIX

Somehow, I made it through the rest of the school day without drawing any more unnecessary attention to myself. The entire walk home, Micah didn't speak a word to me. Instead, he remained a fixed distance of ten feet or more in front of me, almost like a bothersome pet trailed behind as he texted one friend after another on his phone. Already, I felt irritated with his pompous attitude and constant disregard. And here the school counselor thought it would ease my adjustment to place me in some of his classes. Instead, it made things worse. Why couldn't I have lived with Sully instead? At least *he* spoke to me.

The second I walked in the front door, I made a beeline for the basement, dropped my backpack on the futon, and headed back upstairs, intending to go somewhere far away to think of a new plan. I couldn't stay here any longer. Not when Micah's attitude drove me crazy.

I turned to leave my bedroom, but found Micah leaning against the doorway.

"So what was all that about?" he asked, his eyes narrowing slightly.

"Huh?" I muttered, confused. Now he wanted to talk? Then why bother to ignore me the whole way home?

"Today in class. You were acting awfully weird," he continued.

Don't get started, Jordan. Find a reason to go. Now.

So I decided to play ignorant. "I really don't know what you're talking about."

I moved to leave, but Micah's arm spanned the doorway, blocking my exit.

"Fess up," he demanded.

"To what?"

"Something's up. I saw what pages you were looking at... The Chicago Fire, World War II, astronauts landing on the moon."

"What's the big deal?" I asked.

"That's exactly what I want to know. Why were you acting like that?"

I gave an awkward laugh. "Like what?"

"Like they're front-page headlines, that's what. Something's wrong with you and I don't think it's your 'amnesia,'" he said, making quotation marks in the air with his fingers.

His words stung. *Something's wrong with me.* "Maybe I just like reading about history," I retorted.

"No one likes it *that* much. Especially not in Mr. Ta-*boring*'s class."

"Well, maybe *I* do."

"Oh, give it up, Jordan. Lying's not your strength."

Okay. Enough with the insults for one day. I attempted to barrel through Micah's arm, but he locked his elbow to barricade the door.

"Not until you tell me the truth," he said coolly.

"I already have," I barked, my nostrils flaring. I gritted my teeth, fuming. My hands instinctively balled into fists, just in case my rising fury released something I'd regret. I never used my power for anything but defense against The Three, and never once on a mortal, though it seemed a little tempting at the moment. My blood boiled, charging up my veins and threatening to erupt through my palms.

His eyes narrowed to a cold glare of distrust. He grumbled, "Whatever."

I fought to restrain myself from doing something I'd regret, ignoring the breathlessness that choked my throat, sick of his snide remarks, sick of his hatred for me, sick of *him*. None of this would've happened if I didn't fall into the road, if he didn't hit me, if I didn't break my arm and end up trapped here, listening to his complaints about how much I inconvenienced his freedom and complicated his existence.

Spinning on my heels, I marched back to my room and snarled, "Sorry I ruined your life!" I almost slammed the door shut to emphasize the finality of our argument when I heard a small sniffle.

Is that Micah?

Slowly, I turned, doubtful of the source of the sound. Yet sure enough, I noticed Micah's head bent over. His back slid down the doorway as he slumped to the floor. His shoulders quivered in silent sobs.

Oh, God. What did I do now?

I sighed, letting the pent up anger diffuse from my veins before I took a few measured steps toward Micah. He slouched over, his elbows resting on his knees and his palms covering his face. I shifted my weight from one hip to the other, and then I crossed my arms over my chest and mumbled, "Sorry."

He didn't look up or reply.

I took another deep breath, unfolding my arms. That didn't come out as much of an apology. Kneeling beside him, I added, "I'm sorry. I shouldn't have snapped at you. I'd probably feel the same if our positions were reversed."

Micah wiped his nose across his sleeve. "It's not that."

I blinked. "It's not?"

He shook his head.

"You mean, you don't hate me?" I wagered.

He shook his head again, slower and more deliberate this time.

"Then what is it?"

Micah exhaled deeply. "I can't take it anymore. I can't handle the guilt I feel every time I see you."

"Guilt? Why's that?"

He looked up long enough to roll his eyes at me. "Because I almost killed you." The words slid off his tongue with an acid tone.

"But you didn't," I replied casually.

"But I could've."

Holding up my cast, I added, "Really, I'm fine. I can't believe you're so worried about this. It's nothing. Believe me, I've been in worse predicaments before."

Much, much worse.

I expected his mood to lighten, now that my nonchalant attitude officially released him of his guilt. Instead, his head hung lower as a series of sobs raked his body.

He looked so wrought with grief from this whole misunderstanding that I wanted to reach out, to comfort him in my arms and tell him everything would be okay. But I reminded myself this was Micah. And despite what Bethany said, he'd probably react in a hostile way toward me, brushing away my efforts with explosive rage. So I settled for placing one hand gently upon his shoulder and murmured another, "I'm sorry."

He shrugged my hand off. "It's not just that."

Folding my hands in my lap, I sighed in frustration. Afraid to speak or touch him again, I rocked back on my heels, waiting for him to continue.

Long minutes passed in silence before Micah whispered, almost too low for me to hear, "You remind me of what I've lost."

My eyebrows pinched together in confusion. "What you've lost?" I echoed, extremely puzzled.

Micah silently nodded.

Confused thoughts raced through my head, waiting for him to continue.

"It was on March sixth, almost two years ago," Micah finally said in a small voice. "A storm was moving in so it got dark early that night when Dad went out. We didn't think anything of it. He always went for a run after work."

My back grew rigid. Dread filled my gut as I hung on his every word.

A long pause followed before Micah spoke again. "He used to run a lot of marathons— San Fran, Big Sur, LA. So he'd train a lot in his free time. Only that night, his run lasted longer than normal."

My hand slowly made its way to my mouth, smothering the gasp that escaped my lips. All this time, I assumed Micah's parents had separated or divorced — and that explained their dad's absence. Too wrapped up in my own problems, I never bothered to ask. Worse, I had a sinking suspicion I could guess how Micah's story ended.

Micah sighed before continuing, "The driver said she never saw him. He appeared out of nowhere. The ambulance arrived and there was nothing they could do to save him. He died almost instantly."

I blinked, frozen in my spot. Chills ran the length of my spine for Micah, not just for what happened to his father, but for what I did to him.

And then I realized the truth. Micah wasn't mad at me for losing his driving privileges for a month. Not at all.

"Oh, my God," I whispered, everything suddenly crystal clear in my mind. "And then I was in the road…"

Micah nodded.

"And you almost…"

His mouth dropped into a frown. "Exactly."

My shoulders slumped forward as my head fell into my hands. "No wonder Celia was so pissed."

"Bingo."

"I am *so* sorry."

It took Micah a long, long time to respond. And when he finally did, his words surprised me. I didn't hear words of forgiveness as I anticipated, but rather a question for which I didn't have an honest answer.

CHAPTER SEVEN

"You said your family's all gone, right?" Micah asked in a low voice.

I nodded, my eyes glazing over with fresh tears — for them and for Micah.

"How did they die?" he wondered, his words choked with sorrow. "In a car crash?"

I shook my head, unable to verbalize a response. In that instant, memories flooded my mind, like the gushing torrent down a flooded streamed in spring. I visualized our small country house, nestled among the olive groves in the hills outside of Jerusalem so very, very long ago.

The smell of dried herbs hanging in our open windows filled the air. My little sister, Sarah, and I skipped down the dusty road. We'd just visited our neighbor, trading eggs from our henhouse for a fresh loaf of bread, and anxiously returned home for dinner. Sarah happily skipped, her long black hair swaying back and forth. And every time she laughed, she exposed the gap in her mouth from her two missing front teeth.

But when we neared our house, I stopped. Goose bumps scattered across the length of my arms, making my hair stand on end. A young woman, perhaps five years my elder, spoke with our parents on the front stoop. Her russet hair caught the breeze, its tresses blowing wild and unruly upon her head. At the sound of Sarah's giggle, she turned. Her bright green eyes met mine.

"Jordan, this is Gaia. She's come looking for you," my mother explained. "She says she's an old friend of yours."

I bristled, unexpected fear coursing through my veins. "I've never seen her before in my life," I stated coolly.

Gaia's lips turned up in a crooked grin. "Surely you haven't forgotten me already," she said with feigned surprise. "Let us visit for a while. I am certain you will remember."

But her tone made me wary. I reached for Sarah's hand and gripped it tightly. I didn't want her to take another step closer to this beguiling stranger.

My father shot me a reproachful look, disappointed with my rude behavior to our guest.

"Come along, Sarah," Mother said, extending her hand. Against my better judgment, I released my sister, watching her skip the rest of the way toward our house. Never suspecting that would be the last time I saw any of them.

Alive.

Slowly, Gaia turned to me. "For many years, I have been

looking for someone like you."

"Someone like me?" I echoed, confused.

Her bold green eyes regarded me with suspicion. "You cannot possibly believe that I don't know about your powers."

"Powers?" my voice cracked. "What powers?"

Gaia cackled, her head tipping backward in disbelief. "Why, you are an Elemental. One of the four most revered forces of nature." She laughed cruelly. "And when we find the others, we will be unstoppable. Together we can shape the fate of man."

"I have no idea what you are talking about."

"Oh, but you do, I'm afraid," she insisted in a steely tone, extending one hand toward me. "I'll train you to use them. To accomplish grand feats you never deemed possible. All you need to do is leave your family and join me."

I crossed my arms in defiance. "Never."

Her cold, sinister eyes met mine. "Surely you will change your mind. Especially when I offer you no other alternative." She glanced in an assuming way toward my house with my family inside.

In an instant, I understood her presumption. Either I join her now, or my loved ones would perish.

My eyes narrowed. Blood boiled in my veins as I charged the house to warn my family.

Then everything happened in a blur.

Gaia stomped one foot upon the dirt and the ground unexpectedly trembled, knocking me off my feet. My mother's alarmed cries filled the air, adding to the tilting of my world.

I leapt to my feet and sprinted for Gaia, my hands balled into fists. She pounded her foot against the ground once more. Another tremor, greater than the first, rattled the countryside and jolted me off my feet. I heard my whole family yelp in fear. I crawled on hands and knees for the front door, but made little progress before Gaia pointed a finger toward the base of a nearby tree. In an instant, the ground beneath the tree caved. The trunk fell, blocking my family's escape.

Clenching my jaw, I scrambled to my feet and glowered at Gaia, anger consuming the pit of my soul. A gut-wrenching pain filled my heart, tearing at my chest, desperate to break free. Unable to contain the ache inside, it burst from its spot and radiated outward. Within seconds, an unexpected burn flared from my shoulders to my fingertips.

Glancing at my arms, Gaia crowed, "See? I knew you were one of us."

Puzzled, I gaped at my hands in utter astonishment. Flames raged inside my palms as if I brandished a weapon of pure destruction. A frightened gasp escaped my lips.

"Hmm," Gaia snorted. "Perhaps you truly didn't know."

But *she* knew. And that explained her visit. Her threat against my family echoed in my head. In that instant, my initial surprise at finding my hands painfully doused in fire seemed insignificant. I decided I must destroy her before she touched my family.

With an agonizing groan, I raised my hands and pointed them at Gaia's face. Focusing all of my rage outward at my new threat, I shot bursts of flames from my fingertips toward her in a powerful stream.

Yes! I did it, I congratulated myself.

But Gaia dodged the stream, deftly stamping her foot again to rock the ground beneath my feet, making my knees wobble and sending my stream of fire off course. Horrified, I watched helplessly. My molten balls of fire hit the roof of our home instead…and quickly set it ablaze.

A terrifying scream escaped my lips at the panicked cries of my family trapped inside. Sarah's shrieks pierced my ears. I rose to my feet, aiming my hands at Gaia once more with the intent to disable her for good so I could rescue my family from the burning house. Only before I could act, Gaia crushed her foot against the earth once more. Sarah's high-pitched wails suddenly extinguished as the tiled roof collapsed upon my family.

"*No!*" I screeched. My face steamed while blood bubbled in my veins. My eyes burned hot until it felt like glowing embers masked the normal black of my irises. I crumpled to the ground, sobbing uncontrollably, unable to believe what just happened…what *I* did to my own flesh and blood.

"Who are you?" I demanded between sobs. Tears stung my eyes but did little to soothe the grief in my heart.

"The same as you. I am Gaia, the Elemental for Earth. And you are Pyr, the Elemental—"

"For Fire," I finished for her, the words sticking in my throat. I studied my hands, repulsed with what I had done.

"Pyr, I have been searching for you for a long time."

The way my name rolled off her lips, I hated it in an instant. I was Jordan, always and forever.

"Come with me." She extended one hand. "There's nothing left here for you now."

But instead of conceding to her request, I rose to my feet, ignoring her outstretched hand. Fury and determination ran rampant down my spine and planted my feet firmly in the soil. She stole my family from me, so I would steal back that which she most desired.

Myself.

Intense rage coursed through my veins, fueling the fire from within. Immersed in insufferable pain, I aimed my flaming hands at the ground, intending to create my own funeral pyre. I realized only one choice guaranteed she could not cause this type of destruction again. I must actually destroy myself. I stood rigid while flames lashed my body, consuming me with surprising speed. An intense heat wrapped around me and smothered the breath from my lungs. I fought to stand tall and brave while containing my cries of hurt and loss, but the heat grew too great. It burned my eyes, stung my throat, and pierced my nose. I gritted my teeth and dug my fingernails into my palm, forcing myself to appear stoic and defiant to Gaia's demands. Then I shouted, my bold voice ringing clear through the air. "I will never join you. Not in this life."

Her wicked green eyes found mine. She muttered, "So be it."

A small part of me expected Gaia to find a way to extinguish my flames. Instead, she placed her hands on her hips and watched me burn in excruciating misery, her lips turning up in a sly grin.

The world around me faded into blackness, but I had a sickening feeling that somehow I would see her again.

"Was it a car crash?" Micah repeated, louder this time.

I shook my head, ridding my conscience of that atrocious memory. "House fire," I murmured, knowing that explained only half the truth. No need to tell him that Gaia had tricked me into causing it. I buried my face in my hands. Sarah's wail continued to ring in my ears.

Then Micah surprisingly moved closer to me on the floor. He put one arm over my shoulder, pulling me toward him. "I'm sorry, too," he whispered in my ear, letting the confrontation of our original encounters vanish in an instant.

Wrapping my arms around his back, I returned his comforting hug. For a lasting moment, we sat in silence in each other's arms, feeling each other's pain.

I couldn't help but sense some of my emotional burden lift from my shoulders. It didn't excuse what I did. Nothing could ever excuse that. But it's a start. I released a heavy sigh.

Micah squeezed me a little tighter and his sideburns brushed my cheek. For a short moment, I felt safe. And normal. A small part of me wished I could stay and never have to run away again.

Then Micah's phone rang, shattering the silence. Quickly slipping from my embrace, he pulled the phone from his back pocket. Holding it up to his ear, he said, "Yeah?"

Micah listened, his grief-stricken face quickly brightening. Leaning back against the doorframe, he dragged his fingers across his short hair.

"No way. Seriously, she said that?" he exclaimed and leapt to his feet, laughing. "Oh, my God!" Micah headed up the stairs, his voice growing more animated with each step.

My safe feeling quickly dissolved. Letting my head droop back into my waiting hands, I closed my eyes, wishing I could be like everybody else.

CHAPTER EIGHT

In the couple of weeks that followed, I quickly slipped into a routine, making an utmost effort to appear as normal as any other teen—or at least as any other teen who didn't own a phone. At school, I walked down the halls keeping my eyes and ears trained on students' mannerisms and patterns of speech. In class, I quickly learned how to avoid drawing unnecessary attention to myself. Silent, I sat at my desk giving the impression of following the lecture and taking decent notes while avoiding the risk of having to answer a question aloud. And in case the teacher actually called on me, I kept up with my homework so I could provide a believable response. I didn't stand out in any regard; instead, I slid through the day, unnoticed by most, which suited me just fine.

Except one person seemed to notice me more than the others. Most days after school, Sully made his way to our house and included me in whatever they had planned. When he'd arrive, I'd take a break from my assignments to hang out with him and Micah in the basement. They'd set Zombie Dominion to a three-player game and teach me how to prepare my troops for battle. I doubted any of their techniques would ever prove helpful in a real-world application, but I certainly enjoyed feeling normal for a change. And most evenings while Celia prepared dinner and Micah claimed to be studying with Tessa, I'd help Cam finish his homework. Together, we'd sit on the couch and he'd read aloud to me. Then before he went to bed, I'd read one of his favorite stories to him as he snuggled under his covers. His bright eyes reminded me so much of my lost little sister that sometimes I felt like nothing had ever changed and she was still home with me.

Even better, Micah's attitude toward me improved dramatically since he revealed the truth behind his previous animosity. Granted, at times he still seemed a little bitter about missing his driving privileges, but for the most part he stopped ignoring me, though Tessa more than made up for it.

One day when Sully didn't come over, Micah asked me to play basketball in the driveway because he claimed he had "some time to kill" before he and Tessa went to the movies. I'd never played basketball before—but then again, he'd never asked just *me* to do anything before, either—so I couldn't refuse.

Even though I sucked.

"You're going down," Micah taunted. He dribbled the basketball toward the hoop and shot. The orange globe floated high above my head and swooshed through the net without even touching the rim. He rebounded the ball and bounce passed it back to me.

I sighed. Counting that last one, he'd already sunk ten

unanswered baskets and I hadn't managed to steal the ball from him a single time. Mimicking his positioning and offensive stance, I stuck my cast up to block his attack and drove the ball down the middle of the driveway, hoping to get a lucky break this time.

"Hey, you're not supposed to use that thing as a shield," Micah protested when I guarded the ball from his reach.

I smiled with smug satisfaction, then slipped past him and shot one-handed. The ball teetered on the rim before slowly dropping through the net.

"Yes!" I shouted in jubilation. Now I just had to make up those other nine baskets.

"Nice one," Micah said and grinned. He slapped me a high five on my good hand. Funny how it stung, yet felt gratifying at the same time.

A broader smile played across my lips and I readied for his next shot. This time I deflected the ball, sending it rolling across the lawn. I chased after the basketball then passed it to Micah, right as Tessa pulled up in her red Ford Mustang with the top down.

I gave a small wave. She didn't wave back.

"Micah?" she asked, sounding more than a little irritated. "Are you ready to go?"

"Yeah, Tess. After this shot." He rubbed his sweaty forehead against his sleeve as he dribbled back for another attempt. "It's all over now," he told me, too low for her to hear. The side of his lip turned up in a cunning grin.

"In your dreams." I bent my knees, copying the defensive stance Micah used whenever I had the ball.

He aimed and shot. The ball rolled off his fingertips, then sailed through the air. I leapt not quite high enough and missed blocking his shot. The ball had the potential of becoming another sinker. It hit the backboard, then the rim, but didn't go in. Instead, it rolled off one side.

"Sweet!" I said and moved in for the rebound. Micah beat me to it and snatched the ball, dribbling back into position for the lay-up.

"*Micah?*" Tessa called again, her voice more strained than before.

"Just one more," he replied, gearing up for his run toward the hoop.

Out of the corner of my eye, I saw Tessa roll her eyes, shift and turn backward in her seat, rolling the car into reverse.

Micah charged down the lane but I knocked the ball away from him. It rolled into the grass behind the garage.

"You'd better go," I stated flatly. I nodded my head toward her departing car.

"Oh, crap," Micah swore under his breath and sprinted down the driveway. "Tessa, wait!" he called. He leapt over the door and landed in the passenger seat. Mumbling an apology, Micah fastened his seat belt, giving her a quick peck on the cheek. His lips didn't erase the irritated look upon her face.

"See ya, Jordan." He waved. Tessa released the brake and eased the Mustang out the driveway.

"Yeah. See you," I whispered, giving half a wave back. I kicked a stone in frustration before plodding across the grass, begrudgingly picking up the ball from its final resting place.

Just then, Cameron exited the house, his soccer ball tucked beneath one arm. "Wanna play?" he asked, his eyes wide and bright. He batted his long eyelashes twice.

He acted so much like Sarah, how could I say no? So while Cam and I kicked the ball back and forth across the grassy yard, I contemplated my conflicted emotions. Did I feel mad at myself for telling Micah that Tessa planned to leave or at Micah for not electing to let her go?

Late that night I lay in bed. Back in Chicago, I ran across the reaped field on that sweltering Sabbath eve. Only things seemed different this time. When Skye startled me in the barn, I refrained from using my fire in defense, cautious of the destruction it might ultimately bring. I leapt on the bare back of the chestnut mare and sprinted down the dusty street. Then the horse threw me from her back. The Three closed in. I couldn't escape this time.

"Join us, or die," Gaia threatened, her emerald eyes trained on my face.

"Then end it," I spat, masking the fear in my voice. I expected them to drag me off to a fate worse than death like they had done to Skye so many years ago.

Instead, Gaia said in a chilling voice, "As you wish." She removed a dagger from her cloak and lodged its blade deep within my heart.

I flew up in bed screaming as sweat rushed down my brow. My pajamas clung to my clammy skin. Desperate for air, I kicked off the covers.

It took a few minutes to realize I hadn't actually left the basement of Micah's house. Chicago remained a long, long time and place away.

My pulse still thumping in my ears, I meandered upstairs, hoping a drink of water would settle my racing heart. Clutching my glass with two shaky hands, I sank into a chair at the table when a sudden noise outside made panic grip my throat. My eyes fluttered wide.

How could they find me here? Already? Rising to my feet, I aimed my good hand at the door.

Waiting.

The doorknob rattled and then turned. I locked off my elbow, ready to strike. The door pushed open a crack and Micah snuck into the house.

His face paled as soon as he saw me. "What're you doing up?" he hissed.

"I should be asking you the same thing," I muttered, narrowing my eyes.

He shot me a look like, *What's it to you?* Then he gazed at me again, his face softening at my haggard appearance. "Something wrong? You look sick."

I settled back into the chair, rubbing my eyes. "I couldn't sleep."

"The sky's not chasing you again, is it?"

"Wha —?" My face blanched and I gave a nervous laugh. "Where'd you hear something ridiculous like that?"

Micah shrugged. "From you. Well, you said *something* like that. You were kinda freaky when we picked you up on the road." Micah poured a glass of juice before joining me at table.

My heart thudded loudly inside my chest, wondering what else he had heard. Eager to change the subject, I wagered, "Rough night?"

With a heavy sigh he said, "Tessa's pissed."

I wanted to say, *You think? After all, you almost blew her off to finish playing hoops with me.* Instead, I managed an innocent, "Why?"

He sighed again, deeper this time, but didn't reply.

"Maybe you should say you're sorry," I suggested.

"But I didn't do anything."

"So?" I countered. "It couldn't hurt."

He ran his hand over his short dark brown hair. "I dunno."

It took me all of the next ten minutes to convince him to at least speak to her right away the next morning. Oddly enough, I didn't exactly understand why I felt compelled to help.

After considerable effort, Micah agreed to apologize. Flashing me an appreciative smile that surprisingly made my heart skip a beat, he headed for bed, whispering, "Hope you feel better in the morning."

"Thanks," I replied, smiling wider than I should.

But I knew that I wouldn't rest if I went back downstairs. So I stayed at the kitchen table. My eyes finally closed as the distant moon slowly sank beneath the hilltops.

CHAPTER NINE

The sound of persistent knocking woke me. Groggily, I lifted my head from the puddle of drool I'd left on the kitchen table and wiped my sleeve across my mouth. I stretched the kinks from my back and rubbed the sleep from my eyes when the knocking resumed. I rose from my chair and stumbled across the floor to peek out the curtains by the kitchen door. Strangely, Sully stood outside, raising his hand to knock on the glass again.

What's he doing here so early? I unlocked the deadbolt and dragged my fingers through my tangled mess of hair. Stifling a yawn, I turned the handle, careful to keep my pajamas hidden behind the door and slid it open.

"Hey, Jordan. What's up?" he greeted me with a wide grin.

I popped my head out from behind the door and managed a bleary, "What time is it?" Behind Sully, the early morning rays of sun peeked over the hillside, filling the misty valley with a rosy glow.

But before he could answer, the flutter of descending footsteps on the stairs filled the air. Celia burst into the kitchen in a flurry of activity with Cam close at her heels. She flicked on the TV and flipped through the channels until she reached a morning cartoon he liked.

Flinging open the cabinet, Celia pulled out a box of cereal and poured a bowl. She yanked open the refrigerator door, grabbed the milk, and sloshed some on top, then plunked the bowl on the table in front of Cam. "Just sit down and eat. Fast," she instructed Cam who was notorious for dawdling at meals.

Instantly entranced with a show about a boy and his talking dog, Cam slowly made his way into his chair as Celia yelled up the stairs, "Micah, let's go!"

Then Celia turned, noticing Sully.

"Hi, Mrs. T," he said, giving a small wave.

"Sully? What are you doing here?"

He shrugged innocently. "Just thought I'd give Micah and Jordan a ride to school."

"That is so nice of you. I completely slept through my alarm today. Did you eat breakfast yet?"

Sully shook his head.

"Well, have a seat. You know the drill. Help yourself to whatever you can find."

Then Celia spotted me standing concealed in the corner behind the door. "Jordan! Ohmigod, I thought you were already dressed."

I stammered, "Um...I..."

She didn't wait for my response. "Well, go on. You don't

want to be late for school!"

It seemed acceptable to take the morning off to catch up on my rest, but I knew Celia never considered skipping school an option. Rubbing my eyes again, I silently headed for the stairs, my body sluggish and sleep-deprived.

Sully offered me a sympathetic smile before opening the fridge to take out the orange juice. He asked, "What're you having, Cam?"

"Cap'n Crunch," Cam said, absentmindedly swirling his spoon around in the bowl.

"Then Cap'n Crunch it is." Sully poured a bowl and flooded it with milk.

"We're like twins," Cam chirped.

"Except that you're not eating," Celia reprimanded. "That's it, no more cartoons," she said as she reached for the remote.

In desperation, Cam jammed a huge spoonful inside his mouth until his cheeks puffed up like a squirrel hording nuts in autumn, but his efforts were in vain. Celia had already switched the channel to the news to catch the traffic update before she headed into the city.

By the time I lumbered downstairs and threw on some clothes, ran a brush through my tangled black hair, and mustered my way back upstairs, the traffic report had wrapped up and the programming shifted to the weather. I poured a bowl of Corn Flakes and milk, then joined Micah, Sully, and Cam at the table. But when I glanced over at Micah, he didn't catch my eye. Maybe he feared I'd say something and bust him in front of Celia. Again. Whatever the reason, he chose not to speak to me, so I didn't bother to acknowledge him, either.

"You know, Sully," Celia said, sounding a little less harried with everyone dressed and Cam eating. "I was thinking...I haven't seen Karli in a while. Why don't you bring her by our house tonight? I'm making burritos and we always have extras."

Sully's eyes fell to the table. "Thanks, but I don't think so."

"Oh. Okay. Well, how about tomorrow night?" Celia suggested.

Sully shook his head. "I doubt it. We broke up."

I looked up, wondering if the time Sully spent here hanging out with Micah and me had anything to do with it. Then I glanced over at Micah, noticing his face painted in surprise. "Since when?" he asked with sudden interest.

Sully shrugged. "Officially? Last night. But it's been coming for a while."

I knew I should feel bad for him. He'd hardly touched his food — an oddity for him — but my attention lay elsewhere. Wrapped up in the TV, I listened to the meteorologist describe a weather phenomenon that gained strength in Southern California. The rains that started a few days ago had unexpectedly intensified with no end in sight. Several counties had already issued flash flood warnings, advising motorists to use extreme caution when crossing moving water.

My brain ran through some quick calculations. If what they said proved true, that placed the origin of the storm at two weeks to the day after my arrival. Could it be coincidental?

The meteorologist displayed the extended outlook for the Bay Area. Though Sully related the details of his break-up to Micah, I didn't catch a word. Instead, my eyes remained glued to the greenish-yellow mass of storms on the radar, tracking its projected progress up the coastline.

And right toward San Francisco.

I swallowed hard. This couldn't be a normal storm front.

"My God, they're fast," I muttered. My spoon slipped out of my hand, leaving a trail of milk and Corn Flakes before it clattered off the edge of the table and onto the floor.

"What's that, Jordan?" Celia asked. A puzzled expression shrouded her face.

I scooted my chair away from the table, leaving my breakfast half-eaten. Panicked thoughts raced through my mind. Get supplies. Take off. Head for the hills, far away from the coast. This stupid pink cast would definitely complicate things but I could deal with it later. I'd cut it off myself, early if necessary.

"Jordan?" Sully echoed. "What's wrong?"

My dark eyes flashed with fear. "I—I can't stay."

Micah's eyebrows knitted together. "What's the big deal? None of us can stay. Homeroom starts in twenty minutes."

I shook my head, my face filled with fright. "It's not that. It's...it's..." I faltered, unable to form a coherent sentence in my head. Instead, I managed a rushed, "I'm sorry, but I have to go."

I made it halfway across the kitchen floor when Celia placed a firm hand on my shoulder to stop me. I sighed, knowing I didn't have time to listen to her reprimand me for leaving dirty dishes at the table or my used spoon on the floor.

Instead, she said, "Jordan, please." Her eyes flitted in Sully's direction then back at me with a pleading don't-hurt-his-feelings-because-he's-been-through-enough-already sort of look. "He came here to offer you a ride."

I pointed at the TV. "You saw it for yourself. The weather's growing worse. They're even predicting this has the potential to grow into a super storm!"

"So what?"

"It's not normal," I sighed in utter exasperation. "This is all happening...because of..." I took a deep breath, uncertain if I should voice my fear.

"Because of...?" Celia prodded.

I bit my lip, sneaking a worried glance over my shoulder before I responded, "Because of *me*."

While Micah and Sully chortled in the background, Celia studied me with concern. "Because of *you*? What do *you* have to do with the weather?"

My eyes darted around the room, wild with fright, almost expecting Skye to blow open the front door as she did in that old Chicago barn. I dropped my voice an octave before replying, "They're after me."

Micah shot Sully a confused look. "Who is?"

"I—I can't say." The less they knew, the better.

"O-kay," Celia said, her voice filled with disbelief. "And what makes you think these people are after you?"

"You heard him!" I jabbed my thumb at the television set. "That super storm! It's headed right for San Francisco. They know I'm here!"

At that moment, Micah and Sully doubled over in hysterics. Cameron laughed, too, but mostly because he enjoyed laughing.

Celia flicked Micah across the back of his head with a stern, "Stop it, boys!" then turned to me. "This is nothing new, Jordan. It happens every spring. We get a few weeks of some crazy weather and then everything's back to normal. Same old, same old."

I blinked. "But the meteorologist just said that it's the worst storm California's had in over a hundred years!"

"The media thrives on over-sensationalizing everything," she explained in a casual tone. "That's how they improve their ratings."

I crossed my arms over my chest. "Not this time."

Celia raised an eyebrow as she studied me with bewilderment. Or maybe she just thought I was paranoid. "Jordan, you're safe. Who could possibly be after you?"

I frowned. "You wouldn't believe me if I told you."

"Try me."

I tapped my foot nervously on the floor as I pondered her proposal. Finally, I decided, *Fine. Why not? What do I have to lose? Besides, maybe I'd actually feel better once I had a fresh perspective.*

A heavy sigh escaped my lips. "Okay. Here goes." Looking straight at Micah, I began, "You know how you said you didn't believe I had amnesia?"

"Yeah?"

"Well. You were right. It's not amnesia."

"I knew it," Micah said. He smiled with smug satisfaction, pumping his fist to hammer home his point.

I glanced over at Celia, her face shrouded with hurt. I felt really bad. All this time she'd offered me shelter, clothes, food…and I'd been living a lie.

"It's something *else*," I muttered and sank back into my chair at the table. My unsettling tone made Celia eye me with suspicion.

Micah and Sully exchanged a quick glance, as if they'd discussed this multiple times already.

"So what is it? You ran away from home?" Micah started.

Sully chimed in, "Had a run-in with the law?"

"You stole something?"

"Got caught using drugs?"

"You got in trouble for—"

"Boys, please!" Celia interrupted, fuming in part from their lack of seriousness. But I'm sure her rising anger stemmed mostly from the hurt I'd caused her.

I shook my head, swallowed hard, hoping this information wouldn't end up harming them in the end. "You've heard of the Four Elements: Earth, Air, Fire, and Water, right?"

Micah, Sully, and Celia nodded their heads slowly in confusion while Cameron piped in, "I haven't!"

I flashed Cam a knowing grin before uttering, "I'm one of them. An Elemental."

Micah choked on his cereal. Milk shot out his nose.

But before he could think up a witty retort to my absurd claim, I continued, "I'm not really Jordan Smith."

Celia gasped.

"My real name's Pyr. It's Greek for fire. And I'm not entirely mortal, either."

Micah coughed out a word that sounded awfully profane but I pressed on anyway. "I can travel through space and time, jumping from one fire to the next to escape the wrath of the other three Elementals. I don't know how I can do it, but I can." Meanwhile, Sully covered his mouth, yet did a poor job of confining his snicker.

Ignoring him, I continued. "They want me to join them so they'll have unlimited control over the planet. All humanity will bow to their awesome powers. But they can't achieve total control without me. So time and time again, they hunt me down."

For a few seconds, four sets of eyes stared at me incredulously before Micah and Sully busted into uncontrollable fits of laughter.

"I think you nailed it, Sully," Micah chortled. "She *is* on drugs."

"What are drugs?" Cam wondered aloud, though no one bothered to answer.

Celia placed a gentle hand on my shoulder, trying to seem understanding, even though I could tell she thought I was crazy. I quickly stood and banged my chair into the table on accident, then grabbed my backpack off the floor. Crossing the kitchen in three long, angry strides, I headed out the door.

"I thought I was giving you a ride," Sully called, trying to steady his voice between peals of laughter.

"I'll see you at school," I replied gruffly and slammed the door behind me.

But I had no intention of doing such a thing. After ditching my backpack under the cedar in the front yard, I took off down the road as fast as my legs could carry me.

I don't care what they think, I reminded myself while I ran. *I'm worried.* With the massive storm headed this way, The Three would soon arrive. Only a matter of time remained before they found me.

CHAPTER TEN

Pompeii, Italy, August 24, 79 AD

An unsettling stillness hung in the air. The birds and animals sensed my dread. I shuffled down the cobblestone street in my sandals and white tunic with a worn leather bag draped over one arm. Every so often, I glanced nervously over my shoulder, wondering if someone followed me.

Beads of sweat formed across my brow, and the late summer sun burned intensely, even early in the morning. Its rays bore down upon the seaside village swarming with Roman vacationers and hillsides lined with villas and vineyards. The steep flanks of nearby Mount Vesuvius glowed a brilliant shade of peach in the breaking dawn.

The shops had only opened a few minutes before and I had no food for my trip. The road would be long and arduous, filled with danger and hardships, but that didn't seem out of the ordinary for me. Ever since Gaia entered my life, I'd faced similar challenges on a regular basis.

Just yesterday, I'd overheard one of the shoppers in the marketplace mention an Oracle's renowned prophecies in the Greek city of Delphi. I instantly knew the Oracle presented my chance to understand the fate I'd been dealt. A few days walk lay between Pompeii and the Italian port on the Aegean Sea. But with any luck, I could find passage on a boat bound for Greece, then head across the countryside to Delphi.

Slipping around a corner, I dodged in and out of the growing throngs of people and horse-drawn carts on the busy street named Cardo Maximus and stepped into line, peering down the road for any unusual signs of activity. When it was my turn, I placed a coin stamped with a crude image of the Roman Emperor in the vendor's palm in exchange for a flatbread.

I scurried south down the Cardo Maximus, then turned west toward the bustling square of the Forum lined with imposing columns in the oldest part of town. Once I finished here, I would leave town and hastily make my way to Delphi.

Suddenly, I felt a tug on the strap of my leather bag, halting my progress.

A deep voice asked, "Are you going somewhere?"

My heart leapt up my throat as I spun, certain the Roman Guard had found me. My bag filled with stolen coins, I could only imagine what punishment I inevitably faced. However, fear has a funny way of skewing one's perception of reality.

Instead of meeting the stern face of one of Pompeii's protectors, I found my friend, Lucius, studying me with a concerned, almost pained expression beneath his cap of short, black curly hair. His broad shoulders stiffened beneath his tunic and he clenched his chiseled jawbone. His thick black eyebrows narrowed, transforming his typically warm, dark eyes into thin slits.

"You're leaving, aren't you?" His gaze shifted to my bag.

In all the time I'd known him, he'd believed my ruse, that I vacationed here from a distant land. True, it seemed inherently dangerous to forge a relationship upon a lie, only I knew nothing else.

Especially when the truth of my situation eluded even me.

My eyes brimmed with sadness. I hadn't meant to hurt Lucius. I simply thought if I left without informing him, I might spare his suffering on my account. Better he knew nothing of my sudden flight or eventual destination.

"I'll be back. Soon, I hope," I said with feigned confidence, believing my entire future depended on the Oracle's prophecy. She must provide an answer to the myriad questions that flooded my mind. Why did I survive while my entire family perished? How did I end up here in a foreign land, so far from home? And how did my fingertips erupt in flames of rage as a painful fire consumed my body?

"I don't understand. Why would you leave without telling me?" Lucius's face registered a conflict of emotions.

I frowned. "I, um..." I began, unsure of where my thoughts headed. The bag's straps dug into my skin as he tugged harder, expecting an answer.

How could I ever explain the truth to Lucius? Especially when I didn't entirely understand the truth myself. How did I become an Elemental? And what could I do to Gaia as retribution for taking my family from me?

Lucius would never believe any of this if I told him. No one would. I guessed it remained something I must keep to myself until the very end. It was bad enough to spend each day as a fugitive, stealing from the homes of the wealthy in order to survive. One little slip could land me in jail with the Roman guard, or worse…slavery or death.

I couldn't tell what fate might befall him if he discovered my identity. Pompeii proved the perfect place to conceal myself, moving from one unoccupied villa to another before the residents returned to their vacation homes. Yet with convenience came risk. The constant surveillance had made me paranoid, as if I felt watchful eyes forever bearing into the back of my skull.

Biting my lip, I looked away. "I only meant to protect you."

His cold, hard eyes softened. "Protect me?" He chuckled softly. He released the strap of my leather bag. "Why would *you* need to protect *me*?"

I shifted my bag further up my arm and rubbed my red skin, sore from the pressure of his grip. "It's too dangerous for you to be near me. You don't know what might happen."

"Near you?" he repeated with another lighthearted laugh. "So you think it would be better if I knew nothing about your trip?"

"Something like that," I muttered.

The side of his lip curled up in an amusing way. "You underestimate me, my friend. I am better at keeping a secret than you think."

I managed a faint smile.

Lucius slipped his hand into my free one. "Well, if you must depart today, let's make certain you are fully supplied."

"But I—"

Before I could finish my protest, he dragged me off through the crowded Forum. Stopping at one cart after another, Lucius bartered with each vendor, insisting to turn his spare change into a few more necessities tucked safely within my bag. Already I felt better prepared for the journey, thanks to Lucius.

"Anything else?" he asked as we made our way to the end of the busy shopping square on the far edge of town.

I shook my head. My bag dug into my arm, yet I didn't complain. "You didn't need to buy all these things for me."

His mouth opened in a wide grin that exposed all his teeth. "Think of them as something to remember me by... until you return."

"Until I return," I repeated, my heart wishing those words would come true. My eyes held his gaze for a lasting moment. "*Arrivederci*," I said, thanking him. Reaching out for his hand, I gave it a gracious squeeze. Before my eyes filled with tears from his unexpected generosity, I turned to leave.

Lucius's fingers caught mine. He spun me around to face him. "That's it?"

A puzzled look crossed my face. "Excuse me?"

"*That's* your good-bye?"

"Um...yes?" I replied with hesitation. What did I say wrong this time? Searching my brain, I tried to think of another local phrase or custom that I'd forgotten. Nothing came to mind.

A playful smile danced across his lips. "Maybe where you're from. But here in Pompeii..."

He never finished his sentence. Instead, he took one step closer, letting his fingers lightly brush my cheek.

I swallowed hard. He stood so close I felt his breath sweep my cheek. My heart pattered incessantly as my eyes locked with his. For a long minute, my previous worry dissolved.

"And you wanted to leave without saying good-bye," he teased. Lucius's smile lit his face. Bending down toward me, he closed his eyes.

All these weeks, I'd been too preoccupied with my own safety to think of him as anything beyond a friend. And yet when I should worry most, I found myself strangely at ease. I couldn't believe it'd come to this. *My first kiss*. Who better to share it with than kind, unsuspecting, nonjudgmental Lucius?

I closed my eyes, shifting my weight forward slightly onto my toes to meet him. I heard nothing over my thumping heart. Eager to experience something I'd dreamed about for so long, I stood taller, closing the gap. My lips almost reached his when a sonorous rumble rocked the carts scattered across the Forum. The ground swayed unsteadily beneath my feet.

I stumbled, falling into Lucius's arms. For a second, I assumed a sense of euphoria had overwhelmed me. But the panicked look upon his face suggested otherwise.

"What is it?" I asked. The ground shifted a second time beneath my feet. Screams of terrified shoppers filled the air.

His eyes darted around the square, trying to make sense of the turmoil surrounding us. Nearby, columns cracked at their bases, tumbling down upon unsuspecting villagers below. Only the lucky ones dodged out of the way in time. Cries of pain added to the clamor when heavy marble columns crushed the limbs of several shoppers, pinning them to the ground or rolling over them entirely, silencing their screams forever.

"Earthquake, I fear," Lucius replied. He grabbed my hand and darted off, away from the falling columns, right into the thick of people in the center of the square.

I lagged behind him, my overflowing leather bag weighing

me down. Time slowed to a crawl. The Forum swarmed with people fleeing in every direction. A frightened vacationer bumped into my shoulder, making me trip and skin my knees on the hard-packed ground. Lucius pulled me to my feet, dodging bodies as he pushed forward. A terrified horse reared up on his hind legs with a loud whinny. His owner grappled for the reins and the cart full of produce toppled on its side. We ducked out of the way just in time. A fissure opened in the ground before our feet. Lucius paused on the side, and leapt over the crack. I followed his lead but barely made my landing. I hovered on the edge, my heels floating freely over the deep fissure. I saw nothing but an inky black void threatening to suck me in. With a tug, Lucius dragged me safely away from the crack. My stomach flipped, realizing how close I came to meeting my doom.

Then Lucius turned toward me, displeased with my sluggish progress. His gaze met my bag that clunked against my thigh with every burdened step.

"Leave it," he said, helping me drop the straps from my forearm.

"No," I struggled back. "I need this." How could I possibly set off for Delphi without any supplies?

His face hardened. He placed a firm hand against my arm to silence my struggle. "*Leave it.*"

"But—"

"*Now.*" The icy tone in his voice demanded no further rebuttal. Against my better judgment, I let the bag slip off my arm and spill its contents upon the rattling earth.

Satisfied, Lucius grabbed my hand again. His eyes darted wildly across the chaotic Forum, searching for the best escape route.

101

We didn't make it far before a sudden deafening roar smothered all noise in the square. Lucius stopped in his tracks, his eyes bulging with fear. He looked toward the slopes of Mount Vesuvius. I followed his gaze and felt the color drain from my face.

A monstrous gray cloud rocketed out of its summit, towering above the mountain as a ballooning, smoky mass suspended in space.

"Almighty Jupiter," Lucius mumbled, his lips quivering slightly. His hand instantly gripped mine harder, turning my fingers white, then numb.

The massive cloud hung motionless, like a spire reaching high into the bright blue sky. Patches of black, gray, and white gases swirled violently, a visible sign of the immense force that raged inside Vesuvius. Fiery boulders shot from its peak, white trails denoting each path.

In all my life, I'd never seen anything like this. "What do we do now?" I screamed.

Lucius shook his head in confusion. Grabbing whatever they could carry, shoppers dashed toward the sea, away from the danger lurking on the inland slopes. Our hands locked firmly together, we joined the flow, shoving and pushing to avoid being trampled in the mass exodus from the Forum.

Amidst all the commotion, I spotted a figure standing calmly upon the crumbling wall that surrounded the marketplace. Clad in the fine white garments of a village aristocrat, the hem of her silken tunic glinted in the sun, embroidered in glittering gold threads. Her untamed russet hair whisked against her face. Then her wicked emerald eyes met mine, and I shivered in fear.

I knew that face. It belonged to a murderer.

How did she *get here?* But before I chanced a guess, I stopped suddenly and pulled Lucius backward, away from the throngs that fought to escape the Forum. I'd deal with anything to avoid confronting Gaia again.

"What are you doing?" he countered with clear agitation. We had a straight shot to the sea.

"We've got to go back," I shouted as I fought my way through the current of bodies.

For a second, I contemplated letting him go to guarantee his freedom, but the fright of being alone gripped my heart and willed my brain to weave my fingers tighter with his. Who knew that my blissful naïveté mingled with my arrogant, youthful inexperience would prove such a detrimental combination?

Still, Lucius didn't protest. Perhaps he assumed I'd found a better escape route to guarantee our safety.

Nervously, I glanced over my shoulder and spotted the ominous visage of Gaia remaining fixed in her position, the corner of her mouth turned up in a menacing grin. Though she made no attempt to pursue us, I had a sinking suspicion she devised an alternate plan, ensuring our paths would cross again all too soon.

We made our way out of the chaotic Forum and up the main street of the Cardo Maximus leading north through town, the winds shifted, sending the umbrella-shaped cloud drifting toward the sea. The fanning dark mass soon shrouded the bright sun, gradually transforming noon into night. Volcanic ash filled the air, landed like gray flakes of snow upon our hair, shoulders, and bare arms, and choked our every breath.

Pumice rocks and shards of debris rained upon the

stragglers in the crowded street. Fiery lava bombs fell from the sky, igniting everything in their path. People emerged from residences with pillows clutched above their heads. The cushion served as little protection for one unfortunate soul when a lava bomb hit her skull. Her body sprawled upon the ground, engulfed in flames. Frenzied pedestrians saw her body and fled, crying in terror and blaming the wrath of the gods upon Pompeii.

But I knew the truth. Gaia created this catastrophe. And she'd stop at nothing to get me.

The sky darkened, like a heavy velvet blanket draped over the town, pierced with balls of flames that dropped unexpectedly from the heavens. The ash fell thicker now, coating our hair and bodies with a muddy gray paste. Dodging flaming lava bombs, we sloshed up the street against the flow of refugees, and toward the cataclysmic power of Vesuvius.

Lucius and I ducked inside one building after another, looking for a sound place to seek shelter. Nothing seemed impenetrable to the destructive rocks and debris that rained upon the city. Reaching a wide intersection, I stopped, disoriented by the darkness and bedlam.

"Which way do we go now?" I shouted over the clamor.

Lucius frowned. His eyes gauged me with distrust. Moments before, he had successfully led us away from the disaster until I twisted us around, driving us back toward its source. Some leader and friend I turned out to be.

Releasing my hand, he shook his head sadly. He slowly spun on his heels to follow the wave of evacuees. But Gaia stood before him, blocking his escape.

Anger overcame my initial fear of encountering her again. "How did you find me?" I blurted, my eyes filled with hate.

"By your footsteps, my dear," she said in a derisive tone.

My ashen eyebrows knitted together. "Excuse me?"

Gaia released an evil chuckle. "I can feel everyone's feet upon the Earth's surface, of course. Yours happen to stand out more than most."

I cursed myself for persuading Lucius to follow me toward the hills. We would've fared better had we headed out to sea as he originally planned.

Glancing at him, I opened my mouth to apologize when I noticed Lucius looking from me to Gaia and back again in utter confusion. Apprehensive, he backed away.

But Gaia halted his progress. Placing one hand squarely upon his chest, she knocked him to the ground like a shock wave stunning his heart. He lay there, gasping for breath, unable to rise to his feet.

Memories of the recent loss of my family flooded my mind. "Stop that," I screamed, stepping over his crippled body in a protective stance. "Leave him alone!"

Blood boiled within my veins and down into my arms. My palms and fingers throbbed, growing painfully hot. Flames rocketed from my fingertips, aimed directly at Gaia's mocking face.

Amused, she ducked out of the way.

I prepared to launch another blast of fire when I heard a gasp behind me. I turned toward Lucius, expecting him to find relief in my protection. Instead, he blinked, like regarding a stranger.

I'll never forget that look of distrust upon his ash-smeared face. That I betrayed him by withholding vital information, that I alone bore the credit of leading him to his doom.

Tears brimmed in my eyes. "You don't understand. I

never meant to hurt you."

And to prove it, I closed my eyes, focusing my hate for Gaia and her role in murdering my family into a huge surge of energy. An agonizing wail escaped from the recesses of my throat as flames erupted from my palms, stretching from one side of the street to the next to create a wall of fire between her and us.

I looked back at Lucius, praying he'd excuse me now that he realized my intent, when a flaming chunk of molten rock fell from the sky, right above Lucius.

I dropped my hands, forgetting the firewall, and stepped toward him. Before I could shield his immobilized body from the deadly projectile, it landed upon his torso and crushed his ribs. Lucius screamed. His arms and legs writhed in pain and his body convulsed spasmodically. I dropped to my knees, pushing the fiery rock off his chest, but not fast enough. His convulsions had already quieted.

"I'm sorry. So sorry!" I wailed, clasping his hand between mine. For a second, Lucius's head rolled to face me. When his eyes met mine, they softened with forgiveness.

A wicked cackle rose from the depths of Gaia's throat.

"*You* did this?" I yelled, spinning toward her. "Haven't you taken enough from me already?"

My mounting fury made Gaia emit an evil, chilling laugh.

I balled my fists, raising my arms until they pointed directly at her face. "What do you want from me?" I snarled.

Gaia's laugh faded. Her voice sounded deep and guttural when she responded, "What everyone wants, my dear. Power, of course."

My eyes narrowed into thin slits. "Not me. I wanted my family. My friends. And you stole them from me."

My accusations hardly fazed Gaia. Instead, she continued, "Together we can control the future. We possess the power to shape the destiny of man."

Had I expected a similar response from the oracle in Delphi? An explanation for the curse I bore? The prophecy of my destiny?

"What do you mean?" I asked, straining to keep my voice steady.

Her emerald eyes glowed in a terrifying way. She chortled, condescendingly. "It's like I told you before. You are an Elemental. One of the four, chosen as the embodiment of the element, fire. And when we find the others, we will be unstoppable. We will yield limitless power over the forces of nature and the cosmos. Our strength will swell until we can defeat the Fifth Elemental, Aether, from the heavens. Together, we can save the whole Earth from his threat. Mere mortals will bow to us and forever revere our names. They will make us rulers over all."

How does she know all that? And why should I trust her to tell me the truth when she had done nothing but instill fear in my heart? But I said, "So you think that killing Lucius and my family will get me to join you?"

"There is no other way." Her voice turned steely cold. "You will join me. And if you do not, you shall perish and I will find someone else to take your place. Someone more willing to agree to my demands, I expect."

Since neither choice sounded desirable, I knew exactly what I must do. Though I might not have the chance to destroy her for killing my family and Lucius right now, that day would eventually come. With fresh determination, I looked at her, then up to the sky.

She extended one hand, encouraging me to take it. Instead, I stepped backward two paces and glanced up again, spotting a huge lava bomb that sailed toward me through the blackened sky. I stretched up one hand and with a sudden burst of pain, shot a spire of flame at the rock. The immense fiery rock collided with my shoulder, crushing my collarbone and flattening me upon the ashy ground. Flames caught my toga and spread down the length of my body with incredible speed. I howled, thrashing about in the blinding heat, wondering why I must endure such suffering. And wishing I could perish like poor Lucius to halt this recurring torture.

I glanced up at Gaia's ruthless face, certain she knew more than she revealed. Some day, I vowed to unlock her secrets…some day when I could focus beyond this agony. My mouth contorted, releasing another horrific wail while the fire engulfed every inch of my body.

Within seconds, the destruction of Pompeii vanished into blackness, sending me spiraling through time again. In that precise moment, I knew regardless of what future dangers might befall me, I'd never, *ever*, join Gaia.

Instead, I made a solemn promise…to do everything in my power to keep her and the other Elementals from controlling the planet.

CHAPTER ELEVEN

I never made it to the Oracle in Delphi.

I touched my collarbone, remembering the tragedy of that day as I sat upon the California hillside for hours and contemplated my fate. The other Elementals had already destroyed entire cities. What would stop them from annihilating the whole Bay Area?

Nothing. Except me.

And with them too close for my own comfort, I knew I should run clear across the continent, to the far reaches of civilization. Someplace where they could hurt only me and no one else.

I glanced down at my cast. The doctor said I had another couple of weeks before it came off and then I'd have to wrap it with an Ace bandage instead. I doubted Gaia and her crew could make it here that fast.

A few weeks. Then I'd take off on a chase to the ends of

the Earth where we would meet again in battle, just like every other time.

But a voice piped up in my head that said, *You're growing soft. You usually don't stick around this long, you know.*

Stupid conscience. Always knew how to rub things in at the most inopportune times.

"No," I told myself, "it's my arm."

Sure it is.

"Really. It's that and…I'm tired. Tired of running."

Well, let's see how tired you are when everyone you know ends up dead.

I spent the rest of the day in that spot, considering my past and my future. Only when dusk approached did I bother to head down the hillside and make my way back to Micah's house. My stomach grumbled angrily at me for fasting all day but my head felt clearer with the knowledge of what I must do, once free of the cast.

But when I walked in the house, I expected a warmer welcome than the one I received. Celia waited on the phone, her face wrought with grief. The second she saw me, she hung up.

"Where have you been? I've been worried sick about you," she exclaimed, louder and more irate than I'd ever heard anyone before.

"Um…" I began, suddenly understanding how Micah felt that day she interrogated him in the hospital.

Without pausing for my reply, Celia launched into a lengthy tirade about the importance of school and getting a good education to prepare for college. Life was difficult these days because of the recession and many young people in our society vied for the scarce job openings, so I needed to be as prepared as possible for entering the workforce. I should responsibly attend school every day unless I suffered from an injury or lay sick in bed. Skipping school soon spiraled into other problems like underage drinking and drug abuse and pregnancy when teens had too much time on their hands. And she made it abundantly clear that she would not tolerate delinquency or any of those issues in her home.

"So what do you have to say for yourself?" she asked in a threatening tone. "What was so vitally important that you decided to skip school?"

I thought of Mt. Vesuvius with its towering gray cloud of superheated ash. I recalled the flames that devoured Pompeii while residents fled in panic and dodged fiery lava bombs that dropped unexpectedly from the sky. I remembered how Lucius's body writhed in pain. Even though I pushed the molten rock off his chest, I couldn't save him.

Then I looked back at Celia, her normally styled short hair sat askew atop her head. Her deep brown eyes studied me in earnest. Nothing would make her believe the horrors I'd endured. Or what terrors might befall this entire region, all because of me.

Unsure of how to respond, I managed a small, "I went up the hill to think."

"Up the *hill*? Are you out of your mind?"

Who knew my simple reply would instigate a whole new tirade?

"There are way too many crazies out there," she continued. "Someone could have abducted you, out there all by yourself. Or a mountain lion could've attacked you. You do know there are mountain lions around here, right?"

Actually, I didn't. But I felt like I should say, "Yes,"

anyway.

"Don't you ever do that to me again! I was about to call the cops, wasn't I, Micah?"

He nodded, but more out of fear than affirmation. Fear that the blame could easily shift toward him for laughing at me during breakfast. That might explain why he looked so relieved when his phone buzzed to notify him of an incoming message.

"If you skip school again, you can bet your life that I will call the cops, young lady." She crossed her arms to hammer home her point.

Bet my life. What an interesting—yet appropriate—choice of words.

I swallowed hard. Alerting the authorities meant sending up a red flare to The Three pinpointing my exact location.

I opened my mouth to explain and then shut it again. They didn't believe me the first time I told them. What made me think it would be any different now?

Celia heaved a heavy sigh. "Speak to her, will you?" she hissed, facing her son.

Engrossed with his texting, Micah didn't answer.

"Micah?" She waved her hand in front of Micah's face.

Yet Micah still failed to realize Celia spoke to him.

"*Micah!*" she shouted in an exasperated tone.

He glanced up from his phone. "Huh?"

Celia threw up her arms in frustration and marched out of the room, muttering something about how she couldn't take much more of teenagers and our hormonal, adolescent behaviors.

"What was that about?" Micah asked me, slipping the phone back into his pocket.

I shrugged, in no mood for Micah to hound me as well. My appetite forgotten with this new wave of guilt, I headed to the basement and sank into the couch.

He followed me down the stairs and plopped alongside me. But he didn't reprimand me as Celia requested. Instead, he remained quiet. Maybe he was thinking about his last text.

Eventually, I decided to speak. "Has Celia always been like that?"

Micah's silence lasted a long time, making me think he hadn't heard me. When he finally answered, his voice came so low, I had to lean across the couch to hear him. "Ever since Dad died, I guess. She's gotta be the 'heavy' without him around to help."

"Wow." I shivered. "I can see why you didn't want her to know how I ended up in the hospital."

"You have no idea," he snorted in confirmation. "In case you haven't noticed, Mom's a bit overprotective."

I rolled my eyes. "You can say that again."

"Seriously, Jordan. I dunno what it is, but I think you fill a void in her life." He shot me a fast look before adding, "Or remind her of what happened to Dad. Like this is a way to make up for his accident."

I nodded slowly. Part of me could understand her emotions, especially since Cam reminded me of my little sister, Sarah. And after watching my family and friends perish, I felt compelled to prevent all of them from suffering a similar fate. Maybe Celia didn't feel irate with me personally but rather feared losing someone again.

"She'll get over it," Micah smiled softly, his eyes filled with sincerity. "She always does. Eventually, at least." He reached out one hand, placing it gently upon my shoulder. I didn't brush it away.

Instead, I took a deep breath and let my anger gradually dissolve. His warm hand soothed my shoulder and tempered my riled emotions. I looked up at Micah appreciatively, my eyes holding his for a lasting moment.

"Any better?" he finally asked.

"Yeah. Thanks."

"Don't mention it. Consider us even."

It seemed sweet of Micah to care for a change, even if only to pay me back for saving his date with Tessa by halting our basketball game. Shifting closer to him on the couch, I wrapped my good arm over his shoulder to give him half of an appreciative hug.

His body remained rigid and cold with reservation, which made me feel like I completely misjudged him again. Just when it seemed we'd grown closer, he stuck a wedge into our relationship that confounded me all over again. *Whatever.* I berated myself for initiating a hug in the first place. I lifted my arm from his shoulders to avoid annoying him further.

But before I could retreat to my room and avoid this awkward moment altogether, Micah relaxed. Surprisingly, both his arms slipped behind my back and squeezed me with reassurance. "Like I said, everything'll be fine."

I smiled, drawing comfort from his words and his embrace. I wished I could stay there where I felt safe instead of having to run away again and leave him and everyone behind.

Then my smile faded. My back stiffened. Glancing past Micah's shoulder, I spotted Tessa at the top of the stairs with her arms crossed in a confrontational stance.

How long had she waited there, watching us? I didn't even hear her come in the front door.

Instantly, I pulled away from Micah. He fired me a confused look, and then followed my gaze up the stairs.

"Oh, hey, Tess," he said, leaping off the couch faster than a thoroughbred out of the gates. "Jordan was upset so I was just…um…yeah."

"What a nice guy," she said icily, her eyes like daggers trained on my heart.

Micah bounded up the steps two at a time, then took her hand and led her through the kitchen. "So what'd you want to do tonight?"

The front door slammed shut before I heard her response, if she even bothered to speak to him. It might prove a long, long night for Micah trying to climb out of the hole he dug this time, especially when I offered him the shovel.

I sat on the couch, alone once more, wondering why she seemed to rip him away just when I needed him most.

CHAPTER TWELVE

"Ugh," Micah groaned, leaning against the refrigerator door, "will you tell Bethany to quit it already."

Sitting at the kitchen table, I looked up from my US History book. Mr. Tabor had assigned us a killer study packet for our next test that was taking forever to finish. "Quit what?"

"Texting me 24-7. Can't she just call you here instead?"

"She's not trying to get ahold of me," I stated plainly, looking back down at my book.

"What'd you mean?" He cocked one eyebrow skeptically. "She's *your* friend."

"Was," I corrected him.

"What's that?"

"She *was* my friend. Until I figured out she's just using me to get to you."

And believe me, it hurt when I initially made that connection. At first, it seemed like a pointless crush. But

116

eventually I realized whenever I saw her, she only talked about "Micah-this" and "Micah-that." She never cared to get to know me from the start. She just wanted an "in" with him.

"Whatever," Micah disagreed, taking the chair across from me. "Then why is she always asking if you're there?"

"It's just a front," I retorted. The words burned like acid on my tongue. "She just needs a reason to talk to you."

And she used me for that reason. Too pathetically insecure to speak to him on her own, she kept hounding him through the safety of her phone, hoping that maybe one time he'd actually respond.

Micah chuckled. "You're imagining things."

"Like I did the super storm?" I snapped. "You are so naïve. Bethany Donovan is completely, utterly, helplessly in love with you. All she needs is a reason to get you and Tessa to break up. That's why she sends you hundreds of texts. If I were Tessa, I'd be a little suspicious to say the least. All she has to do is catch wind of it."

Micah's jaw clenched. "You wouldn't." He shifted uncomfortably in his chair.

"No. *I* wouldn't," I countered. "What do *I* have to gain? But Bethany…she might."

"You're lying."

"Don't put it past her. At least if I were her and wanted you that bad, I would."

He narrowed his eyes, glaring at me.

So what did I do? Glared back.

After a long moment, he said, "You hate me, don't you."

"No. I don't hate you." Though I felt pissed at him right then. Why wouldn't he just leave me alone and find someone else to annoy?

"Then what is it? Why the hostility? Shouldn't *I* be the one pissed at *you*?" He muttered under his breath, "I can't believe it. A whole month without a car."

"It's almost over." I turned away. "Besides, I'm not trying to be hostile."

I just felt a little stressed.

I'd spent the last two days glued to the Weather Channel, listening to meteorologists describe how this atypical storm system grew worse. Ten inches of rain fell on some parts of Southern California over the last two days as the front made its way up the coast.

I really needed to get this cast off *now*. Unfortunately, the doctor said I had to be patient and wait another week.

Micah blew the hair out of his eyes. "Whatever. Would you just get it out already, for God's sake? I'm tired of all your cryptic remarks."

"Fine," I spat, my eyes filled with anger. "You really want to know?"

"Enlighten me," he replied, heavy on the sarcasm.

God, did he burn me up sometimes. Gritting my teeth, I mumbled, "I'm jealous."

"What's that?" He leaned a little closer, waiting for me to repeat it in an audible tone.

"I'm jealous, okay?"

Micah snorted. "Jealous? Of who? *Me?*"

Rolling my eyes, I snipped, "Oh, don't look so surprised."

"And why shouldn't I?"

"You've got everything." I unfolded my arms, gesturing to the whole room. "A home. Friends. A family."

"Yeah? And so do you. Didn't you hear Mom say you don't have to leave after your cast comes off? You're free to stay as long as you need."

"That's the problem." My anger faded. My eyes dropped to the floor. "You don't get it."

"You're right. But it's kinda hard to 'get it' when you never tell me what *it* is," he fumed.

Tears clouded my vision. I slipped out of my chair and slumped down the stairs. I couldn't look at him, couldn't speak to him. I just wanted to be alone.

"Great," Micah called from his spot at the kitchen table. "Don't answer. Like that's really mature." I heard his chair shuffle across the floor and his footsteps follow me downstairs. Standing in front of me, he jammed his hands deep into his pockets, waiting for me to continue. But when I didn't respond, his defensive tone softened a little. "Jordan? Are you okay?"

Sniffling, I shrugged my shoulders.

Micah sighed again before joining me on the couch. "What is it?"

I shook my head, knowing I couldn't tell him the truth. The danger loomed too near.

"Come on. You can tell me," he said, slowly placing one hand on top of mine.

Trying to ignore my pattering heart when he willingly touched me, I managed a reply, "I'm not safe here. It's not safe to have me stay."

Micah chortled. "Get real, Jordan. This is *Pacifica*, not South San Francisco or downtown LA. In case you haven't noticed, not a helluva lot happens here."

But it will, I thought, wiping a tear from my face.

"Come here." He extended his arms, wrapping them around me in a soothing hug. "You're trembling," he commented.

I tried to calm my emotions but my anxious heart fluttered. Certain things would worsen if Tessa found us again. I tried to wiggle free of his grip yet he held me tighter, refusing to let go.

My initial fury with him and Bethany still pulsed through my veins, making me hesitant to accept his reconciliation. But my tears slowly faded in the comfort of his embrace and my anger followed suit. I rested my head against his shoulder, hoping my nose wouldn't drip onto his clothes. Squeezing my eyes shut, I leaned into his chest, seeking comfort and warmth from the horrors that filled my mind, wishing I could feel truly at ease.

After a long moment of silence he whispered, "You're safe now." He sat so close, his words brushed my hair. "There's nothing to worry about anymore."

I closed my eyes, a shiver racing down my spine. Biting my lip, I responded in a chilling tone, "I hope to God you're right."

And if not…I'd find out soon enough if my arm had truly healed enough to take on The Three alone.

CHAPTER THIRTEEN

Car after car passed as I walked home from school the next day, mulling through the events of my last class. How could I be so careless as to get into a heated debate with Mrs. Bernard—in French, no less—over whether or not Queen Catherine de' Medici's strict policies against the Huguenots resulted in the Paris massacre of thousands under her sons' rule? What did ancient history matter? I certainly shouldn't risk my cover over something so far in the past. I chided myself to show greater restraint from this day forward.

Or I'd pay dearly for my mistakes. Just like every other time.

As I berated myself, a red Honda Nighthawk motorcycle chugged to a stop on the shoulder beside me. I turned, my heart suddenly gripped with fear, half expecting to see one of The Three.

Instead, the moment the driver lifted up the face shield,

I recognized his pale, blue eyes. I sighed with relief. *It's just Sully.*

"Want a lift?" he asked.

Why not? My backpack weighed half a ton and I still had several blocks to go.

"Sure." I smiled.

He reached behind him to unbuckle a spare helmet and passed it to me. Running my fingers through my hair, I slipped the helmet over my head. Then I threw one leg over the back seat and squeezed onto the tiny space remaining, careful to leave as much distance as possible between my body and his. I searched for a safe place to put my hands and feet to keep them out of the way.

"Your feet can go on those pegs back there," he pointed at these pieces of metal sticking out by the back wheel. "And stay away from the muffler. It gets pretty hot."

I nodded, relaxing a bit. Heat I could deal with. It wasn't the first time I'd been burned and I doubted it would be the last.

"Anything else?" I asked, still wondering where to find the passenger handles on this thing.

"Um..."—Sully chuckled in an amused way—"you're probably gonna want to hang on." He raised his arms to offer his waist.

Well, as long as he didn't mind.

I slid down the seat, my body resting against his back. I settled my hands lightly on his hips, wondering how he managed to get out of bringing a backpack full of work home today.

"Ready?" he asked and lowered his face shield.

"I guess," I replied.

He pushed my hands tighter around his waist, and then twisted the throttle to increase our speed. He shifted his weight to slide from the shoulder onto the road. I followed his lead, trying not to disturb his balance. It seemed like the slightest movement might upset the bike.

Each time he twisted his wrist, our speed increased, making scenes from my familiar walk home pass by in a blur. Within no time at all, we'd reached my street.

"Thanks for the ride," I said when my street sign appeared around the corner. But Sully didn't slow his bike. How could he forget where I lived when he came over practically every day?

"Sully?" I said, louder this time to ensure he heard my voice over the wind. "You missed my turn."

"How's that arm doing?" he replied. "Are you able to hang on?"

"Yeah, I suppose so. But—"

"And are you in a rush to get home?"

I thought about that for a minute. Most likely, Tessa had already come over. So I'd end up locking myself in my room until Celia got home from picking up Cam at daycare. Or go for a long walk, just to get out of the house. How did going for a ride with Sully seem any different? At least I'd have something to do to pass the time.

"Not especially," I admitted.

"Okay, then. Do it."

My eyebrows pinched together as I asked, "Do what?"

He revved the throttle. "Hang on."

I imagined that crooked grin of his lurking beneath his helmet and locked my arms in place. I tried to ignore the weight of my backpack straps that dug into my shoulders as he zoomed down the road toward the beach, before turning to go south along the coastline. We flew up and down hills and around the bends, the arid hillside whizzing past. A gasp escaped my lips. I squeezed my eyes shut, keeping myself close to Sully while he leaned in and out of each curve in the winding road.

"Do you always drive this fast?" I shouted over the roaring wind.

He gave a loud laugh for his answer and revved the throttle again, rocketing us around the next turn at an incredible speed. I tightened my grip, clinging desperately to his waist until my white knuckles turned numb.

After my heart made its way out of my throat, I dared to open my eyes again. Dazzled by the spectacular scenery of the rocky coastline and the vast Pacific that unfolded before me, my fears surprisingly subsided. Sunlight shimmered off the deep blue sea and danced upon its rippled surface. Waves rolled toward the exposed cliffs, rumbling and crashing against jagged boulders and outcroppings. Overhead, gulls swooped and soared on the rising currents, cackling to each other with glee.

For a brief moment, I rested my head against Sully's back and forgot all my worries. The chance of the other Elementals finding me after a minor class debate seemed very insignificant all of a sudden. I closed my eyes again, this time to feel the rush of the wind against my clothes, the power of the engine beneath me, the warmth of his body warding off the chill in the air. Even in the rush to escape Chicago on horseback, I'd never felt such a thrill like this. Probably because I'd never gone this fast before.

And I had to admit, I liked it.

I glanced over at the speedometer and saw the red needle push seventy on the straight stretches. A small part of me knew I should worry when little protection existed between our bodies and the black ribbon of asphalt that wound along the precipitous sea cliffs. *Give it a rest, Jordan. You've had enough to worry about for one day.*

So I did. Give it a rest, I meant, and allowed myself to soak up the scenery, the speed, and the briny sea air.

Eventually Sully slowed the bike and pulled off at a lookout point at the top of a steep cliff. When he removed his key, I loosened my grip, my muscles stiff from hanging on so tightly and keeping my legs locked in the same position. It took a minute to regain enough blood flow to my extremities that I could straighten my limbs.

Sully set his kickstand in the gravel at the edge of the lookout, then climbed off. I let my heavy backpack slide off my shoulders and land on the ground in a heap, eager to rid myself of the straps that dug into my shoulder and reminded me of how much I had to complete before tomorrow. I felt sick and tired of all the additional work I endured in my desperate attempt to blend in with society and remain unnoticed. So I walked over to the railing and joined Sully.

He took off his helmet and tucked it beneath one arm. A wide grin filled his face. "This is one of my favorite places," he said, leaning on the railing to gaze out across the dizzying heights.

"I can see why." To say the scenery looked spectacular was a gross understatement. Far below, waves rumbled against the rocky cliffs in a constant challenge of strength and perseverance. The coastline stretched for miles in each direction until its muted periwinkle shades of distant slopes faded with the sky. On the rocks below, raucous sea lions battled for the best sunning spots, changing their tiny nearby island into a moving mass of complaining tan and brown blubber.

Sully climbed over the railing, positioning himself on the side of the cliff for a better view.

"Do you always like living on the edge?" I asked, reflecting on the speed of the ride and now his proximity to the edge. Personally, I thought the railing sat close enough to the drop-off to make my stomach lurch.

"You only live once, right?" He chuckled and tapped the ground in an invitation to join him.

Interesting choice of words. I sucked in a breath and straddled the railing. The ground seemed to sway beneath my unsteady feet. Throwing my other leg over the rail, I quickly sat down, eager to keep my center of gravity low to the earth. It felt like the slightest of breezes threatened to sweep me over the edge.

Sully smiled again, pleased I took him up on his dare. "This isn't too far from where Micah and I found you, you know."

I nodded.

"Y'know, I probably passed this place about a hundred times growing up. But when I got my license, I found myself coming here more and more. Look out there," he said, pointing to a few black, glistening figures dressed in black suits that clung to their bodies. They waited patiently on long, smooth boards that bobbed on the rising swell. "You can see the big wave surfers."

We watched one of the black figures paddle his board swiftly toward shore as the wave grew in magnitude behind him. The surfer rose, staggered his feet on the board, and then barreled down the face of the wave. The frothing crest towered far over his head, threatening to engulf him at any moment.

"The waves get bigger than this sometimes," Sully added. "But I still think it's pretty cool to watch."

Awestruck, I nodded, imagining the rush of adrenaline that shot through that surfer's veins as he risked his life to conquer such a behemoth and come out intact on the other side.

"Someday I'd like to try out these waves," he said dreamily. "Some day."

"That sounds a little crazy to me," I admitted.

"Maybe a little. But it'd still be cool." Then he turned to me. "How about you? Do you surf?"

Though the sport appeared exciting, I knew I couldn't take the chance of ever entering the ocean again. Not after what happened to Skye and me after fishing in ancient Polynesia. And especially not with Hydros so close. The beat of my heart would travel toward her in a matter of minutes, like a homing beacon that alerted her to my current location.

So I fudged a little lie, "No. I don't swim."

"Really?" he said skeptically. The look on his face suggested he didn't buy it. "Not at all?"

I shook my head and looked away. "Nope. Never."

"What about skim-boarding?"

Puzzled, I glanced back. "What's that?"

His smile lit his eyes. "It's where you take a thin board and ride on top of the water that rushes up the beach. Like you're skimming over the surface."

My forehead crinkled. "So you still get wet?"

"Just your feet. But you stay on the sand."

I thought about that for a minute. It sounded kind of

fun—but at the same time, unnecessarily risky. "Thanks, but I still think I'll pass."

"I know a nice beginner beach in town," he continued. "The waves are nothing like here."

"I really don't think I should."

Apparently, Sully had no intention of letting up that easy. "And you can borrow my board."

I frowned, knowing I needed to end this. So I admitted, "I'm scared of the water."

"Oh," he said, disheartened. "Well, if you change your mind, the offer still stands. Just think about it."

"Fine." I smiled in concession. "I'll think about it."

We sat in silence for a while, watching one surfer after another challenge the immense waves. The breaking crests swallowed up a few, engulfing them in a sea of white. One actually rode through what Sully called the "tube" and came out unscathed on the other side with his fists raised in jubilation.

Then Sully sighed as if something weighed heavy on his mind. In a small voice, he said, "By the way, sorry about the other morning."

I forced my attention away from the next rider's attempt at tackling the massive incoming wave to mutter a confused, "Huh?"

Sully sighed again, deeper this time. "Y'know, when Micah and I laughed at you."

Though they definitely infuriated me, how could I possibly expect anyone to believe my tale? I knew I should've kept my mouth shut in the first place, but I didn't. Now it seemed in my best interest to forget the incident entirely and focus on bigger concerns. "Don't worry about it. It's in the past."

"Still, we shouldn't have laughed."

I looked at him, puzzled. Since when did Sully sound so genuinely concerned about his actions? "Did Celia put you up to this?"

"The apology, yes. But not the kidnapping," he admitted sheepishly. "You don't mind, do you?"

"No...it's actually nice to get away for a change. To forget..." I trailed off as a finger of clouds obscured the sun. The wind carried a sudden nip that sent a shiver down my spine. As amazing as it appeared, sitting here atop this stunning panorama, I couldn't help but glance over my shoulder at the clouds building in the south. I hoped this weather pattern was typical for this time of year.

Because I couldn't help but believe otherwise.

"Are you cold?" Sully asked, snapping me from my thoughts.

I shook my head. Not cold. More like *frightened*.

Behind us, the clouds collected over the mountaintops and obscured their peaks in a thick layer of fog.

Following my gaze, Sully frowned. "Looks like rain. I should probably get you home."

"Yeah. Probably," I agreed, surprisingly disappointed by the prospect all of a sudden.

Climbing back over the railing and onto the bike, I slipped my arms through my backpack straps and pulled the helmet down over my head, then adjusted my grip around Sully's waist. Perhaps the incoming clouds—or perhaps the disappointment of returning home to Micah and Tessa—made the ride back seem twice as long. By the time we reached our street, I shivered with fear. I could forget about the Elementals far more easily with the storm stationed hundreds of miles away instead of on the brink of town.

When Sully stopped in the driveway, I pulled off the helmet and said, "Thanks for picking me up today." I surprised myself at how well I masked the fear in my voice.

Shooting me a wide grin, he nodded. "Not a problem. See you tomorrow."

"Yeah. Sure," I replied, wondering how many tomorrows remained.

With a quick wave, he backed down the driveway and into the street. Even after his bike disappeared from view, I could still hear the rumble of his engine roaring down the road.

I glanced back up at the sky, growing gray and cold with the approaching storm. I shivered again before heading inside. Thankfully, Celia and Cam hadn't returned yet. At least I wouldn't get in trouble for skipping out again.

CHAPTER FOURTEEN

After school the next day, Micah slammed open the front door and dumped his backpack in the middle of the kitchen floor, grumbling, "I can't believe I got a 67 on my French test."

"At least it's passing," I said.

Micah shot me a spiteful look. Why couldn't I remember to hold my tongue?

"You don't understand," he griped and paced back and forth across the kitchen floor. "Mom's gonna freak. She always does when I get less than a B. You know why?"

I looked at him blankly.

"College," he sighed. "Everything's always about college with her."

"She just wants the best for you."

He rolled his eyes, "Thanks for the encouragement."

"I'm just saying…"

"Well, you can stop right there." He opened the fridge

door and yanked out a half-gallon of milk, drinking right from the container. I crinkled my nose in disgust and made a mental note to have a glass of water at dinner tonight.

I settled down at the table and opened my backpack. Last I heard, a meteorologist said the super storm had stalled indefinitely along the coast, making me question if the weather was truly a result of the Elementals or merely a natural phenomenon. So while I waited a little longer for my cast to come off, the ruse continued of blending in to remain hidden. Which meant I had a heap of work to complete…again. And if I didn't start now, I'd never get through it all before I crashed tonight. With a sigh, I cracked open my History book and pulled the lengthy assignment from my folder on President Woodrow Wilson's persuasion of the Democratic Congress to pass the Clayton Antitrust Act and create an income tax as home front reform in the years leading up to World War I.

I frowned. Sounded thrilling.

Micah closed the fridge door with a bang. I looked at him in surprise and noticed his eyes lighting up. "I almost forgot," he said, suddenly optimistic. "How'd you do?"

He said this as if I earned a lower grade, perhaps Celia wouldn't come down so hard on him.

I shrugged. "I dunno," and returned my attention to the book. Anything to change the subject. Or avoid it altogether.

"Aw, c'mon. Tell me," he prodded as he pulled out the chair next to me and turned it around backward, straddling like a rider on a horse. "Seriously. What'd you get? It's not like Celia's gonna ground you or anything. You just got here. She'll understand you've gotta catch up first."

I shook my head. "Drop it, okay?"

"Come on. Tell me." He reached for the folder lying under

my textbook. "Is it in here?" He quickly slipped my papers from the folder and sorted through them.

"Hey, give that back," I cried, trying to grab my French test. A wide grin formed across his face as he scooted his chair away from the table, safely out of reach.

I flew out of my seat to snatch the sheet, but he slid off his chair and dodged one way then the other through the kitchen, giggling to himself in an irritating way.

Conflicted emotions of annoyance and amusement flooded my mind, unsuccessfully struggling to regain control of my test paper. When I grabbed his wrist, he wriggled free. When I reached around his back, he spun the other way. I wanted to be mad at him but found it impossible when he snickered in such a lighthearted way. Instead, I found myself joining in with his laughter while attempting to wrestle the test from his grasp. Only each time, the little weasel managed to escape. How could someone be so infuriating and so comical at the same time?

Finally, I managed a strong lock on one of his forearms, twisting it high behind his back. With my cast, I reached around his chest. "Ha, ha," I taunted and yanked my wrinkled test from his hand when Celia marched through the door with Cameron.

My smile instantly faded. So did Micah's. Sheepishly, I released my grip and slid my cast out from around his chest, and then took a huge step away from him.

Celia gave us a sideways look.

"Micah just wanted to see my French score," I said flatly, passing him my crumpled test.

Micah smoothed out the paper, exclaiming, "A 92! What the...? But how'd you...? You weren't even here for the whole unit."

I shrugged. I should've gotten a 100 percent since I used to live in France. But Sixteenth Century Renaissance French sounded far different from the modern conversational French Mrs. Bernard taught us in school.

"And how'd *you* do on that test?" Celia turned toward Micah. She set her purse and keys on the kitchen, then poised her hands on her hips, waiting.

His playful demeanor quickly faded. "Not as good as Jordan, that's for sure."

"How '*not as good?*'" she asked while her fingers formed quotation marks in the air.

He passed his test to Celia. Her amused smile quickly wilted.

"Okay, young man. You know the drill. Hand it over."

"C'mon, Mom. It's not like—"

She stuck out her hand. Waiting.

Micah protested, "But I didn't—"

"*Now.*"

Micah pouted like a petulant toddler and fished his phone out of his jeans' pocket, dumping it in Celia's outstretched palm.

"Now you go wash your hands before dinner," Celia told Cam and ushered him out of the room. "And you," she said, pointing her index finger at Micah, "start on your homework."

With Celia out of earshot, Micah crossed his arms over his chest. "I still don't get it. How'd you do that good?"

The truth? I had a choice—either learn French or die. However, that minor detail remained another fact Micah didn't ever need to know.

So I gave a noncommittal shrug. "Let's just say I don't

have as many distractions as you."

Micah bristled. "And what's that supposed to mean?"

"Whatever you want it to mean," I retorted.

His face flooded with anger, his hazel eyes burning into me before he stormed from the room in stony silence. Suddenly remorseful, I followed him up the stairs only to have his slammed door greet my face.

Why can't I just keep my mouth shut? I slumped back to the kitchen and flopped into a chair, burying my face in my hands. *Why do I always manage to mess things up?*

A few minutes later, Cameron tugged on my sleeve. "Micah said he's too busy, so can you play soccer with me?" His bright brown eyes twinkled, wide and innocent like a baby deer, and impossible for me to refuse.

Pushing thoughts of Micah to the deep recesses of my mind, I managed a small smile. "Sure, buddy. Sounds good."

CHAPTER FIFTEEN

Finally his phone can't consume his constant attention, I smiled. I'd have a chance at reconciliation without interruption.

And that probably would've happened, if Micah actually elected to speak to me. But he didn't the rest of the night. Or the next day. Or the day after that. Each time Sully came over to play Zombie Dominion in the basement, I made a show of taking Cameron outside to practice soccer so they didn't feel like I hovered over them and dampened their fun.

Because that was precisely how I felt—as if Micah regarded me as the biggest nerd who'd rather spend all my time with my nose in a book.

He didn't understand the truth...that I only knew that stuff because I *lived* it. At least for a while before they found me again. Languages had to come easy for me. No other option existed.

I couldn't tell if Micah seemed mad or jealous. I didn't

get it. What did he have to worry about? I had to leave. And besides, Micah and I argued too much to ever think of progressing to another level.

The following afternoon, Celia returned Micah's phone privileges before she dropped Cam off at a birthday party and got her hair done. "You two will be all right while I'm gone?"

Before answering, I snuck a glance outside. The sky appeared a uniform shade of muted gray that threatened to open up at any moment. I guessed taking a walk to get away from Micah was out of the question. So I nodded halfheartedly.

With a wave, Celia led Cameron out the door with the present he had clumsily wrapped with lots and lots of extra tape and the card he'd drawn using colorful markers. I had helped him spell *Happy Birthday*. He added two exclamation points and turned the dots into eyeballs, adding a smile underneath. She opened the car door and steered Cam inside when Micah charged out behind them, calling, "Hey, Mom, can I have a few friends over?"

Celia sighed, buckling Cam into his booster seat.

"Please, Mom," Micah begged in the sweetest voice I'd ever heard him use.

Pushing the hair from her eyes, Celia sighed heavier this time, as she did whenever she rushed to get someplace on time. She climbed into the driver's seat and jammed the keys in the ignition.

"Fine," she conceded. "But only a few."

"Thanks, Mom," Micah said before whipping out his phone.

Celia rolled her eyes. She slammed the door shut and backed down the driveway.

What a manipulator. I tromped downstairs to grab a jacket.

I couldn't stick around here. Rain or not, I felt a sudden urge to leave.

By the time I made it halfway back upstairs, I heard a car pull up. *Probably Tessa*, I figured and slid my arms into my jacket sleeves.

I slipped on one of my shoes and another car pulled in. *Great. That one's probably Sully.*

Then I heard another car. And another.

What is Micah thinking?

Without bothering to tie my laces, I found him in the yard. Only I sounded bossier than I intended when I reminded him in front of Tessa, "Celia said a couple of friends."

Micah glared at me. "What's the problem?" he asked in a condescending tone. "Will we be too loud for you to study? Hey, I've got an idea…why don't you go run off to the library and *leave us alone.*" He slipped his hand into Tessa's, as if he deliberately tried to make me feel worse.

Tessa giggled at his remark and dragged Micah off to their growing group of friends.

"But your mom said—" I called after him.

Micah turned, his hazel eyes cruel and insensitive. "You worry too much. They'll be long gone before she gets back."

Though he wanted me to leave, I decided I'd stay. Micah might not appreciate my efforts, but I knew he'd need some major help to pull this off without Celia catching wind. Especially when Isa Estes walked over to the stereo and cranked up the volume. And Mark Wagner started unloading six-packs of beer from his trunk.

I twisted the volume down a notch and then raced over to Mark's car. "Put those away. Celia'll be back soon."

Mark looked at me in a confused way. Then his face

slowly lit with recognition. "Hey. You're like in my science class, right?"

I rolled my eyes. I'd been here over a month. "Yeah. That's right."

"Cool." A leisurely smile formed across his face. "And what's your name again?"

"Jordan."

"Jergen?" Mark asked in sluggish tone and reached for another six-pack.

"Jordan," I repeated, understanding why Mr. Horowitz grew so irritated in class every time Mark asked a question about something he had just explained. "And you can't bring that here." I removed the cans of beer from his hands and set them back in his car, then slammed the trunk shut. "Micah will get in a heap of trouble."

"Gotcha," Mark nodded with a knowing wink. "So are you and Micah like…" He made an obscene gesture with his hands, insinuating that Micah and I were "together."

"*What?*" How clueless could he be? "No," I exclaimed with extreme repulsion. "I *live* here."

"Ohhh." He nodded again. "Well, in that case, would you like to…?" He jabbed his thumb in the direction of the front door.

Eww! Completely disgusted, I spun on my heels and marched away, reminding myself to avoid him for the rest of the day…or the rest of my life. Whichever came first.

Headed far away from Mark, I brushed past Karli McDonald talking to Justin Doyle, her arms wrapped loosely around his waist. *It sure didn't take her long to find someone else,* I thought, wondering how Sully felt about that…and if he even knew. I looked around quickly, expecting to find him sitting with a bunch of people, oblivious to Karli and Justin's blossoming relationship.

Instead, I spotted him off by himself in a corner of the yard, his face buried in his hands.

Yep. He knew all right.

I glanced over my shoulder, wondering if Micah had noticed Sully in this state. Then I spotted Mark Wagner. He gave a casual wave as he took a step in my direction.

Eager for any excuse to avoid another painful conversation with Mark, I made a beeline for Sully and pulled up a chair beside him. "Hey," I said. "How's it goin'?"

Sully shrugged a reply.

I should be too pissed at Micah and Mark to actually care about anything beyond the issues I had to deal with right now, but I'd never seen Sully like this before. I should say something to cheer him up. He'd do it for me.

While I racked my brain for a helpful response, I gazed down at the ocean. Maybe I would've been better off spending the day at the beach — even with the inherent risk involved — than policing everyone's behavior here at Micah's impromptu party.

And then I remembered Sully's offer the day he picked me up on his motorcycle. He claimed that only my feet would get wet. Hydros couldn't find me from that small amount of contact with the ocean, right?

"Hey," I asked. "Does your offer still stand?"

He lifted his head from his hands. "Say what?"

"About going skin-boarding? Are you still up for it?"

A faint smile played across his face. "You mean *skim*-boarding?"

"Oh." I bit my lip. I felt my cheeks grow warm. "Right."

"Yeah," he said, his face gradually returning to its normal sunny disposition. "The offer still stands."

I smiled. My plan worked.

Then he added, "You know, Jordan, I was thinking. I haven't seen you in a while."

I shot him a surprised look. "What're you talking about? You stop over every day."

"Yeah, but you're always so busy with Cam."

"So? He's got his first game coming up. He's a little nervous about it."

"Oh, *that's* it," he said unconvincingly. "And here I thought you were just trying to avoid me."

"Not you," I muttered. "More like Micah."

Sully raised one eyebrow high on his forehead. "Really? Why's that?"

I took a deep breath. "Let's just say it's been a long, *long* couple of days."

He jabbed me lightly in the ribs in his "cheer-up" sort of way. "Don't worry about it. Micah's like that. He gets over stuff pretty fast."

"Not this time."

"So what'd you do?"

"Beat him on a test," I grumbled.

"That's not too hard to do," Sully laughed. His smile grew so wide, I couldn't help but chuckle, too. Perhaps I *had* blown this whole thing out of proportion.

Sully and I talked about anything and everything that he'd beaten Micah on over the years. Video games, card games, sporting events, spelling tests…the list went on and on. Listening to his stories erased my worries with doses of laughter.

The sun sunk lower in the sky when Sully placed a gentle hand upon my shoulder. "Hey. Tell you what. Tomorrow after school, why don't we plan on—?"

I raised my index finger in front of his face as my ears perked up. "Hold that thought," I told him, whipping my head around, certain I heard another car pulling into the driveway. *Who'd be coming this late?*

When the car door angrily slammed shut, I knew my answer—an uninvited guest.

"Oh, God. It's Celia," I gasped. So exhausted from my job of crowd control, I never noticed how late it'd gotten.

"Already?" Sully said with a trace of disappointment in his tone.

I turned to him, my voice desperate. "What time is it?"

"I dunno." He pulled out his phone to check but I pushed it away.

"Oh, never mind. Just help me find Micah."

While Sully headed off in one direction through the crowd, I darted in the other, hoping to catch Micah before Celia did. Not that it really mattered. We both should expect some serious trouble.

Furious, Celia marched up the driveway. In thirty seconds flat, she'd shut off the music and ordered everyone home, including Sully. He caught my eye, almost as if he feared I'd be grounded, too.

"I can't believe you!" Celia roared after the last car turned out the driveway. "How dare you have a party when I'm gone!"

"But I asked if I could have a few friends over," Micah argued.

"A few! This is *way* more than a few. You abused your

privileges, young man, and you know it. Perhaps I've been too lenient." She aimed an accusing finger at Micah's face. "Maybe this time I should ground you until your graduat—"

"It's not his fault," I shouted, stepping between Micah and Celia.

They both paused, looking surprised I'd come to Micah's aid.

"Micah was just trying to make me feel better," I blurted before I lost my nerve. "I'd been so depressed these last few days because I felt like I didn't have any friends at school. He thought if he invited some over, it'd help me out." Celia's irate face made my voice trail off. I envisioned myself grounded for the next two weeks as the Elementals' super storm closed in to surround the Bay Area. Maybe I should've kept my mouth shut.

Out of the corner of my eye, I saw Micah's jaw drop for a second. But he corrected it before Celia noticed.

"Make me feel better, you know," I added, softer this time.

For a long moment, Celia stared blankly at me. Finally, she blinked, my words sinking in. She opened her mouth and closed it again without uttering a sound. Then she turned to Micah, "You were?"

Micah nodded slowly.

Celia pressed her fingers to her temples to fight off a migraine while she debated between punishing him and thanking him.

Eventually, she heaved a deep sigh. "I just wish you would've told me first."

"He did ask if it was okay to have a couple of friends over," I reminded her in a congenial tone.

She sighed again. "Well, thanks to Jordan, it seems you're

off the hook. *This time.*" She stepped in the garage to grab a huge garbage bag. "But you still have to clean up."

Cam tugged on my shirt, eager to show off the prizes he won at the birthday party. "You should've been there!" he beamed and described the piñata, games, soda, cake, and pizza. Then he ran off into the house to add the toys to his collection. I had a feeling with that much excitement and sugar, he'd crash early tonight.

Me on the other hand…

I looked around the trashed yard. Without a doubt, Micah needed some help.

So I walked into the garage and grabbed another garbage bag. Bending down to place one plastic cup after another in the bag, I sensed Micah's eyes upon me. I hesitated to meet his gaze and have him mad at me for being right.

Only once we finished cleaning up the driveway and the yard did I finally look him in the face. He continued to stare at me in a funny way.

"What?" I asked, narrowing my eyes defensively.

"You didn't have to do that, you know." Micah's tone remained cool, but at least it lacked hostility now.

"Do what?" I asked, feigning innocence.

"You know. Cover for me. You didn't have to."

With a small shrug, I said, "Consider us even."

A faint smile flickered across his lips. *A step in the right direction.* I returned his smile.

CHAPTER SIXTEEN

The next afternoon, Cameron and I passed the soccer ball back and forth in the front yard when Sully pulled up. An unexpected flutter filled my heart. He stepped from the car with a quick wave, making me freeze in my tracks, my face fixed in a quirky smile. Cam's ball rolled past my feet. Blushing, I chased it down, and then kicked it back to Cam.

"Busy today?" Sully asked, intercepting my pass. He trapped the ball with the inside of his foot, before tapping it to Cam.

"Not too much," I said, avoiding Sully's face. "We're almost done. Right, Cam?"

Cam's lip turned up into a cute little smirk that he must've learned from Micah. "Next goal wins," he giggled, then dribbled the ball, trying to scoot past Sully.

Sully maneuvered his body to block Cam, faking left then right, but letting Cam past at the very last second.

"Yay!" Cam exclaimed. He raised his arms in the air when the ball rolled between the pair of old tennis shoes that marked the goal.

"Nice one, bud," Sully grinned, rustling Cam's curly hair. Then suddenly, Sully blinked, as if noticing me for the first time. "Hey...your arm!"

I glanced down at my forearm, wrapped neatly with an Ace bandage. "Yeah. I got my cast off this morning. The doctor said I need to keep it in this for another week." Which explained why I didn't leave town a few hours ago, or so I told myself.

Sully made a poor attempt at hiding the disappointment written upon his face.

"What's up?" I asked him.

"Oh," he sighed in a very un-Sully-like way. "I just stopped by to see if you were up for some skim-boarding. But I guess it can wait until your arm's all better."

I almost agreed with him when I remembered his wounded face at the party after he saw Karli joined to Justin's hip. Plus the timer in my head counted down the days until my full recovery...and my necessary departure. *No more excuses*, I reminded myself.

True, he graciously offered me a way out with no reservations. And deep down, I knew I should accept since my arm still needed time to heal and the doctor told me to take it easy.

But I couldn't stop my pulse from quickening when Sully's pale blue eyes held mine, waiting for my response. My heart leapt unexpectedly, realizing he came over today just to see *me*. So it didn't come as a complete surprise when I found myself replying, "As long as I don't fall on it, I should be okay. I'll go grab a towel."

"Sweet." Sully's smile broadened, brightening his entire face. "I can hang out here with Cam. See if he can beat me this time."

Cam's face wrinkled with determination as he dribbled the ball forward, trying to get past Sully again.

Walking through the house, I kicked myself for allowing my emotions to wield such control over my mind that my personal feelings prevailed over things like logic and reason. Why should I risk my safety just to spend a little more time with him? Or with *any*one for that matter?

Then again, maybe the Elementals hadn't even arrived in this time. Maybe they really had no idea I was here at all. Throughout the morning, the sun had broken through the clouds at intermittent intervals, leading me to conclude nature truly accounted for the origins of this storm. I began to think I had overreacted to the whole mess when I should've listened to Micah and Sully instead.

Deliberating over my mixed feelings, I opened the hall closet to grab a beach towel. But when I turned to shut the door, I found Micah standing on the other side.

"Where are *you* going?" he asked, though it sounded more like an accusation than a question to satiate his interest.

All the joy from Sully's unexpected visit vanished in an instant. Why did he care? It wasn't like I needed to ask his permission or anything.

"Sully's taking me skim-boarding," I replied coolly and tucked the towel under my arm.

Micah's face clouded. "*Sully's* here?" he asked, sounding hurt that his best friend would choose me over him. Not like Micah didn't do the same to Sully on a regular basis, letting

Tessa take precedence over everything in his life.

"Wanna come?" I felt suddenly obliged to ask. Not that it really mattered. Of course, Micah would say no. Surely, he already had weekend plans.

Micah grabbed his phone from his back pocket to check the time.

Wait for it, I told myself. I folded my arms over my chest, expecting him to refuse so I could leave.

Instead, Micah slipped his phone into his pocket and grinned. "Sure. I'll be right there."

As Micah raced to his room, I blinked with surprise that he voluntarily chose to take time out of his day to spend with us. *You're overanalyzing it,* my conscience reproached me. *He just wants to hang out with Sully.*

Yeah. That made sense. But a small part of me still felt wary. As if he decided to tag along to keep me in check so I didn't steal his best friend without his consent.

Whatever, Micah. I shouldn't be a worry to him for much longer.

I walked back outside and announced to Sully, "Micah said he's coming, too."

"Oh. Okay," Sully agreed.

I dwelled on every word they said the whole way to the beach. Dwelled so much, in fact, that I didn't speak to either the entire ride.

When we reached the parking lot, I climbed out the back, wondering why exactly I had agreed to come. The sun had disappeared behind a new set of gray clouds that hung low across the sky and fused with the sea. A penetrating chill rode on the back of the strong breeze. Though Sully and Micah didn't seem to care, I couldn't help but think the weather had again taken a turn for the worse.

When I drove past this beach the first day of school, the sea appeared placid with gentle waves rolling into shore and brushing foam against the sand. But today the sea looked angry, swirling in a stormy broth from the surge preceding the storm.

Sully seemed to notice my skepticism. Giving me a reassuring nudge, he grinned. "It's perfect." Then he pulled the skim-boards — thin boards shaped like a small surfboard but completely flat on both sides — from the trunk and passed one to Micah. With a wink, Sully raced down the beach, tucking his board under his right arm.

Sully neared the water's edge, holding his board in front of him with both hands. His feet left soggy impressions in the sand with each step. Then he tossed the board across the shallow water and leapt onto it to skim across the thin layer of water on the top of the sand. But he didn't stop there…instead he headed straight toward the sea. The tip of his board caught an incoming wave and he rode up its face. At the top, he flew through the air for a moment, and then dropped with a splash into the crashing surf.

"Show off," Micah muttered under his breath. He and I walked down the sand to join Sully.

After fishing the board from the surf, Sully jogged back up the beach, his face happily lit from the thrill of the ride. "Your turn," he said. He flashed me a wide grin and handed me his board.

Normally, a smile like that would've stopped my heart altogether. But I reflected on the insanity of his actions long enough to keep myself in check.

"You're outta your mind," I said, shaking my head and

pushed the board back toward him. "There's no way I can do that."

"Okay, then. What about over here?" He walked into a few inches of water and pointed out a path that paralleled the beach. "Just go along the shallow water. You can try cutting into the waves later if you'd like." He handed me the board again.

I doubted that. Reluctantly, I reached for his board. I took a few hesitant steps closer to the sea, where the next wave broke, washing up the sand and enveloping my legs up to my shins. Suddenly, I discovered a new meaning of pain as the icy water wrapped around my ankles and instantly shocked my skin into a feisty shade of red.

"Ohmigod!" I shrieked, dashing up the beach away from the water with Sully's skim-board tucked under my good arm.

"What's wrong?"

"How can you stand it?" I stared at him, befuddled at how he voluntarily dunked his entire body in water that felt only a few degrees above freezing. "Don't you wear suits like those big wave surfers or something?"

Sully shrugged. "Nah. It's not so bad once your body turns numb."

My jaw hit the ground. "Seriously?"

"Seriously," he replied, nonchalant.

Okay, then. I headed back for a second try so I didn't look like a complete wimp. I braced myself when another wave raced up the beach and encircled my legs once more. Within seconds, thousands of needles pierced my skin, jabbing me incessantly. Long after the water receded, my skin still prickled in pain.

Frowning, I looked back at Sully and mouthed, *No way.*

Dripping wet, Sully smiled back and gave me a thumbs-up.

I rolled my eyes. *Okay, here goes. Think warm thoughts, think warm thoughts.* I closed my eyes, willing my body to project out whatever heat I could muster in a desperate attempt to alleviate the pain. Steeling my nerve, I tossed the board in front of me and splashed through the water. Then with a deep breath, I leapt onto the board and extended my arms for balance, standing up like the big wave surfers, only on a flat section of beach without any waves.

I kept my balance for a few feet before I leapt off its side. I glanced at Sully and Micah for approval.

"Not bad," Micah admitted.

Surprisingly, I found myself smiling. The warmth of a blush rose in my cheeks. Since when did Micah offer *me* a compliment?

I handed Sully back his board but he refused to accept it. "Give it another try," he suggested with a clap on my back.

With an exaggerated sigh, I waited for the next wave to rush in, then took a few running steps and tossed the board across the top of the water, jumping on its surface and riding further than the last time.

"Sure you're not ready to try the bigger stuff?" Sully called.

"Are you nuts?" I yelled back. What did he think? I hadn't even perfected riding the board here on the flat ground.

Micah jabbed Sully in the ribs. "Don't push her. She's probably scared."

My jaw dropped as his previous compliment vaporized from my recent memory. Why had I bothered to invite him along? I so did not need this. "Am not." I glared at Micah, dangling my bandaged arm in the air. "Remember?"

"Whatever," Micah said as he grabbed his board and walked toward the sea. "If you need me, I'll be over here," he called to Sully over his shoulder.

I bit my lip, so easily infuriated with him. All this time I wondered what Micah saw in Tessa. Now I couldn't fathom what Tessa saw in him.

"Forget him," Sully said encouragingly. "Go on. Take a couple more rides."

So I did. But between waves, I glanced over at Sully's pathetic attempt to stop shivering in the blustery breeze. Returning his board, I suggested he join Micah in the larger surf. This time, Sully didn't object.

Meanwhile, I plopped down on the sand and watched Micah and Sully take turns popping their boards up over the waves. Sully's laughter carried over the surf. After a huge wave pummeled him into the sand, he stood slowly on wobbly legs to scrape his body off the beach. I looked at him and shook my head. That boy sure had a warped sense of humor.

Micah poised, ready to hit the next wave as it broke. He rocketed up its side then zipped over the top and landed in the breaking water with a huge splash. When he surfaced, he shook the water from his ears. Despite the pervading chill in the ocean, he wore a huge smile upon his face.

Suddenly, I felt excluded and very alone. A small part of me actually wanted to try and to prove Micah wrong. And another part of me wanted to impress Sully, though I knew that shouldn't really matter. I couldn't afford to have him like me back.

Still, why not? It looked fun and I'd love to show up Micah. How dare he think of me as scared and wimpy?

I got off my butt and walked toward the boys. Sully readied for another dash into the sea when I blurted, "Can I try?" before I lost my nerve.

Sully paused mid-stride to hand me his board but Micah beat him to it. Thrusting his board in front of my face, Micah said, "Go on. It's all yours."

I blinked. Why did he have to act so confusing? One minute he detested me, and the next he seemed generous and helpful. Did he simply enjoy egging me on?

"Thanks," I said flatly. Though the waves looked much larger here than they had from my spot twenty feet away, I definitely couldn't chicken out now.

I watched the next wave build. The midnight blue ripple grew in size until it swelled, threatening to break on top of me. Swallowing hard, I raced to the sea and released the board in front of me like I practiced, and planted my feet upon its smooth surface. With my arms extended and my knees bent, I hit the wave and immediately jetted up the sheer face of liquid power. At the top, the crest curled over, white and frothy as it spilled toward the earth. For a moment, I hung motionless. The earth seemed to stop spinning beneath me, frozen in time.

I dunked beneath the surface. Adrenaline coursed through my veins as the icy water quickly engulfed me. It still hurt this time but didn't feel nearly so cold. Using my good arm to pull myself up to the surface, my mouth turned into a huge grin. I grabbed a quick breath before declaring, "That's awesome!" Then the wave dumped me on the shore. I staggered out of the surf, searching for Micah's board. Spotting its colorful form floating up the beach, I quickly snatched it before the current dragged it back to sea.

Tottering back up the beach, my legs shook as a flood of

adrenaline rushed through my veins. *I can see why Sully's so into this sport,* I watched him zoom down the beach, ready to catch another wave.

"Y'know something. You were right. That was pretty cool," I told Micah and handed him the board.

But Micah didn't reply. Instead, he stared at me. His jaw grazed the sand.

Was I really that good?

Micah blinked twice before exclaiming, "Jordan, you're smokin'."

Wow. That sounded like a huge compliment, especially coming from Micah. "Thanks," I replied. Strangely I couldn't seem to keep from beaming, despite the pain in all my extremities. "Hey, d'you hear that?" I called to Sully as his head broke the surface. "Micah says I'm smoking."

Sully climbed out of the water and jogged over with his board. "That's great!" he exclaimed. But when he neared, a baffled look clouded his face. "Oh, my God, Jordan. He's right."

"Oh, please. You didn't even see me, did you?"

"No, seriously, Jordan," Sully said, his voice uncharacteristically grave. "You're like *steaming.*"

"Really," Micah chimed in. "Look."

I glanced down at my arms, realizing I didn't deserve his compliment. Micah meant every word. Literally.

Because right then, in the plain of day, steam actually rose off my body. I immediately turned the heat from my core down to nothing and let all evidence drift away with the breeze.

"Weird. Guess I just worked up a sweat or something," I said, trying to blow it off. In my mind, I knew I was dead.

How could I be such an idiot?

"Or something," Micah replied, his eyebrows twisted in a quizzical way.

I never should've gone in the water. The steam was a huge warning sign—in bright neon lights and all.

"At least you didn't fall on your arm. You're fine." Sully said, shooting Micah a fierce look to drop the issue. "Besides, you only live once. Right, Jordan?"

"Yeah. Something like that," I muttered. I felt the color drain from my cheeks.

Sully shot me a sympathetic look. Then he wrapped his arms around his chest and shivered, though it seemed deliberate this time. "Why don't we head back? I think I'm done for today."

"Sure. Whatever," Micah said and nodded. He picked up his board and headed back to the car.

Sully waited until Micah stepped out of earshot before he threw one arm over my shoulder and asked in a low voice, "You doin' okay?"

"Yeah," I sniffled. "Never better."

He gave me a quick squeeze, then bolted ahead to unlock the doors. When I reached the car, Sully tossed me a towel. While I dried off, I glanced up at the sky. Dark storm clouds rolled in from the south, circling overhead, practically pinpointing my current location.

And though I might've helped Sully forget about Karli, I never should've agreed to come to the beach. Now Hydros knew my exact location.

CHAPTER SEVENTEEN

"Remember, keep both hands on the wheel," Mr. Mendoza, my Driver's Ed teacher, reminded me. Again.

"Right." I replied, trying to hide the frustration in my voice.

"Adjust your rearview mirror," he added.

"Check."

"And the side-view mirrors."

"Okay."

"Is your seat a comfortable distance from the pedals?"

"Yep."

"Your seat belt's fastened?"

"It is."

"And your mind's clear from all distractions?"

"Uh-huh." *As clear as it can get with my life at stake.* I couldn't believe I was stupid enough to risk a dip in the ocean. Who cared that I proved Micah wrong or showed off for Sully?

None of that mattered while I tried to act like things were normal, sitting behind the wheel.

Not that I didn't want to take off right after we got back from the beach with a soaked Ace bandage. But Celia sat me down and told me how proud her late husband would've been to know I was safe living with them. Then she read the newspaper headlines aloud to remind me of all the horrors that might befall me on the streets. I peeked out the window while she read. The sky looked less threatening, so I figured I still had time to devise a plan before The Three arrived.

"Now, then, are you ready to begin?" Mr. Mendoza asked calmly, breaking my thoughts.

I wanted to scream that I'd been ready for the last five minutes. Instead, I settled with a, "Sure," followed by a dramatic rolling of my ebony eyes. Mr. Mendoza gave the same litany every time. What a tedious job he had, repeating those directions all afternoon. Why didn't he just record his voice on a CD and press Play instead?

"Okay, Jordan, you may place the key in the ignition," he said as if I prepared to complete an extremely complicated task that required great dexterity and skill, like performing open-heart surgery. I'd seen Celia and Sully drive tons of times. How hard could it be?

I rolled my eyes again and turned the key, giving it a little gas to resuscitate the idle engine. Gradually, the old Chevy Malibu chugged to life and I shifted from Park into Drive.

Pulling out of the parking lot, I braked to a full stop at every stop sign, hoping he wouldn't harp on my rolling stops like he did last week.

A light drizzle coated the windshield and Mr. Mendoza advised me to turn on the wipers. "Roads are slippery in these types of conditions," he said. "So you should use extreme caution as you would in any adverse weather."

"Of course," I replied.

Isa Estes, Karli McDonald, and a sophomore named Stef Hirsch giggled from the backseat, knowing Mr. Mendoza's propensity for extremism. Why worry about a little rain?

I pulled up to the last stop sign in the school parking lot when Karli pointed at Micah and Sully hanging out by Sully's car. Wondering where they were headed and why Karli cared since she made it plainly obvious that she liked Justin, I turned for a quick glance and forgot to stop on the white line.

Right when another car zipped in front of us.

Mr. Mendoza slammed his foot on the teacher brake by his passenger's seat, lurching us forward into our seat belts. Then we spent the next five minutes parked in this exact spot, listening to him lecture me about the utmost importance of remaining completely focused on my task every time I got behind the wheel. Driving needed total concentration. No distractions.

"Can you agree to that, Jordan?"

I loathed his patronizing tone. Especially when it elicited a bunch of stifled giggles from the backseat.

I gritted my teeth, agreeing to devote one hundred and ten percent of my energy into driving the Malibu safely from this moment forward. Satisfied, Mr. Mendoza instructed me to cautiously proceed out of the parking lot and take a right up the street.

No more mistakes. Okay, Jordan? I told myself and flipped on my right turn signal. I couldn't let Celia down again, not after everything she'd done for me. She'd already mentioned on more than one occasion the expense of behind-the-wheel training and I should feel lucky my guidance counselor could squeeze me into the popular class. I offered to drop out and save her the cash but she refused, insisting I needed to learn to drive safely at some point in my life and there was no time like the present.

So here I sat, essentially wasting her hard-earned money. Why bother preparing for the future that might not even exist?

Taking the turn slowly, I headed uphill, careful to keep my hands in their proper positions at all times.

"You're doing great so far," Mr. Mendoza encouraged me when I anticipated the red light and coasted to a stop. When the light turned green, I scanned the intersection for pedestrians before continuing. I manipulated the car smoothly in and out of the hairpin turns up the hillside, making Mr. Mendoza's face light up into a genuine smile. I grinned back, satisfied with my improvement. Maybe I'd make Celia proud after all.

And then I saw something that sent a chill down my spine.

Up ahead, a flash of lightning illuminated the sky. And on the top of the hill, I spotted a figure, silhouetted against the gray storm clouds, her spindly arms raised to the sky. Her long blond hair caught the wind and lashed her face.

I gasped, immediately recognizing that pose, those arms, that hair. I didn't even have to see her face to know they belonged to Skye.

Panic gripped my throat, squeezing the breath from my lungs in a horrific scream. The noise startled Mr. Mendoza so badly he jumped out of his seat and hit his head against the roof of the car. Slamming my foot on the gas pedal, I whipped the car around, pulling a U-ey in the middle of the street. Zooming off in the other direction, our tires squealed when I fishtailed on the slippery roads. The entire time, Isa, Karli, and Stef screamed madly, begging Mr. Mendoza to make me stop.

Jostled around and frozen in shock, Mr. Mendoza couldn't get a solid foothold on his teacher backup brake. I peeled around one corner after another and the girls in the backseat shrieked. I pressed my foot harder against the accelerator to weave in and out of traffic, narrowly missing other cars. Behind us, the sounds of skidding tires and crunching metal filled the air. Two more cars swerved out of our way as we flew across the intersection beneath a red light.

Finally gathering his wits, Mr. Mendoza placed one hand firmly on the steering wheel and veered us onto the shoulder while applying full pressure to his brake. Screeching to a halt, the car slid into the side of the hill and smashed its bumper.

I glanced over my shoulder with wild eyes, frightened we hadn't made it very far from the hill where I saw Skye. Wondering if I could escape the rest of the way on foot, I peeked over my shoulder again.

Only this time she had disappeared. The hillside stood empty.

Mr. Mendoza breathed heavily, clutching his chest like he staved off a heart attack. He looked frazzled times ten, his toupee disheveled and askew. Then he launched into a tirade of the ginormous number of mistakes I just made. How I ran a red light. Sped. And caused not just one accident but *three*. His face boiled like steam inside a pressurized cooker. He threatened to report me to the police for negligence, vehicular misconduct, and destruction of school property. I didn't know if those were actual crimes or if he just made stuff up in his agitated state, but he sounded pretty convincing.

Not that it mattered much. Between Celia and The Three,

I was as good as dead.

Trying to maintain composure, Mr. Mendoza ordered me out of the car so we could switch places.

Slipping into the passenger's seat, I buckled my seat belt and glanced through the rain-streaked window at the barren hillside. Had I imagined the whole thing?

Still, I swear I saw her. At least I thought I did.

CHAPTER EIGHTEEN

It didn't surprise me when Mr. Mendoza dumped me off in front of the school by myself. After the car rolled away — forty-five minutes before the scheduled end of my class — I plopped down on the curb, letting the intensifying rain soak my hoodie and jeans until I transformed into a human puddle. The chilling dampness soon penetrated deep into my core and reminded me of another time I felt this wet and cold.

Bora Bora, February 17, 465 A.D.

The rain came fast and hard. It was one of those unexpected showers that suddenly drenched the valley. Only a few hundred feet from the mouth of our cave, Skye and I ran, hoping to make it to shelter before the rains completely soaked us.

Yet we weren't that lucky.

Pushing the hair from my eyes, I squinted into the downpour, trying to keep up with Skye as she dashed down the overgrown path. My waterlogged sarong clung to my legs with every stride. My arms grew tired from carrying the heavy basket of fish we'd caught by the reef. I didn't know how Skye could keep her pace.

Finally reaching our protected hideout, we ducked under the hanging liana vines that obscured our entrance and dumped our catch of fish upon the ground.

Skye's long blond hair lay plastered flat across her face as she wrung out a corner of her soaked sarong. Pouting grumpily, she mopped the strands from her face, like a drowned cat desperately trying to groom itself. It probably didn't help that I took one look at her and broke into hysterics.

"What?" she declared. Her testy voice sounded ready to snap.

"You," I said, still chuckling. "You look so funny."

"Like you're any better," she snipped. A rush of wind zipped through the entrance of the cave, swirling the dried leaves from the floor into a dust devil that encircled me.

"Come on." I smiled, shrugging off Skye's sudden mood change. "Let's get these cleaned. I'm starving."

I certainly didn't intend to escalate Skye's anger. Especially now that I'd found someone like me. I stumbled upon her soon after I survived another near miss with Gaia. Not that it seemed too hard—on an island full of deeply tanned Polynesians, a towhead like Skye clearly stood out, born without the normal dark pigmentation to handle the intense sun exposure of the tropics.

I suspected another reason. Watching her tend the taro crops and pound the tapa cloth, I noticed the wind mimicking her mood. When she appeared happy, a serene breeze carried off the sea. But when she grew mad, the wind howled and knocked over everything in her path.

Skye might anger easily, but lucky for me, she calmed down quickly, too.

The wind gradually died as Skye's frown faded. Satisfied I'd appeased her for the moment, I stacked the kindling into a pyramid by the mouth of the cave and ignited it with a short, painful snap of my fingers. Normally, I avoided using my powers and contending with the pain that ensued, but today I felt too ravenous to care. When the kindling caught flame, Skye and I set to work, drying our clothes by the firelight while we scraped off the filets with a couple of sharp rocks.

Whistling a sad tune, Skye hunched over her fish, her wet hair hanging like a veil that shrouded her face. I peeked at her for a moment, wondering if she enjoyed her life with me or if she'd rather be back with her punitive aunt. Skye's mother had died in childbirth, leaving her father with more mouths to feed than he could manage. So he gave the infant to his childless sister to raise. All those years, Skye's aunt treated her as an outcast, making her labor long hours each day while insulting her...and often driving her to anger.

So when I realized Skye's identity, I offered to have her come and live with me, like sisters. Though she accepted, I wondered if now she regretted her hasty decision. We moved to the other side of the island, far away from her tyrannical aunt. Here we gathered our own fruit, caught our own fish, and traded with the locals for taro and other essentials.

I questioned if I had been too selfish in asking her to come. Did I really hope to save her from Gaia? Or to save myself by forming an alliance? Or did Skye simply remind me of the sister I lost long ago?

So far, Skye hadn't really complained. But I couldn't tell if she was truly happy.

Studying her while we worked, I suddenly heard hushed voices over the falling rain outside. "Shhh," I whispered to Skye, motioning for her to drop her rock and follow me to the dark recesses of the cave.

The rain suddenly lessened. Soggy footsteps sloshed through the mud to pause at our entrance. A figure peered around the corner, spotting our abandoned piles of filets and tools by the blazing fire. Even with her feisty russet hair drooping against her wet cheeks, I recognized the face immediately. My stomach knotted. I inched toward Skye and hugged her protectively.

"Who is it?" Skye whispered, her voice trembling with fear. She'd never seen me so frightened before.

I couldn't answer. Gaia had found me again. And worse, I led her to Skye. Then again, maybe the two of us could destroy her and end this hunt.

At the mouth of the cave, Gaia motioned for her willowy companion with long, dark brown hair and startlingly blue eyes to approach, declaring, "They're here, Hydros."

Uh, oh.

Apparently, Gaia had discovered another Elemental, too. The *last* one, to be precise.

Hydros. The name sat like poison on my tongue. In the past, I'd struggled to escape Gaia alone, but now the challenge had doubled. I quickly understand Hydros's potential, finding it decidedly convenient the rain stopped upon her arrival. I wondered what else she could accomplish.

Well, at least I had Skye to help. Two versus two. That

seemed fair, right? Only a slight problem remained. Skye didn't believe she had powers…and I barely knew how to use my own.

"Remember how I started the fire?" I murmured in Skye's ear.

She nodded her head slowly. Silently.

"And remember when I told you that you can control the wind? That you're also an Elemental like me?"

She shot me a skeptical glance.

"Well, you are. And so are these two." I swallowed hard, adding, "And they're looking for us."

"Us?" Skye trembled. "Why?"

I opened my mouth to speak but the words garbled inside my head. How could I explain to her what I didn't entirely understand myself? Why could I produce fire, yet feel extreme pain? Why must I endure the agony of dying each time I exited this world? With so many questions unanswered, how could Skye ever believe in something I knew so little about? My face filled with trepidation and Skye shrunk beside me.

"Don't let them find me. Don't let them hurt me," she said in a soft voice. Panic filled her smoky gray eyes and she shivered with fear.

"Never," I promised, soothing her long blond hair flat against her back. "You're safe with me."

But deep down, I knew I shouldn't have hid here with her. Concentrating our auras made us an easy target. That must explain how they tracked us down so readily. The instant we entered the ocean, we notified Hydros of our presence, like a beacon attached to our souls. Maybe Skye would've been better off with her aunt. I started to think we didn't stand a chance.

Unless I could make Skye mad.

My eyes narrowed. In my sternest voice, I goaded, "And this is all *your* fault."

Skye turned on me, a fierce stormy look in her silvery eyes. She pulled away from my protective embrace. "What are you talking about? It was your dumb idea to come here." Her voice rose, piercing the calm following the rainstorm. "Some hiding spot you chose. Like a couple of hanging vines make a good cover." The wind stirred, rusting the tree branches.

"This is definitely the place," I heard Gaia tell Hydros. Entering the mouth of the cave, a sly grin crept across her face.

Keep it up, Jordan, I encouraged myself, thinking up more stinging words to rile Skye.

"I wish I never met you," I continued, my voice low and harsh.

Skye's face drooped into a deep, saddened frown that brimmed with hurt. Outside, the wind gathered in strength. I heard it whistle through the treetops, prepared to burst in at any moment.

My plan worked. Just one more comment, then I'd channel her fury at Gaia and Hydros. They wouldn't stand a chance.

What devastating remark could I say to set her off? The same thing that drove me over the edge. Something about her family—her mom, in particular. How Skye had caused her death, much like my whole family had perished... inadvertently...

Because of *me.*

"You want to know why your mom died in childbirth?" I sounded like a nasty child taunting a dog with a bone.

Skye whipped her head around. Her wet fair blond hair stuck to her cheeks. She studied me incredulously, expecting the truth.

The corner of my mouth turned up in a cruel, calculating way. "It's because of you. You and your freakish powers. You were the one who killed her."

There. That should cover it. I congratulated myself for successfully enraging Skye. Now to harness that energy and direct it against Gaia and Hydros.

Skye paled, shaking her head in disbelief. She backed away from me. "You're lying," she breathed through her quivering lower lip. A sudden roar of wind burst through the cave entrance and unsuspectingly flattened the other two Elementals.

"Excellent," I snickered, bracing myself against one wall as a precaution. I aimed my hands at Gaia's startled face. The wind swirled in strong gusts and suffocated the fire with a sudden swoosh. Served her right for taking my family and Lucius from me. A broad grin filled my face when I saw Gaia lying helplessly upon the ground.

This would prove easier than I imagined.

"Now hit them again," I told Skye while I summoned a fireball to send their way to finish them off. They couldn't hurt anyone else I loved.

Ever.

Only Skye glowered at me, her face registering the hurt I had caused. Before I realized her intention, she raised her hand and aimed her palm at my heart. Her eyes glimmered like quicksilver. A sudden blast of straight-line winds nailed me against the rocky cave wall. My head whipped backward, smacking a protrusion at incredible speed. Bolts of pain shot through my skull and neck before I crumbled to the ground in a heap.

"I hate you," Skye spat. She pointed a finger at my skull and a second blast of wind tore through the cave, crushing my face against the rock once more. Blood oozed from fresh wounds on my cheek.

"Not me, you idiot," I exclaimed through the rushing wind. "Get them. They're the ones who want to hurt you."

Skye blinked, her face torn with confusion. The wind outside died in her puzzled state. Gaia and Hydros scraped themselves off the ground and seized the opportunity to strike.

"I never meant to hurt you," I shouted, pressing one hand to my cheek to stop the bleeding, desperate for Skye to see my point of view.

Skye shook her head, biting her quavering lip to control the tears.

I wanted to tell her I lied, that her powers hadn't caused her mother's death. But time was unkind.

Regaining her strength, Gaia rose to her feet, stomping her foot on the cave floor. Around us, the ground trembled. Loose rocks tumbled down the slope outside and blocked part of the entrance.

"Skye, do it again," I shouted. "Call the wind."

But Skye continued to shake her head, dropping to her knees in defeat. Hydros neared her side and placed a slender hand upon the girl's shoulder.

"Don't take her!" I screamed at Gaia and struggled to my feet. Blood dripped from my wounds. "She's mine."

Gaia's eyes gleamed. "Not anymore, my dear. You've done more than we ever could have asked for."

"What do you mean?" I snarled. "I'd never help you and you know it."

"Oh, but you have. You've done a wonderful job of helping us turn Skye against you."

Oh, my God. *I did.*

The blood drained from my face. "Skye, don't listen to her!" I shrieked in desperation. "I just needed you to help me fight them. You're powerful when you're angry. So that's what I had to do. Make you angry."

But at this point, it didn't matter what I said. Skye didn't believe me. Not anymore.

Reading my face, Gaia cackled an evil, chilling laugh that sent a shudder down my spine.

I'd lost this battle. And possibly the war.

So it didn't really surprise me that the air outside remained calm and still when Hydros wrapped her spindly fingers around Skye's arms and led her from the cave. Instead of using Skye's power to confront Gaia and Hydros and guarantee our safety, I'd effectively crushed her spirit and relinquished her trust.

Then Gaia grabbed my arms, pinning them behind my back. She directed me toward the mouth of the cave. Stepping over the loose rocks that littered the entrance, she pushed me after Hydros and Skye. For a safeguard, Hydros split the sky with another drenching downpour, ensuring my fire could cause them no harm. At that precise moment, I realized Gaia had trained Hydros well already, while I did nothing to prepare Skye for this day.

They led us down the forested trail in silence. The rain pelted our skin like painful shards of glass. Then they dumped us in separate pits, each at least ten feet deep. The smell of damp earth filled my nostrils. I scanned the walls, searching for a handhold or a root to aid in my escape.

Unfortunately, I found none.

I sank to the floor and buried my bloody face in my hands, regretful for saying all those horrible things. I spent a sleepless night shivering in a growing pool while my blood congealed into a jagged scab across my cheekbone. Meanwhile, the torrential rain continued. I wondered when phase two of their torture would begin.

When the morning light touched the valley floor, the water level in my pit had already reached mid-thigh. Above, I detected a pair of footsteps that signaled Gaia and Hydros's return. Next to me, I heard a splash in Skye's pit followed by a frightened scream. Perhaps now she'd realize my true intentions. I glanced up to see Hydros's lithe form perched at the edge of my pit. She dumped a basket over the side while a sinister grin lit her gaunt face.

I edged toward one wall. My eyes scanned the water, uncertain of what exactly had entered the pit. In the dim light, I spotted a slithering form that undulated through the water. It neared the surface and I caught a glimpse of its black and white stripes before it ducked beneath the dark water again. I swallowed hard, recognizing the shape and coloration in an instant.

The deadly sea krait.

If I held perfectly still, perhaps the snake wouldn't strike. *Don't move, don't move.* I willed my body to remain calm.

Skye screamed again. Judging by her tone, she'd also discovered the identity of our new companions.

"*Jordan!*" she screamed, begging for help.

Unfortunately, I couldn't even help myself. I held my breath while the krait slithered toward me, wrapping its cold scaly body around my calf. Afraid to exhale, I gritted my teeth with fear and wondered what they planned for us next. If I survived that long.

CHAPTER NINETEEN

"Jordan?"

Subconsciously, I touched a finger to my cheek, remembering the pain when Skye had slammed me into the rocky cave wall.

"Jordan?"

Funny. I didn't remember her calling my name more than twice.

"Jordan!"

Maybe because this voice didn't belong to Skye. Instead, it sounded male. And familiar.

I blinked, letting my eyes focus through the sheet of rain as a white Toyota Corolla stopped by the curb. Inside, I recognized the baseball cap turned backward and the wide, infectious grin.

I gave Sully a small wave.

"Thought you had Driver's Ed?" he said.

I shrugged, unsure of how he knew my schedule, unless Micah had told him. Which again made me wonder how much they talked about me.

"I did," I replied. "Until today."

His brow crinkled. "Huh?"

Wiping the rain from my face, I approached his car. Not like anyone else could overhear, though I still felt embarrassed to admit, "I flunked out."

"Seriously?" He hooted. But his laughter instantly faded. "I'm sorry," he said, struggling to keep a straight face. "So what happened?"

I shrugged again. Raindrops slid down my face. "They dropped me off here. I told them I'd walk home. Only—"

"—you haven't made it too far," he finished for me. "Get in. I'll give you a lift."

Dripping wet, I climbed in, my clothes clinging to my skin. I sank into the passenger side.

"Here. Take this—you're soaked," he offered, passing me a dry jacket from behind his seat.

Slipping out of my soggy hoodie, I slid my arms into his jacket sleeves, wrapping it tightly around my chilled core. His jacket smelled like laundry softener, fresh and clean…with an added hint of Sully. I inhaled a deep breath and then dragged my fingers through my wet hair. "No motorcycle today?"

Sully shook his head. "My parents won't let me drive it in the rain. They're afraid I'll do something reckless, I guess."

"No. Not you," I said, feigning surprise.

Sully laughed. "Wouldn't you think they'd know their own son by now? I don't know what I ever did to get such a bad rap."

Sully headed out of the school parking lot. Instead of

turning down the residential street to take me home, he continued into town. I glanced at him in confusion. Was this another one of his detours?

Pulling into the strip mall, he parked in front of the Old Chicago Towne Pizzeria. A sign hung in its front window, its neon lights spelling Open.

"What's this?" I blinked at the idea of him...and me... sitting down to eat. Inside my head, I couldn't help but think this had "date" written all over it.

"You hungry?"

I nodded. Sure, I felt hungry, but a part of me didn't really object to the whole *date* thing, either.

He held the door for me when we walked inside, then asked, "So what would you like?"

"Anything—as long as it's hot."

While Sully stepped up to the counter to order pizza and drinks, I crossed my arms over my chest, shivering from the cold when I noticed something familiar about the restaurant's décor. Sepia-tinted photos of scenes from old Chicago town suddenly drove up powerful memories. I stretched one hand toward the wall, reaching out to touch the side of a church's steeple. The very same one I passed as the chestnut mare and I fled down the street.

I couldn't help but think back to what I read in Mr. Tabor's class, about how I had unintentionally destroyed it all.

A shudder traveled down my spine. My face paled as I bit my lip, remembering that ill-fated night.

Holding two drinks, Sully appeared by my side. "Something bothering you?"

"No. I'm good," I fibbed, pushing the images to the back of my mind.

Sully blinked. "Are you sure? 'Cause you look like you've seen a ghost."

I shook my head, snapping my thoughts to the present. "Sorry, just tired, I guess. You were saying?"

He handed me a soda. "They're all out of coffee."

"This is fine." I smiled and took a long swig off the straw. The soda's sugar, caffeine, and carbonation traveled straight to my brain.

Finding a small booth in the corner, Sully sat across from me and perched the number placard for our pizza order on the edge of the table. Then he stared me straight in the eye, biting his tongue to keep from laughing. "So how exactly did you flunk out of Mr. Mendoza's class?"

He didn't help me feel much better.

"I take it this doesn't happen very often," I muttered.

Sully shook his head, letting a confined guffaw escape. "Are you kidding? He's got a reputation of being the softest teacher at school."

Wringing my hands in my lap, I admitted, "Let's just say I kinda freaked out."

Sully cocked one eyebrow high on his forehead. "This doesn't have to do with the storm you saw on the news?"

I looked away.

"About the Four Elements?"

"*Elementals*," I corrected him. "And it was just one."

Sully placed his hands on the top of his ball cap and leaned backward against the booth's burgundy padding. With a sympathetic grin, he added, "I'm all ears."

I sighed. I shouldn't do this but he had heard it before. Plus he hadn't believed me then, so he probably wouldn't now either. If nothing else, it would help get things off my chest. Give me a new perspective.

At least I told myself it would.

So I explained about Skye up on the hill, her hair flapping wildly in the breeze. Then I related what happened afterward…how my reckless driving and running a red light caused multiple accidents until Mr. Mendoza stopped the car and took over.

Sully stared at me, speechless, his jaw reaching the floor. Only this time, he didn't laugh. "That's it? You saw a person standing on the hillside?"

"Yes—with her arms raised, like she was shaping the air to her whim."

Sully's face relaxed. "Lots of people go up on the sea cliffs to practice yoga or Tai Chi."

"In the rain?"

He shrugged. "This is California. Haven't you heard it called, 'The Land of Fruits and Nuts' before?"

I couldn't help but chuckle. I must fit right in.

Just then, our hot, steaming pizza arrived, topped with pepperoni and sausage smothered in piles of melted cheese. I dug in, never realizing how starved I felt. Maybe Sully was right. Maybe I had imagined the whole thing. How could something as little as a momentary dip in the ocean guarantee they found me already?

Sully downed his first piece in about three bites. Reaching for a second slice, he asked, "How's the pizza?"

"Really good." And I meant it. Somehow, the food and his reassurances made the whole Driver's Ed fiasco seem insignificant in the grand scheme of life.

We ate our food, never once mentioning the weather or the Elementals again. I wished I could stay there forever, nestled inside our little booth, laughing at Sully's stories, and forgetting everything else that went on in my life. After finishing three-quarters of the pie and boxing up the rest, Sully paid the bill and tip and drove me home.

When I entered the house, I found Celia waiting at the kitchen table, livid. "Where have you been? I've called everywhere. You had me worried sick."

Sully stepped in. "It's my bad, Mrs. T. I saw her in the rain, so I gave her a ride home. But she was so cold, I took her out for pizza, y'know. To warm her up first."

Celia narrowed her eyes. "Sully, I understand you were trying to help. But still —"

"I know," he interjected. "I should've called. I'm sorry. Really. I totally forgot."

Will someone please explain to me what just happened? Did Sully just voluntarily help me out again?

Celia released a heavy sigh. "Next time, Sully, promise me you'll call."

"Sure thing." He turned to leave, giving me a knowing wink. "See you, Celia. See ya, Jordan," he called on his way out the door.

Suddenly, I found myself seeing him in a whole new light.

CHAPTER TWENTY

Before I went to bed, I caught a part of the late-night news where the TV meteorologist likened this unrelenting storm to the Winter Super storm of 1861 that dumped ten feet of rain in the Central Valley over a period of forty-five days.

When I crawled under my covers, I couldn't help but think the whole thing would end abruptly — with my inevitable capture.

It wouldn't be the first time. I remembered the three days I spent in that pit back in Bora Bora, staring up at pinpricks of light that dotted the black velvety sky, wishing for a different existence. The sea krait skirted threateningly close to my legs and Hydros's addition of blood-sucking leeches feasted on my flesh. Three days spent listening to Skye's muffled screams as Gaia and Hydros subjected her to various types of torture, each more hideous than the previous one. Her will finally broken, she begged for mercy. So when they offered her the

179

chance to escape her loathsome hole by joining them in their insatiable quest for power, she succumbed.

On that same night, Gaia ordered a couple of island men to throw down a rope and drag me out of the pit. In the light of their torches, she surveyed me with my sunken eyes, my wrinkled and sallow skin, and my jagged scab of dried blood across my cheek. In my weakened, passive state, I no longer seemed a threat. Perhaps with rest and recovery, I could prove a valuable ally.

Then Hydros had the audacity to offer me the same option as Skye—join them or else.

I glanced over at Skye, more terrified and pale than ever. Wet and cold, she shivered on the ground, clutching her trembling legs. *This is all my fault.* Pity filled my heart. Maybe I could still help. Something I could say to make her change her mind.

"Skye—it's Jordan. Remember me? Your best friend?"

Skye didn't look up. She simply rocked back and forth.

"I love you like a sister," I continued in earnest. "Doesn't that mean anything to you?"

But Skye stared into the distance through blank eyes. No flicker of recognition remained. Not a single smile painted her lips, recalling the many times we'd fished together and gathered fruits. Nothing remained to show she ever knew me at all.

Nothing…because the spirit of Skye was dead.

So instead of mustering a verbal response, I spat in Hydros's face. In retrospect, a more civilized response might have spared other innocent islanders their lives. Then again, maybe not. Like Skye, Hydros's temper flared quickly.

Hydros wiped my spittle from her eye, her face flushing

red with mounting fury. Nearby, I heard the loud rush of water from the sea, swelling far beyond its normal limits. The surge pushed inland, flattening everything in its path. Frightened, the islanders dropped their hold on my arms and their torches as they fled.

"Idiots!" Gaia exclaimed as their forgotten torches fell about my feet, lapping my heels with fiery tongues that quickly grew with my aid until they consumed my entire body in an agonizing inferno.

Soon, the receding wave encircled the village men and dragged them out to sea. Their drowning cries echoed in my ears as I left that world for another, fearful of what The Three might achieve…now that they had united against me.

I might have lost a friend that day, but I'd gained an enemy. And a powerful one at that. Which left only me to stop them from annihilating mankind.

I shot up in bed, shivering with sweat. Glancing around the room, I struggled to make sense of my surroundings. The red glow of the clock read 11:15 but meant nothing to me until the familiarity of the walls and furniture settled my racing heart. I'd suffered another nightmare, that's all. Only someday, the nightmare would undoubtedly come true.

Even once my arm completely healed, I'd never be enough to stop them. I could only run away so many times before they'd win.

So why stay here? I knew I wanted stability and a family again. I felt like I had that now, especially with Micah acting nicer toward me.

But at what cost?

Outside my window, I heard a car pull into the driveway. Only this time I didn't panic because I recognized the rumble of Tessa's engine pulling to a stop and the tinny sound of her doors slamming shut.

She and Micah walked to the front door, speaking in hushed tones, too low for me to discern. Periodically, Tessa would burst into a muffled fit of laughter, then for a long time I wouldn't hear either of them at all. I guessed his lips had silenced her voice.

Why does this bother you so much? They were together before you even arrived. Besides, even if she wasn't around, there's no telling he'd pick you.

Not when he had the lot of the junior class to choose from.

"It's not that," I told myself.

Then what is it? What do you want?

"To be normal."

That's it? Well, don't get your hopes up. It'll never happen.

I envisioned Tessa and Micah standing on the stoop, wrapped in each other's embrace as they shared a passionate kiss good night. I heard the door close before Micah locked the dead bolt behind him. He tiptoed across the kitchen floor, and then Tessa's car backed down the driveway.

I rolled over in bed, pulling my covers tight under my chin. I had a family and shelter. What more did I need?

"Okay, it's not *just* that," I whispered to myself. "I want to be loved."

CHAPTER TWENTY-ONE

The next day after gym class, I passed Karli, Tessa, and Isa in the locker room. Karli gave me a wave, but her face had a phony smile written all over it. *Whatever*, I shrugged and stopped at my locker in the next bay to change out of my sweaty gym clothes. Spinning my combination lock, I overheard Karli grumbling to the other girls. It took me a minute to realize she was grumbling about *me*.

"She's a real piece of work," she muttered. "Where'd Micah find her anyway?"

I heard Tessa give a reply, too soft to catch her exact words.

Then Karli let out a forced laugh. "Get real. So she's like what...homeless?"

"Why do you think she's always wearing Micah's old clothes?" Tessa chuckled. "Like her hoodie...did you know his mom pulled it out of the donation pile? He hasn't worn it since like freshman year."

"So sad," Isa commented, a hint of sarcasm in her tone.

I bit my lip, restraining the tears that instantly welled in the corners of my eyes.

"Those are Micah's?" Karli scoffed. "And all this time I thought she was just fashion-deficient. No offense to Micah, of course."

"None taken," Tessa sniggered.

Isa chimed in, "Remember what happened in Driver's Ed yesterday? It was crazy, wasn't it, Karli?"

"*Really* crazy," she said, her laughter coming out like a stifled snort. "She totally freaked out." Eager for an audience, Karli recounted the details of our harrowing trip through town that ended with Mr. Mendoza making me crash into the hill.

Aside from the minor exaggerations — I believe I only ran one red light, not several, Karli — her accuracy in recalling the order of events surprised me, especially when she had screamed the entire time.

When Karli concluded her tale, all three girls broke into high-pitched laughter...at my expense. And to think I had begun to feel pretty normal around here with a home, family, and friends.

Honestly, how is this any different than when you bump into the other Elementals? At least these girls didn't intend to *kill* me.

My lip trembled with hurt. I didn't care if I got detention for skipping Mrs. Bernard's French class. They had no idea what I'd been through. And no idea of what I still must endure in order to save their lives...at the expense of my own.

I spent the whole French period hiding out in the locker room, unable to face Micah in front of the rest of our class. At dismissal, I avoided him and chose to walk home alone, taking a long, deliberate detour. The girls' conversation replayed in my head, making me angrier with Micah, the one who started it all.

When I finally decided to return home, I barged through the front door and flew down the stairs, my face reddening with bottled fury when I found him sitting next to Sully on the couch. "You told Tessa I'm homeless?" I screamed at Micah.

But Micah's attention remained focused on his Zombie Dominion game. He didn't bother to respond, like he never even heard me in the first place. Instead, he built hordes of the undead to wage war against unsuspecting bands of pirates, aliens, and politicians. So I tore off Micah's hoodie and launched it at his face. The sound from the video game suggested I made him lose another life. Big deal, that happened to me way too often...only for real.

"What the — ?" Micah said. He muttered a string of curses under his breath, attempting to regain control of his characters.

I moved right between him and the TV screen so he had to look around me to see his game. "How could you?"

Micah glared at me. "How could I what?"

"You told her. And now Tessa's off blabbing to her friends that I'm homeless. Look, I don't need any charity handouts. You can have your stupid hoodie back." I picked it back off the couch and threw it in his face again.

Micah lifted one arm to block the assault when Sully said, "Easy, Jordan."

What a nice friend to cover for him. *Wish I had one too.* I glared at Micah. *Instead of someone who spreads lies about me behind my back.*

"Don't worry about Tessa," Sully continued, pushing a few buttons on his controller to maneuver his zombies through the incoming band of senators. "She's just jealous."

"Jealous?" I gasped. "What does Tessa have to be jealous of?"

Sully actually stopped playing for a moment to stare openmouthed at me. "How would you feel if someone who looked like...well, like *you*...moved into your boyfriend's basement?"

I placed my hands on my hips in defiance. "And what's that supposed to mean?"

"Aw, come off it, Jordan," Sully said from his spot on the couch. "You're gorgeous. And Tessa knows it." His gaze quickly shifted back to his video game, sparing a pair of zombies from certain doom.

I opened my mouth, ready to sling back some witty retort when Sully's words sank in. *He really thinks I'm gorgeous?* Oh, please.

I glanced over at Micah to gauge his thoughts. Though he refused to meet my gaze, the blush rose pretty darn high in his cheeks.

Gorgeous, huh? That single word magically dissolved my anger.

"Oh," I said and plopped down on the couch, suddenly feeling a little silly for launching into a tirade. Plus I felt a little chilled having thrown my hoodie — I mean, Micah's — away. I rubbed my arms for warmth, too stubborn to take the clothes back.

Soon Sully noticed me shivering. "Hey. I've got an idea. My sister Vanessa's off at college."

"Vanessa? What does she have to do with anything?"

"What I mean is her closet's still pretty full. She maxed out the space in her dorm, so everything left here she doesn't really need. Why don't you borrow some of her clothes? You guys are about the same size."

I rolled my eyes. "So I go from one charity handout to another?"

Sully shrugged. "Except this time, no one will ever know."

He did have a point.

"I figure her stuff's fair game," he continued.

Still, I shot him a skeptical look. "I dunno."

"It'll be fine. I've raided it before."

Though Micah seemed completely oblivious to my complaints, this comment drove him to hysterics.

"Okay. That came out all wrong," Sully explained. "I was only looking for her —"

Now Micah guffawed even harder, preventing Sully from finishing his sentence.

"Oh, come on. Will you shut up already?" Exasperated, Sully stood up to slap Micah across the back of his head. Keeping his attention focused on his zombie battle, Micah ducked out of the way and missed the blow.

Sully dropped his controller on the coffee table and joined me on the couch. He draped one arm around my shoulder. I felt warmer already.

"C'mon," he said, giving me a little squeeze. "It can't hurt to take a look."

"Why not?" I shrugged, rising to my feet. "And you're sure your parents won't mind if I come over?"

"Nah. Besides, Mom's at her book club tonight and Dad's in Denver on business. You won't be bothering anyone."

I raised a skeptical eyebrow. "Okay, I guess. As long as I'm not a bother."

"Not a bit." He placed one hand against the middle of my back, which made me shudder, but in a good way, and guided me up the stairs. I glanced over my shoulder once, noticing Micah intent on his game. At least it appeared like he was playing even though none of the characters actually moved. Almost like Micah stared blankly at the screen. Why did he have to be so irritating and confusing?

When we hopped in his car, Sully said, "You really shouldn't let Tessa get to you. She probably just feels threatened by you."

"By me?" I crinkled my nose in confusion.

"Sure." He started up the car. "Why else would she go out of her way to say those things in front of everyone else?"

While he backed down the driveway, I couldn't help but think how Sully had a funny way of making me feel better and worse at the same time.

We headed down the darkening road, a part of me thinking I should thank Sully for helping out—again—but I felt too frustrated with Micah and too cold without his warm hoodie to say anything. Sully dished me a few concerned glances. Each time he looked like he wanted to speak, but my defiant attitude seemed to silence him before he could begin.

We pulled up in front of his beautiful stucco home. Funny, for as long as I'd known him, I had never come here before. He unlocked the front door, and we entered his foyer where a crystal chandelier dangled from the lofted ceiling. When he slipped off his shoes and left them on the mat inside the front door, I followed suit.

"Her room's upstairs," he said, his eyes flitting toward the upper level. "Come on." He grabbed my hand, which made my heart skip a beat, and led me up the hardwood stairs. At the top, he turned to the left and entered the first door.

Not that my basement bedroom didn't seem adequate, because I appreciated Celia's generosity in welcoming me into their home, but Vanessa's room looked...well...*amazing*. My eyes swelled at the sight of her queen-size bed with its fluffy comforter and silky pillows, bottles of makeup lined neatly across her desk, and framed posters of pop singers staggered artistically across her chocolate-colored walls.

Sully, on the other hand, barely seemed to notice. Making a beeline for the closet, he slid the doors wide open and gestured to the contents. "Like I said before, it's all yours."

I gasped in astonishment. Clothes filled the closet from wall to wall. How much stuff did she own with her dorm completely packed, too?

Glancing back at Sully, I asked, "She really doesn't need this?"

He shook his head. "She probably doesn't even remember it's here."

I looked back at the clothing. "Still, I'd feel a little better if we just say I'm borrowing it."

"Fine. Borrow it."

"And you promise you'll let me know if she wants it back."

A grin lit his face. He wrapped his arm around my shoulders again and gave me a little squeeze. "You'll be the first one I call."

"Okay, then. As long as we've got that straight."

"I'll just be down the hall if you need me," Sully said. A wide grin flashed across his face and he readjusted his baseball cap on his head. "Take as much time as you'd like." Then he gave me a small wave and closed the door behind him.

"Thanks," I called. And I meant it. Sully had gone out of his way to make me feel comfortable, while Micah didn't bother to say a thing. Not even an apology for telling Tessa all those hurtful things.

My anger eventually faded while I flipped through coat hangers and gauged the possibilities. Like Sully had guessed, Vanessa seemed about my size. But her clothes looked a little more revealing than I preferred. Her jeans had only a two-inch zipper that rode low beneath my hip bones. Worse, I felt certain my butt crack would show the second I bent down to sit at my desk. I looked for something long enough to cover my waist, but her shirts either had low cuts in the front or accentuated my midriff…or both. Even when I yanked them down, they didn't hide my waist. I sucked in my breath just to zip the jeans to the top. Why did clothes have to be so complicated? Even though all the girls at school wore stuff like this, I didn't mean to draw this much attention.

Don't worry so much. You'll blend in. Isn't that what you want?

Yes. Blending in sounded good and made me less likely to spot. Plus the girls couldn't make fun of me for wearing Micah's clothes anymore. I posed in front of the mirror, trying to let the self-conscious feelings dissolve.

It didn't work.

Digging through the back of Vanessa's closet, I found a zipper-down sweater to cover my waist. I slipped it on and yanked it lower over my hips.

There. That's a little better. But I still needed a second opinion. Maybe Sully could help me out. I pushed open the door a crack. I didn't see him in the hall, but I heard music coming from his room, two doors down.

Taking a deep breath, I tiptoed through the hall and knocked on his door, yet received no response.

I knocked again, louder this time. Maybe he couldn't hear me over all the noise.

"It's me," I shouted and cracked the door open. "Can I ask you something?"

"Sure. Come on in."

I pushed his door wide, wincing at the full blast of his blaring rock. Sully lay stretched across his bed, texting on his phone.

Unlike Vanessa's neat and orderly room that looked untouched for months, Sully's room looked like, well, like it hadn't been cleaned in months. Piles of clothes lay strewn across the floor. How he determined which were clean and which were dirty befuddled me. His iPod, car keys, surfing magazines, and other miscellaneous items cluttered his desk. His backpack rested on the chair, probably in the same condition it was when he brought it home earlier that afternoon.

"How can you think when it's this loud?" I shouted over the music.

"Huh?" he asked. He reached for his iPod and turned the volume way down.

With the music at a tolerable level, I amended my question. "So…what do you think?" I crossed my arms over my chest and leaned against the doorframe.

Sully slipped his phone into his pocket and sat up on the

bed. His blue eyes widened to the point of bulging and his eyebrows rose so high they disappeared under his baseball cap. His mouth opened into a "wow," though he didn't say a thing.

"Well? Do I look okay?" I asked, feeling the need for some sort of verbal affirmation.

"More than *o-kay*," he confessed. He scooted off the bed to take my hand and led me into his room, then closed the door behind him. He stopped in front of his wall mirror.

"See, wasn't I right? I told you you'd look great," he smiled. "No—better than great. Make that *hot*."

I blushed. Usually I looked pretty hot right before I perished in flames and reentered this world in another dimension of the time continuum, but I didn't think he meant that type of "hot."

"I dunno," I said, still self-conscious. I ran my fingers through my shiny black hair until it fell straight against my shoulders. I shifted my hips one way, then the other to model in front of the mirror. Everything seemed so formfitting, providing nothing to hide behind. Still, if everyone else wore stuff like this…

Sully squeezed my hand for support. "You look great. Seriously. And no one will ever know. It'll be out little secret."

"And Micah's," I added.

"Sure. And Micah's," he repeated, sounding more than a bit disappointed I chose this time to mention his best friend's name. Should I worry that he had closed his bedroom door? Or that his mom wouldn't return for a while?

Instead, I smoothed my hands over the tight jeans and studied myself in the mirror, scanning my body from head to toe.

Sully said I looked great. He called me *hot* and *gorgeous*. Micah would never say those things.

A small grin made its way across my face. "Thanks, Sully. And thanks for helping me out. That's sweet of you." I looked up at him with genuine gratitude.

"Never a problem," he replied and turned to face me. His pale blue eyes held mine for a long moment. Until then, I hadn't realized just how much his eyes resembled the color of the sea. Not bright and bold like Hydros's wickedly deep blue ones, but placid and soothing, like on a calm, sunny day. I blinked to rid Hydros from my thoughts and stared into his eyes, glad to feel safe again. Happy, even.

Though I realized Sully still held my hand, I didn't pull away. It felt so warm and comforting. In fact, everything felt normal for a change.

So when he lifted one hand toward my face to caress my cheek, I let him. I closed my eyes, feeling the soft touch of his fingers gliding across my skin, the soothing heat of his palm resting against the back of my neck, and the brush of his breath against my mouth as he slowly pulled me toward him.

And when his lips met mine, I didn't step away. Because, like everything else, I wanted to feel normal...and loved.

His lips touched mine hesitantly at first, waiting for a sign to proceed. So I kissed him back softly, tenderly. My lips broke from his momentarily and then rejoined, eager to reunite once more.

But this small, sweet kiss didn't last long.

Before I had time to think if my actions might jeopardize his relationship with Micah (or mine), I kissed Sully back with greater intensity. A flood of adrenaline coursed through my veins. I pressed my lips to his with heightened passion. My fingers skimmed through his short hair, accidentally knocking his cap to the floor, but he didn't seem to mind. He wrapped his arms tightly around my back, drawing me closer to the warmth of his core.

Sully's hands made their way down my back and settled on my waist. His tongue explored the recesses of my mouth, touching, twisting, entwining with mine. Pulling me toward him, he strode backward while we kissed, one step after another, until eventually we tumbled onto his bed.

As remarkable as it felt to have someone love me again, I couldn't help but flash back to the only other time I shared a kiss like this.

CHAPTER TWENTY-TWO

Salem Village, Massachusetts Bay Colony, June 8, 1692

Under the cover of darkness, I cast a nervous glance over my shoulder before I stole behind a one-room log cabin. Pulling my cloak tighter around me, I shivered more out of fear than from the chill in the air on this early summer night. I knocked softly at the back door of the cabin, afraid to wake the children or alert anyone to my presence. When no one responded, I cracked open the door and slipped inside, shutting it quietly behind me. The hearth long extinguished, I used only the scant light of the crescent moon that filtered through the thick, glass windows to navigate my way across the Spartan room. With his straight brown hair spilling into his face, William Mills had fallen sound asleep at the table while awaiting my return.

Dressed in the same ragged cotton shirt and dirty woolen pants with suspenders he'd worn all week, William might have been two years my elder but appeared considerably older. And rightfully so. His mother died while delivering her stillbirth baby boy nearly a year ago, leaving his father grief-stricken. Even before the elder Mills succumbed to smallpox this past winter, William had taken over much of the responsibility of raising his three younger siblings, Clarissa, Beatrice, and Thomas. Though William would never admit it, I believe he secretly felt grateful the baby didn't survive — he'd only have been another mouth to feed. While William spent early mornings in the field, tending to their crops, his nine-year-old sister, Clarissa, cared for the two younger ones and readied them for school, but it never seemed enough. Even with all her tasks to complete, little Clarissa, wise beyond her years, insisted on teaching me to read by candlelight. Neither one ever muttered a complaint but deep down I knew they had more responsibilities than they deserved.

Still, William somehow managed to find time for me. Perhaps he hoped to one day take me as his wife and alleviate his burdens. In my heart, I knew he loved me, but I doubted affection sat foremost in his mind. William truly needed another soul to share his growing workload. So I did what I could to help. Besides, it provided a good excuse to see him every day.

But he'd never call me his wife. Especially not since Hydros arrived in Salem a day ago. She was the sole reason I must now hastily depart from the life I'd known these past six months.

I tiptoed across the hard earthen floor, laying a hand upon his shoulder. "William," I whispered in his ear. "It's time."

"Jordan? Is that you? But I...I didn't think you'd still come." His voice sounded groggy, filled with perpetual exhaustion. I felt awful for waking him; he rarely got a decent night's sleep. It was selfish of me to stop here, just to say good-bye.

"Shhh…" I pressed a finger to his lips, my voice a strained whisper. "I don't have much time."

"Don't go. Please," he implored, his body unusually clumsy and drugged with sleep. He staggered from the table. Wobbling once, he reached for my hand to clasp between his. "I'll protect you."

I detected an earnest tone to his voice, a fierce conviction that he wouldn't let harm befall me.

I wanted to believe him, and I felt desperate to hold him, to experience the warmth of his arms around me one last time and his tender lips pressed against mine. But I couldn't. I didn't have much time.

I pulled my hand away. "You don't understand how strong she's become. If I don't leave now…" I was unable to verbalize the truth. Once Hydros captured me for good, no one would stop them.

No one.

"I'm sorry," I whispered. This seemed far harder than I imagined. I berated myself for swinging past his home on my way out of town.

"Listen, Jordan," he said, rising from the table. "I need you. Promise me you'll stay."

I wanted to. I'd love to. And I merely needed to reply with a small, simple "yes" to satisfy this desire. Why did Hydros have to ruin everything I'd worked so hard to achieve?

My eyes found the floor. "I can't," I mumbled. The words stuck inside my throat. William had no idea of the dangers that lurked with every passing minute. *Leave now, Jordan,* I

197

reminded myself, *before she finds you…and him.*

William placed both hands behind my head, forcing me to meet his gaze. His deep brown eyes held mine with desperation. "I love you, Jordan. I do."

"Oh, God, William. Don't do this to me," I begged. It was hard enough to leave without his profession of love, something he hadn't declared until now.

"Please," he implored, "say that you will."

Swallowing hard, I managed, "Will what?'

A soft smile filled his face. "Marry me."

I shook my head as tears welled in my eyes. I wanted to explain everything to him, but I couldn't. I knew I should at least answer his question, but I wouldn't. Agreeing might mean imminent destruction for his entire family. And declining would leave him wondering if I truly loved him in return. Because I did. The only power I possessed to demonstrate that love was to actually leave the premises.

Now.

My eyes filled with sorrow as I pulled the hood of my traveling cloak over my head and turned for the door. I reached for the handle, when I felt his hand slip inside my palm, wheeling me to face him. A gasp of surprise escaped my mouth. Before I could speak, his lips met mine. For a brief instant, the fear and panic of Hydros finding me evaporated. Against my better judgment, I relented, allowing him to shape my mouth to his will. My arms sought his body, clutching him tightly to mine, a buffer from the fear and uncertainty that surrounded me. He kissed me longer and deeper. Every part of me that screamed to escape grew silent. For what seemed an eternity, just the two of us existed in this time and space. Nothing else mattered.

But love has a funny way of deluding me and dulling my senses with its euphoric bliss—so much that I neglected to hear the footsteps that approached outside.

Suddenly the front door to the Mills household slammed open with a resounding bang. William immediately separated from my embrace. He stepped in front of me in a protective stance to shield me from the multitude of fierce eyes that trained on my face, ready for my demise.

I knew with the manic fear of witches running rampant throughout Salem Village, it didn't take much to rally the townspeople. Still, the numbers Hydros gathered in support startled me—including faces of those I had trusted and considered friends since my arrival.

My eyes darted around the room I knew so well, searching for something to aid in our escape. I thought of shooting flames from my hands as a diversion but what good would that achieve? I'd end up torching the entire place, leaving William and his siblings without a home. Despite the initial confusion, the crowd would quickly track us down, even if we could get the slumbering kids out in time. Plus, who knew what punishment he'd face for conspiracy to witchcraft?

No. Bide your time, Jordan. I took a deep breath to calm my shattered nerves. My brain calculated another avenue when Hydros entered the room.

"There," she declared, pointing a long index finger in my direction. "That's Jordan Young."

I'd had many different surnames in the past, usually choosing a commonplace that sounded discreet after every jump through time. It didn't matter much to me what I selected. *Anything* was better than *Pyr*. So when I arrived in Salem, "Young" seemed like a good fit, but now it sounded entirely wrong, like it bore a sentence to death.

Two men bound my wrists behind my back. I knew I shouldn't fight as it would only make things worse.

"That one, too," Hydros commanded, nodding her head in William's direction.

A confused look passed over William's face. Two others reached for his wrists and lashed them behind his back.

All complacency left my body in an instant. "Let him be. He's done nothing wrong. It's me you want."

"It is," Hydros agreed, her lips turning up in a wicked grin. Her intense blue eyes gauged me with scorn. "But I think I'll keep him a little longer." Her long, evil fingers traced the length of his jawbone.

William lunged at her in defiance, but his captors restrained him.

Hydros's eyes gleamed maliciously. She added, "He might prove...*useful*."

They pushed us out the front door. I feared for little Clarissa Mills when she discovered her brother missing in the morning. I knew she possessed the strength to manage for a day until we resolved this whole mess. Then I'd leave the village and William could return home. Besides, it wouldn't be long before he found another suitable girl to call his wife.

Still, anguish seized my heart at the thought of him finding true happiness with someone else.

It's the only way, Jordan. It's always the only way. I would never have a normal life or a normal future. Never.

I spent a long night locked in a cold cell adjacent to William, unable to speak to him, unable to explain. I wondered how I let myself get into this predicament.

Worse, how I got him involved as well.

I knew I should sleep. I'd need my strength and sharp wits to save William but the strain of anticipation proved too great to endure. What would she do to me? Would I withstand her torment another time?

A few hours after daybreak, the guards arrived. I stood, ready to meet my fate. Instead, they unlocked William's cell and led him down the narrow hall.

Before long, I heard his cry pierce the eerie stillness of the jailhouse. In an instant, I realized her plan. Hydros chose to torture him instead of me, hoping to break my spirit.

Well, it wouldn't work.

"Release him!" I shouted and leapt to my feet. I shook the bars of my cell door. "He's innocent."

"*Silence*," a burly guard spat.

"Please! You must believe me," I implored. "He's done nothing wrong!"

By the look on the guard's face, I could tell he didn't approve of my outburst. Gruffly, he stalked over to my cell, raised his club high over his head, and whacked it on my door.

Luckily, I jumped backward in time to avoid him crushing my fingers. My hands created fire, my only defense. I couldn't risk injuring them when they were my last opportunity to save William.

You'll have your chance, I reminded myself and silently sank upon the filthy, bug-ridden mattress in my cell.

All day long I waited, listening to William's cries grow weaker and weaker. My guards passed by periodically but never once offered me a thing to eat or drink. My head spun, weak with deliria and dehydration, weary from lack of sleep.

And fearful of what had become of William.

The next morning, sunlight filled my cell, but I still hadn't seen or heard William return. Did Hydros torture him to gain information? If so, her actions seemed pointless since I told him nothing of value to her. Or did she torment him to the point of death? I bit my lip, thinking about the poor Mills kids, first orphaned and now abandoned — all because of me.

Later that morning, two guards unlocked my door and ushered me from my cell. I craned my neck, hoping for a glimpse of William when they guided me down the hall to the courtroom. Only his cell stood vacant. I prayed to God he remained alive.

The guards pushed me into the crowded courtroom, leading me past jeering citizens, eager for the judge's verdict. I looked across the crowd and recognized a few faces — Reverend Stephen Billings, the old widow Millie Parish, and the cuckold Gabriel Stern who looked on with pity.

Unfortunately, there was no sign of William.

Chief Justice Stockton and his court of magistrates and jurors stood at the far end of the courtroom, imposing in their long black robes. One of the jurors, Samuel Cornwall, the village blacksmith, peered down his hawkish nose at me with scrutiny and scorn.

"Bring forth the afflicted," Chief Justice Stockton called.

Hydros led in a girl, perhaps four years my junior, by the name of Amy Charles. I didn't know her personally but I recognized her. She was the niece of Eli Charles, the doctor who made a house call to William's father when he first contracted smallpox.

Amy looked up at Hydros with trepidation then walked

down the courtroom aisle. Hydros raised one hand to silence the crowd and flashed Amy a cunning smile before presenting the girl to the court. Having been here such a short time, the amount of power Hydros wielded in this small community amazed me. Then again, fear acted as a powerful motivator. And Hydros possessed quite the proficiency of generating fear in others.

"Doctor Charles hath recently diagnosed his young niece, Amy, with a case of bewitchment," Hydros bellowed for all to hear. "As is customary in the court, Amy will now identify the source of her affliction."

I rolled my eyes. Amy looked completely healthy, if you asked me. I wondered what bribe Hydros offered her family in exchange for this act of betrayal. Food? Firewood? It seemed so menial a reward to exchange for a person's life.

Then Hydros nodded her head—an understanding to proceed.

Amy stood still for a moment before her eyes rolled back into her skull. She dropped to the floor, kicking and thrashing madly in front of the entire courtroom. Her hair spilled onto the ground like slithering snakes and she rolled wildly.

Several witnesses gasped in shock and horror at the abnormal behavior of the niece of such a prominent citizen. Hushed accusations floated through the crowd. "It is obvious she hath been bewitched by someone, but who?" The witnesses, magistrates, and jurors perched on the edge of their benches. Their ears strained to hear the name cried of the accused.

"Her spirit enters my room at night," Amy wailed. Her body continued to thrash upon the courtroom floor. "It pinches me and torments me and bites me. Make it stop. *Make it stop!*" She displayed a fresh bite mark across her forearm, one she likely had inflicted upon herself for effect.

A few startled gasps carried through the audience. The low din of frightened whispers rose in alarm.

I had to admit, Amy put on a good show. Especially when I suspected how Hydros arranged for this to end.

Hydros hovered over Amy's unruly body. She placed one hand upon the girl's shoulder to silence her motions. "Who hath committed such atrocious crimes? Sayeth her name, young girl, loud enough for all the court to hear."

Amy rose to her knees and ran one hand through her tangled hair, then peered into the crowd. Then she turned toward me. Her accusing finger trembled as she pointed, "It is her. Jordan Young."

The back of my neck prickled at the sound of my name. Meanwhile, the courtroom filled with the commotion of a multitude of voices that whispered animatedly at once.

Hydros released Amy's shoulder, a sly grin spreading across her lips. She stepped up to the stand. "Admit it," her voice rang clear through the crowded courthouse, silencing the crowd with the fear she instilled. Her bold blue eyes bore into my skull. "*You* are a witch."

"I am not!" I screamed in protest, though I knew nothing I said would sway the crowd after Amy's accusation. They came here for a hanging and a hanging they would get.

Before I could utter another word in my defense, Chief Justice Stockton leaned toward his magistrates and jurors who nodded their heads in unison. He turned back to the crowd, announcing, "The court finds Jordan Young guilty of witchcraft. Her sentence shall be carried forth immediately."

Two guards grabbed each of my arms and brusquely led me out the double doors of the courtroom and up the nearby Gallows Hill with the crowd at our heels. Compared to the cool night of my capture, the day's bright noon sun felt insufferably hot. While the guards bound my hands behind my back and draped a noose around my neck, I scanned the crowd, still searching for William. Where could he be?

On the gallows stood another citizen accused of witchcraft — Abigail Howe, a leading scholar in the community who occasionally instructed the older students at Clarissa Mills' school as a guest lecturer. Abigail stood, brave and stoic, despite the rotten vegetables the crowd tossed at her feet. One hit her in the face, another in the gut, yet she paid no heed. Her lips moved in recitation of a prayer to help her pass to the next life.

I wished I could do the same, to help me end this agony. But my fate lay elsewhere. I glared down at Hydros, the one responsible for this unfortunate turn of events.

Hydros glared back. "Admit it," she gloated. "You are a witch."

"I'm no different than you," I sneered in return. *An Elemental*, though I couldn't actually confess that to the crowd. The word meant nothing to them.

My response did not sit well with Hydros. Her eyes narrowed to thin slits. She commanded, "Bring him forth."

Her words made my heart leap into my throat. *He was alive.* I breathed a huge sigh of relief though short-lived. When two guards dragged out William, I barely recognized him. His eyes looked black and beaten. His legs appeared so weak — perhaps broken — he could barely stand without aid.

Guilt washed over me like the heavy spring rains, consuming me fully. I never should have fallen in love. Nothing justified this type of suffering, to watch the person you adored endure such undeserved pain.

Though New England law prohibited captors from torturing criminals awaiting trial, they had never charged William with a crime. Which meant Hydros probably found a way to convince the others that his torture would lead to my conviction.

"Leave him out of this!" I pleaded. "He's innocent. Haven't you done enough to him already?"

"Hold him," she commanded. Hydros removed a knife from her cloak, letting the bright midday sun glint off its sharpened blade. Her eyes flickered steely cold and calculating when she raised the blade to his throat.

"Join us," she said, loud enough for only me to hear. "Join us and he lives. It's your choice." Her face turned smug, certain I'd surrender this time.

Then William raised his head to look me straight in the eye. "No," he mouthed, his expression determined and resolute. "Don't."

His selfless act weighed heavy on my soul.

"I'm sorry," I confessed, my eyes brimming with tears, "for everything."

Only one option remained for me to save him, an action that would prevent The Three from jeopardizing the future of all mankind. Of course, it meant I must die and would never see William again, in this life or the next.

I looked back at Hydros, my lips turning up in a cunning, crooked smile. Pleased with myself for foiling her attempts, I declared in a sharp voice, "I *am* a witch."

In an instant, I felt heat glimmer in my ebony eyes. A sudden, sharp pain spread from my heart outward and down through my bound arms. I snapped my fingers together behind my back to burn my cords and free my hands from the ropes.

The crowd gasped in alarm and Hydros's smugness instantly faded. She shot me a fierce, venomous look. For a brief second, I thought she would release William until her lips curved up in a wicked grin.

Then reality struck. She had a backup plan, too.

"*No,*" I screamed, reaching out to stop her.

I didn't make it in time. William's head slumped forward, her blade slicing his neck from ear to ear. Crimson soaked his ragged cotton shirt. Through my tears, I saw the image of those sweet Mills children, orphaned again.

I screamed in horrific agony, my skin scorched with anger. Flames shot from my hands, directly at Hydros's face, making the townspeople shriek in alarm.

"She is a witch!" yelled one.

"Hang her," cried another.

The chant spread quickly through the crowd, like wildfire across scorched prairie grasses, "*Hang her! Hang her!*"

But their wish would not come true that day. I'd already torched my gallows, sending flames high in the sky. Next to me, Abigail Howe stopped praying. Her face studied mine with confusion and fright. Tongues of fire wound around my form, paralyzing my body with an unbearable pain that ignited the loss in my heart.

I howled from the intensifying heat of the flames compounded with William's unfortunate fate. "*I hate you,*" I cried, glowering at Hydros through lethal eyes, determined to seek vengeance for all she stole from me.

Furious, Hydros thrust both arms toward the heavens. Like fast motion, clouds rolled in to darken the sky. Thunder boomed and a sudden downpour soaked the earth, drenching the onlookers. Most ran away in fear, cries of my devilish witchcraft fresh on their lips. Not a soul suspected Hydros.

Muddy puddles soon filled the square, but couldn't squelch the raging inferno I'd created that rapidly sucked the life from my soul. William Mills' lifeless eyes met mine, his blood mingling in a pool of mud before I vanished from Gallows Hill in a fiery blaze.

CHAPTER TWENTY-THREE

Sully kissed me deeper, his tongue investigating every inch of my mouth. While one of his hands ran through my hair, the other traced my tight-fitting jeans.

Then a new set of nightmarish images entered my brain, squelching the pleasure I derived from Sully's sensual kiss.

I stood back on Gallows Hill in old Salem Village. The weight of the thick noose hung heavy on my shoulders. Once again, I boldly defied Hydros, refusing to declare my association with witchcraft.

Only when she commanded the guards to bring forth her captor, I didn't see poor, innocent William, sole supporter of his household of siblings.

Instead, I imagined Sully wearing faded jeans, a charcoal gray T-shirt, and his baseball cap turned backward. Battered and bruised from Hydros's torturous acts, his pale blue eyes studied me with bewilderment and fear.

I gasped. *How did* he *get here?*

I shook my head, knowing that information was irrelevant. It only mattered that I prevent him from suffering the same fate as William. I could not—*would not*—let history repeat itself.

Before Hydros had a chance to remove her silvery blade, I snapped my fingers behind my back, gritting my teeth through the pain and burned the ropes that bound my wrists.

Amidst the cries of confusion that echoed through the crowd, I leapt off the gallows and landed right between Hydros and Sully. My hands erupted into balls of flame aimed directly at Hydros's depraved face. The crowd screamed louder but I paid them no heed. My attention remained focused on Hydros alone.

"Leave him alone," I demanded. "He's nothing to you."

I turned for a second, asking Sully, "Are you okay?"

He opened his mouth to respond when Hydros whipped out her knife and dragged its blade across the length of *my* throat. For a fraction of a second, I looked into her evil blue eyes, knowing that despite my efforts to save him, she chose Sully for her next victim. A gargled scream escaped my lips, *"No!"*

Then everything turned black.

The nightmare dissolved into the clarity of Sully's room. Suddenly dread consumed me, knowing I shouldn't stay here. Not for the inherent risk involved.

My heart seized with terror and I broke away from his kiss. Sweat drenched my brow. I tried to catch my breath, uncertain if the scream I issued was real or merely existed inside my head.

Sully used this opportunity to kiss my neck instead, his

lips brushing the soft skin of my throat until they reached my mouth once more.

Only my lips remained rigid. With all my strength, I pushed his chest off mine, my body overwhelmed with a desperate urge to escape.

Sully sat upright. His face appeared shocked. Confused. And hurt.

"What is it?" he managed, trying to understand what he did wrong. Because in all fairness, I hadn't shown any signs of regret until now.

I glanced over at the clock, biting my lip. I quickly devised a valid excuse. "Ohmigod. Is it that late already?"

Sully blinked. The face read a quarter after eight.

"I've gotta go...I promised Celia I'd put Cam to bed tonight." Though I tried to sound believable, Sully saw right through my lie.

"Oh. Okay," he said in an unconvincing way.

"I'm sorry." I leapt off his bed and ran my fingers through my tangled hair then dashed back to Vanessa's room to grab the clothes I wore here. Before I could leave, Sully stood in her doorway, his hands jammed deep in his pockets. By the expression on his face, I couldn't tell if he seemed sad, disappointed, or angry. Probably all three, I guessed.

I frowned, tears clouding my vision. "I'm sorry," I repeated in a whisper. "Really."

Sully allowed himself a small smile. The back of his hand caressed my cheek to wipe away my tears. I closed my eyes, wanting his arms to hold me tight and wishing this never happened at the same time.

Uncertain of what I should do, I flitted my eyes open and gazed at his face. The Sully I saw appeared beaten with black, sore eyes and split, bruised lips. Blinking again, I erased that image from my sight. But not from my memory.

Sniffling once, I moved to leave. Yet Sully stopped me, gently pressing his lips to mine once more. And though it seemed as sweet as the very first time, now the fire had vanished.

This time, I wouldn't let myself kiss back.

I bolted out Sully's front door and headed toward home where I invented some lame excuse to get out of reading a bedtime story to Cam. Intentionally avoiding Micah, I headed straight downstairs. I couldn't look at him much less speak to him, not after I essentially signed a death warrant for his best friend.

I grabbed my pajamas, then ran back upstairs two at a time to jump in the shower and turned on the water so hot it stung like painful pellets against my skin. Because I needed exactly that—intense pain to snap me back to my senses. And to make me realize what could happen the second I let down my guard.

Even after the shower, my brain remained a mess, my stomach a knotted whorl of conflicted emotion. What did I think, leading Sully on like that? He'd been nothing but nice to me since I arrived. Then I decided to get close to him just like I did with Lucius and William…the same closeness that unintentionally led to their demises.

I couldn't love Sully. I forbid myself to get involved with him or with anyone else ever again. That was why I always preferred to live on my own. I felt no guilt when only I died.

It's still not fair. Micah had Tessa. Karli chose Justin. Even Jake had asked Isa out last week.

Except me…I'd always be alone. How I could ever truly

love another person when The Three posed such a threat?

I pulled on my pajamas and slipped into bed when I heard a knock on my basement door. Dragging myself off the mattress, I opened the door to find Micah looking genuinely concerned about me for perhaps the first time ever.

"Sully just called. He wants me to check on you. He sounded pretty worried," Micah said, his eyebrows knitting together. "Is something wrong?"

I managed to keep all expression from my face and shook my head.

"Are you sure?" he pressed.

Biting my lip, I nodded slowly, though my eyes found the floor. I wished he would leave before the tears came. I doubted I could hold them back much longer.

"Will you speak to him?"

I squeezed my eyes shut and shook my head again.

"Fine." Micah sighed with exasperation. "I'll tell him you've never been better," he added with a heap of sarcasm.

After he shut my door behind him, I heard him give Sully some excuse about me being in the middle of Cam's favorite bedtime story and I'd have to wait to talk to him in the morning.

Why does everyone have to be so nice to me? Fresh tears poured down my cheeks, knowing I had nothing but pain to return.

That night, it seemed impossible to fall asleep. When I finally drifted off hours later, my dreams mixed with reality.

Haunted by my kiss with William, I relived the instant the townspeople barged through his door again in my mind. He would've been safe if I hadn't stopped there to say good-bye.

Suddenly, I found myself burning on the gallows again.

213

Only this time when Hydros brought forth her captive, I saw the lifeless eyes of *Micah* stare up at me through the dancing flames.

I shot up in bed, drenched in a cold sweat and consumed with guilt. Regardless of his sweet personality and my irrepressible teen urges, I shouldn't have targeted Sully. Not when the merciless Three would stop at nothing to harm him to get to me. He was my friend, he trusted me. Though life seemed difficult and unpleasant and unfair, I couldn't afford to make the same mistake again.

Then I thought about Micah. I remembered my confusion of anger and humor when we wrestled over my French test. How he almost missed his date with Tessa so he could finish crushing me in our one-on-one basketball game in the driveway. How he hugged me in sympathy after I shared the story of my family's death. How he made up a convenient excuse to cover for me with Sully.

Then I saw the Micah from my dream—his body lying in William's place and his blood mingling with the mud and rain on the crest of Gallows Hill.

Suddenly, I knew the other reason I couldn't let myself get physically close to Sully again. Deep within the confines of my heart, my love lay elsewhere. Somewhere along our rocky path to friendship, my feelings changed. Why must the heart always want what the soul couldn't have?

Worse, I could never, ever, let anyone know. Not him. Not Sully. And definitely not the Elementals. Unfortunately, they had a way of finding these things out...which worried me most.

CHAPTER TWENTY-FOUR

I woke the next morning, consumed with guilt. Why did I kiss Sully? Especially when I had fallen for Micah?

I guess I didn't want to admit that Micah's irritating, obnoxious behaviors had grown on me over time. Not that it really mattered now. The fact remained I'd become too comfortable and relaxed here. Even if I could stay, Micah wouldn't break up with Tessa for me. So I struggled to contain my emotions, watching them hold hands on the way to homeroom together, wishing it could be *us* instead.

I didn't have much time to dream of the impossible. Just then, Sully sidled up and slipped his arms around my waist. A pit opened in my stomach when he leaned to kiss me on the lips in greeting. I quickly turned my head so he grazed my cheek instead.

A weird expression passed over Micah's face, almost like I'd dished up a plate of hurt with a side helping of betrayal.

He shot me a fast look like, *Since when did this happen?*

I shrugged and turned away.

"You left in such a hurry, you forgot to bring the rest of Vanessa's clothes home with you," Sully whispered in my ear, too low for anyone to hear. "Remember, it's our little secret."

I swallowed hard, reminded of dangerous secrets that threatened everything I held dear.

"Maybe I'll swing by later," I replied sullenly. At that moment, clothes seemed the least of my concerns when just the sight of him made me sick with fear. I felt brainless and selfish for letting him get too close.

"You feeling okay? You look worse that you did last night." Eyeing me with concern, Sully placed his palm to my forehead. "God, Jordan. You're burning up."

I felt the color drain from my face. I looked down, half expecting to see my clothes ablaze, just like so many times before.

"How about I walk you to the nurse?" he offered.

I frowned. *Sweet as usual.* My stomach twisted into a giant knot.

"Don't bother. I'll be fine," I said and slid out of Sully's reach. On my own, I headed to the nurse's office, eager for an excuse to get away from the awkwardness of being around Sully and Micah together, now that my true feelings had revealed themselves.

After lying down in the nurse's office for all of homeroom, she took my temperature, claimed it appeared normal, and told me to go to my first period class. Unfortunately, Sully's class stood next door to Mr. Horowitz's Environmental Studies, so I asked if I might rest for a little while longer until my stomach felt better, which miraculously occurred at the bell to signal the end of the period.

I spent the rest of the morning avoiding Sully. When I spotted him waiting for me by my locker after math, I quickly turned the other way—hopefully before he saw me—and took a circuitous loop down a different hallway to get to art.

When he caught me after art class, I said all of two words to him before ducking inside the girls' room. Regardless of a tardy in British Lit, I didn't dare emerge until after the final bell rang.

My luck ran out by lunch. As soon as I entered the cafeteria, Sully waved me over to the seat next to him. I couldn't do anything but join Sully...empty-handed, of course. My stomach remained a whorl of emotions, way too conflicted to eat. So I sat beside him, unable to meet his gaze.

"What's up, Jordan?" he asked.

I shrugged as I stared at the empty table in front of me.

"Having a rough day?"

"Something like that," I admitted in a flat voice.

Sully sighed. "I don't get it. I mean yesterday you were like...you know."

I did know. And I enjoyed the "you know" part, but hated myself for getting carried away. No—not just for getting carried away. For letting things begin in the first place.

"And today...?" he continued, adjusting his baseball cap on the top of his head. "I just don't get it. What did I do?

I took a quick glance and noticed his wounded face. I never meant to cause him this grief, never meant to like Micah, and certainly never meant to create future harm should The Three suspect they could use him to get to me. Even though my feelings toward Sully had changed, I'd never want anything to happen to him.

"It's not you," I reassured him.

His brow knitted. "Then what is it?"

I couldn't respond. When I looked at him, I could only see the face of William Mills lying in the mud. His kind, loving eyes devoid of life, a pool of blood growing around his throat. I buried my face in my hands, wishing an end to the nightmares.

I heard Sully sigh, and then felt him place a soothing arm around my shoulder, pulling me toward him in a sympathetic sidearm hug. Suddenly, I found myself wishing Sully could hold me, wrap his arms around me, and take me away from this place.

Scratch that. I really wanted *Micah* to hold me reassuringly and promise me that everything would be okay.

But I couldn't take that risk with either of them, so I kept my backbone rigid like a washboard. Without another word, I walked away from the lunch table, forcing myself to lock my emotions deep inside in a place The Three could never reach.

My mind wandered through all of American History, unable to focus on anything with Sully and Micah in the classroom. When the bell rang, I ambled aimlessly down the hall until Micah dragged me off toward the gym.

"I'm not feeling too good," I told him. "I think I'm just going to go home instead."

"Oh, no you're not! We've got ballroom dancing, remember?" He said this in a faux British accent, though it didn't sound very convincing. Slipping his arm through mine, he led me down the hall. "Tessa's at a choir lesson so you've gotta be my partner today."

I blinked. He really wanted *me* for his dance partner? An unexpected smile lit my face.

Then Micah continued, "Otherwise I'll be stuck with…" His voice trailed off as he quickly glanced over each of his shoulders. He finished his sentence with a shudder, "…Bethany."

Oh.

The part of me that felt suddenly important was squashed in an instant. I couldn't believe I actually thought she wanted to be my friend when I first arrived. In reality, I provided a convenient excuse to get closer to Micah.

Then I reminded myself that it didn't matter how Micah felt about me. In fact, he'd probably be better off if he despised me outright. Sully, too, for that matter. I made a mental note to do whatever it took to drive Sully away. He could get over having his feelings hurt, but he couldn't get over being dead.

The boys' class and girls' class paired up for our ballroom dancing unit. I saw Bethany Donovan snake her way through the crowd, straight toward Micah.

"Help," Micah whispered to me and slipped his hand into mine. My heart made a sudden leap up my throat.

"So what do you say, Micah? Ready to be partners today?" she asked in her fake-nice voice.

"Thanks, Bethany," Micah responded as he held up my hand wrapped in his, "but Jordan already asked me."

"Oh. Okay." She frowned and shot me a pointed look. "Well, maybe tomorrow."

"Yeah, maybe," Micah said, waiting for her to leave until he added, "…*not.*"

Like a precaution, he kept his fingers tightly woven with mine as Mrs. Riviera and Mr. Swenson demonstrated the first few steps of the box step, counting for the boys to lead the waltz: left-two-three, right-two-three.

I looked down at our entwined hands, my mind driven mad with anxiety. I couldn't chance staying here another day, spending every second wondering when they'd catch me again or take Micah and Sully away forever.

Mrs. Riviera instructed us to take our partner's hand — which we already had covered — and to place our other hand on our partner's hip. The second Micah's palm touched my waist, perspiration beaded across my brow and pooled in my armpits. Unfortunately, Vanessa's tight clothes left little room to hide this fact from Micah or the rest of the world.

The music began and Mrs. Riviera counted like a metronome, "Left, two, three. Right, two three," Micah's eyes found mine. I expected him to look half as flustered as I felt with us positioned this close together. Instead, he griped, "This stuff is so lame. When will we ever need to use this?"

"Oh, I dunno. Maybe if you're invited to the coronation of King Henry III," I replied offhandedly while attempting to contain my conflicted emotions deep inside, keeping them hidden from him and everyone else.

Micah looked at me sideways. "*What?*"

"Hypothetically speaking, of course," I added and let my eyes find the floor. Truthfully, I only received an invitation to the coronation of the favorite son of Catherine de' Medici and King Henry II because I worked as a palace servant at the time. I thought that job would keep me isolated and protected while I learned the French language. And the guests probably considered it more of a sixteenth century French Renaissance dance than a true waltz, but it seemed close enough to me. Not that I could stay and enjoy the night of festivities anyway. Not with Skye there, at least. Dressed in her opulent scarlet gown that emphasized her narrow corseted waist and her bodice cut in a low, squared-off neckline, Skye blended in well with the other regal guests in attendance. Even with her long blond hair pulled back in a bun and adorned with glittering jewels, I recognized her immediately. Across the crowded room, her silvery eyes caught mine.

So before I knew it, I fled again—awkwardly, I'd admit—in a corset and full-length dress.

Micah snorted, interrupting my memories of the event. "Honestly, Jordan. I don't know where you come up with this stuff."

I shrugged. "You know me. The history buff, right?" I tittered, reminding myself to keep my stupid mouth shut.

Micah returned my nervous smile, growing silent as he stepped left, two, three, right, two three. After a long moment, he finally spoke, "About last night."

I raised one eyebrow high on my head. Did he expect an explanation after covering for me on the phone? I held my breath and waited for him to continue.

"I think Sully likes you," Micah admitted.

Suddenly, my palms turned cold and clammy. *How much did Sully tell him? Was it last night on the phone? Or this morning after I left for the nurse?* Then I wondered if guys even talked about stuff like that.

I felt my face turn pale, convinced Micah could see my heart beating wildly beneath Vanessa's tight shirt. What did I think, wearing this outfit today?

"Oh, please. He was just helping out," I said, struggling to keep an even tone. "Making me feel better, that's all. So I didn't throw another fit."

"Well, I'm glad you took him up on his offer." He swallowed hard. "Her clothes look good on you."

My heart skipped a beat. I couldn't believe he just said that. Then I remembered a scene from my nightmare, where Micah's lifeless eyes stared up at me from Salem's muddy Gallows Hill. I buried my feelings again, knowing I shouldn't take the risk.

Trying to sound casual, I retorted, "Whatever. You're just happy to have all your stuff back."

"No, seriously," he started.

For some strange reason, I found myself hanging on his every word, hoping for another compliment. *Get a grip, Jordan. You're becoming pathetic and insecure like Bethany.*

"I meant to tell you this last night," Micah continued, "but..."

Despite Mrs. Riviera's methodic counting, my feet stopped moving in an instant.

Was he jealous of Sully? If so, would he actually declare he liked me? More than the annoying girl his mom took in and eventually became somewhat of a friend?

"I mean, I know it's none of my business, but..." Micah shifted his eyes away from my face.

Then my heart seized up. Suddenly, I had a sinking suspicion I wouldn't appreciate what he was about to say.

"When you didn't come back right away...I mean, I know it can take a long time to try on clothes but..."

"*But...?*" I asked. My pulse thudded inside my veins.

"Well, I just thought." Then he shook his head. "It's nothing. All I'm saying is *if* you and Sully...you know."

"There's nothing going on," I said coolly. He was right. It was none of his business.

"No, I'm serious. He's a great guy. Don't get me wrong but..."

Okay. Enough with the buts already. "There's *nothing* going on," I repeated, my eyes drawing thin. And to think just a moment ago, I actually chastised myself for blushing at his kind words.

"Fine. But suppose that there was," Micah simpered. "Just don't say I didn't warn you."

"So what are you now," I snapped, "like my overly protective big brother?"

His eyes hit the floor. That came out harsher than I intended. Still, he had no right to assume anything serious actually happened between Sully and me.

Dropping his hand, I marched straight across the gymnasium floor, leaving Micah standing there alone and confused — something I seemed to have mastered recently.

I didn't even look back when I heard Mrs. Riviera call my name, demanding to see my pass to leave class. Without acknowledging her request, I blew through the double-wide doors and cruised down the hallway, needing a breath of fresh air to clear my mind.

To be honest, all those thoughts had crossed my mind at some point last night when Sully and I lay on his bed, alone in his house, wondering how far to take this new development in our relationship. Because I liked Sully, I really did. Until I'd flashed back to Gallows Hill.

Mostly, I feared Micah could read me to see what bothered me the most. That something changed inside of me, making me realize I liked *him*. After what had happened to Lucius in Pompeii and William in Salem Village, I couldn't bear to live with the grief of another unnecessary death burdening my soul.

CHAPTER TWENTY-FIVE

I turned down the hallway, heading for the main doors, hoping no one would spot me.

Then I heard a voice say, "Where do you think you're going, young lady?"

Dang it. Nabbed by the hall monitor, I quickly whipped up a story. "I've got a doctor's appointment that I completely forgot about because I was so busy taking notes in Mr. Horowitz's class and now I'm gonna be late."

She eyed me skeptically and I knew my story didn't cut it with her today, even with my arm still wrapped in an Ace bandage. "May I see your pass?"

I jammed my hands into the tiny front pockets of Vanessa's jeans. "Oh, I don't believe it," I grumbled in my most convincing voice. "When did it fall out of my pocket?"

"Well, stop by the office on your way out and they'll contact your parents."

"But I'm already five minutes late and my mom's waiting outside," I pleaded, gesturing to a vehicle conveniently parked along the curb, just outside the front door.

"And the office already knows?" she asked.

"Yep." I nodded vigorously. "Told them first thing this morning."

The monitor's eyebrows remained in a fixed position high on her forehead, but the desperate look in my eyes must have worked because she let me go.

Good thing, too. This way I'd have enough time to pack up a few things and get out of town before Micah returned home.

I raced the whole way back to the house. The slate sky looked angry and volatile, but it didn't open up. While I dumped my backpack's contents on the kitchen table, I flipped on the TV and turned to the Weather Channel. The storm cell swelled to enormous proportions, completely engulfing the entire Bay Area plus the lower half of the state. Which meant I needed to head east and north—ideally away from any populated area so I couldn't unwittingly subject anyone else to harm.

My bag now emptied, I pulled out a Post-it note to scribble Celia an explanation for my sudden disappearance. Only the words stuck as if ink clogged my pen. How could I ever thank them for everything they'd provided on a hot pink Post-it note, no less? Or apologize for what might happen if I didn't leave at once? Or to tell them not to look for me, that somehow I'd manage on my own?

Dropping the pen on the table, I left the hot pink square lying there, unused. Maybe I'd call them later, after the storm followed me far inland.

I ran down to the basement and tossed a few sets of clothes in my backpack. Then I spotted Micah's old hoodie lying on the floor. I never realized he'd given it back yesterday after I got so mad at him for what Tessa had said. I grabbed it to stuff inside the backpack, too, when I noticed a soccer ball lying underneath.

Oh, crap. I completely forgot about Cam's first game tomorrow morning. I promised him I'd be there. I frowned, knowing that Celia, Cam, Micah, and Sully would never understand my reason for departing unexpectedly. But having them mad at me forever, I could live with.

Them not having a forever…not so much.

After tossing a jacket, toothbrush, and toothpaste on top of my clothes, I raced up the stairs and grabbed some food from the cabinets and fruit from the fridge. I closed the fridge door and saw a new drawing held in place with a magnet clip. Using a different color for every object on the page, Cam had drawn himself in blue, me in pink, the soccer ball in orange, and a goal in purple. He kept the grass green.

I blinked, my throat feeling tight. Maybe I was making a huge mistake in departing without telling anyone. Maybe I should at least thank the family who'd been kind enough to host me.

Then again, if I stayed, it might be too late for them. Some thanks that would be.

Steadying my resolve, I took one last look at Cam's picture, a memory to hold me when on the run, and slung my backpack over one shoulder. With a wistful look at the Trudeau home—one of the few places I'd ever felt safe—I headed out.

When I reached the door, I heard car tires approach.

Peeking out the kitchen window, I spotted Vanessa Sullivan's white Toyota Corolla pull up the driveway. An expletive slid off my tongue. I *so* did not have time for this.

I slipped my other arm through my backpack strap, thinking up a good excuse to get out of talking to Sully and reached for the door handle. Only it turned from the outside.

I blurted, "Sully, I'm really sorry but I have to—"

Then I stopped and took a startled step backward.

Sully hadn't come to check on me. *Micah* had.

"What happened?" Micah exclaimed. "You didn't come back for French class."

I hung my head. I couldn't bear to look him in the eye.

The next thing I knew, he pressed the back of his hand to my forehead. I paused for a moment, feeling a bit safer with him near. I closed my eyes to remember the feel of his touch against my skin once I was far away and alone again.

Jordan! I screamed at myself for getting distracted again. *Just go.*

I brushed his hand away. "I'm not sick," I confessed. My weak voice trembled. "I...I'm sorry, but I have to leave."

He placed one hand on my shoulder to stop me. "What're you talking about? Leaving? But I thought you said you didn't have anywhere to go?"

"I, uh..."

"You already said that everyone you know is gone," he reminded me.

"Yeah, but..."

"Come off it, Jordan. Why don't you just come to grips with the reality that *we're* your family now?"

Suddenly, it didn't matter that he loved Tessa. He admitted that he wanted me to stay, which only made my decision that much harder.

"I'm sorry. I have to go. It's what's best," I said in a soft voice.

"Best for who? You? And what about me?"

"What about you?" I echoed.

"What if it were me instead of Sully?"

My heart skipped two beats at his suggestion. I forced myself to ignore it with a dramatic roll of my eyes to hide the effect his words had on me. "Oh, please. You're so whipped. Tessa's got you wrapped around her finger and you know it."

On cue, I heard Micah's phone vibrate in his pocket. I readied for him to check the text so I could dart through the door. Instead, he pulled the phone out of his pocket only a hair to glance at its screen, then slipped it back inside without reading the new message.

So much for my easy exit.

"I can't stay," I continued. "It won't be long before they find me."

He sighed. "Jordan, you're safe. I've told you that a hundred times. No one is chasing you anymore. What will it take to convince you?"

"I can't take that chance." I walked past him, right out the door as a drizzle leaked from the heavy sky.

Micah grabbed my wrist tightly and spun me toward him. Defiant, I struggled to pull free of his hold. He gripped my good wrist tightly and then placed his other hand on my cheek, forcing me to meet his gaze.

His expression changed when he saw the sadness and confusion that warred inside me, the pain I'd experienced countless times before. More importantly, the peril I caused other innocent friends, all because of my folly. I refused to let that happen again. Not to Micah or Sully or Cameron. Not to anyone. I'd overstayed my welcome and nothing he could say or do would change my mind.

Nothing.

"I'm sorry, too," he said and took a meaningful step closer.

Except for that. I held my breath, waiting with anticipation.

I heard his phone vibrate inside his pocket again. It sounded irritated like an angry swarm of bees defending their hive. For once, he completely ignored it, his eyes locking with mine.

He leaned an inch closer, then another. My heart jumped up my throat. I found myself surprisingly short of breath. How many times had I wished for this to happen? For him to focus his attention solely on me? To look at me with the care and concern he doted on Tessa?

His eyes burned into mine. Fixed in his gaze, I couldn't move. He stood so close, I felt his breath on my lips. I stopped resisting and consciously let my heavy backpack drop to the floor. His fingers released my wrist and laced with my hand instead.

Remember, it's time to go?

Right. But what harm could come of a little good-bye kiss?

Do I need to remind you of what happened to Lucius? Or William? my conscience scolded.

I closed my eyes tight to block the pain. Never again. I wouldn't let that happen.

At that precise moment, I heard the sound of tires peeling down the road. I turned a fraction of an inch to see the tail end of a red Mustang drive behind the wall of junipers at the end of the neighbor's driveway.

I could be mistaken. Many people owned red Mustangs.

But I felt pretty sure I knew what I just saw.

Tessa's car.

Don't worry, Jordan, I convinced myself. She didn't see a thing. And a large part of me thrilled in the fact I wouldn't have to worry about enduring her verbal abuse at school ever again. I'd be gone. Micah could patch things up with her afterward.

A small part of me wished she actually had something to witness besides Micah holding my hand. And that afterward, Micah wouldn't want to fix his relationship. Though the thought seemed selfish, I couldn't stop it from existing in my mind.

Suddenly, I heard a different car pull to a stop as more footsteps came running up the driveway. My heart leapt up my throat again and stole my breath. *Oh, God. The Elementals!*

Only the footprints sounded soft, too small for The Three. I pulled away from Micah to watch Cameron dash up the sidewalk. "I'm home," he declared. "Did you miss me?"

I couldn't help but smile. With everything troubling my soul, Cam's sunny disposition always brightened my mood.

Micah managed to squelch it. "Why don't you tell him?"

"Tell me what?" Cam chirped.

I frowned, unable to verbalize the truth. So Micah helped me along. "Jordan's leaving."

"What?" Cam exclaimed. His head turned sideways and his voice reached an impossibly high pitch. Tears instantly filled his big eyes. "But you promised you'd watch me play in my first game. It's tomorrow, right, Micah?"

Nodding his head, Micah said, "See?" He stepped away and gave me a meaningful glance that might signify, *How can you say no to a face like that?* Or maybe it meant, *Promise me you won't leave without saying good-bye.* I couldn't be sure of his exact intent.

I looked into Cam's innocent, brown eyes, hating Micah for using him to get to me. I found it extremely difficult to say no to a six-year-old, especially a sweet one like Cam.

"Promise," Micah whispered so only I could hear. He squeezed my hand tighter.

I closed my eyes, the strain and burden of my curse growing impossible to bear. When I opened them again, he still stared at me, refusing to let go.

So that confirmed it. He wanted me to say good-bye to him. Alone. "Fine," I mouthed back with reluctance and forced a small smile.

His eyes kept a wary look. Finally, he released my fingers from his grip.

I'd give him one more day. One day to find a way to say good-bye, then I'd take off for good. With no looking back.

Micah turned to follow Cam into the house. *It's better this way,* I reminded myself, even if I must sacrifice everything I care about. Besides, he still had Tessa. He didn't have room for me in his life.

On the doorstep I looked upward. A darkening storm front of low-lying clouds advanced from the south. A chill hung in the air. I rubbed my hands up and down my arms to keep warm, hoping I could escape their wrath in time.

That night I volunteered to read Cam his favorite bedtime story, *Fox in Socks,* though I didn't tell him this marked the last time my tongue would twist in such ridiculous knots. I didn't mind helping Celia a little, especially since she looked so frazzled from work today. I also felt glad for one last chance to spend with Cam who slipped from wired to tired in

3.9 seconds flat. I pulled his blankets over his shoulders and planted a small kiss on his forehead, whispering, "Good-bye, Cam." Deep inside, I'd miss him more than he'd ever know.

Closing his door on my way out, I sniffled, kicking myself again for getting too involved. From this day forward, I needed to stick to myself.

I didn't see Micah the rest of the night, though I suspected he hid in his room. I wanted to knock on his door and get this over with, but knew that wouldn't solve anything. Micah purposefully avoided me so I'd make it to Cam's game. I crawled into bed early, unsure of when I'd get another chance at a decent night's sleep once I hit the road. Exhausted and emotionally drained from the day's events, I tucked myself deeper under the covers. I squeezed my eyes shut, willing a peaceful sleep to find me, if only for one night.

I tried to forget the past, but nightmares continually resurfaced, grim reminders of the awesome power The Three wielded in shaping the fate of humanity.

CHAPTER TWENTY-SIX

Saturday morning, the phone rang early. Celia's office called and needed her to come in to work.

"But you'll miss my first game!" Cam protested.

"I know, I know. Oh, Cam, I'm so, so sorry. But I'll make it up to you. I promise. And Micah's agreed to take video of the whole thing for me so I can watch it when I get home."

I looked at Micah, murmuring, "*You* did?" Since when did Micah volunteer to do anything that didn't directly benefit himself?

He gave me a nonchalant shrug, then jammed his hands into his pockets and looked away. Fine, avoid me again. I still planned to leave right after the game.

I tried to appear happy and lighthearted when I pulled Cam's high black socks over his shin guards and tied his cleats. But I had a hard time masking the fear and uncertainty that shrouded my every thought.

Then Sully walked in, carrying Cam's soccer ball from the porch. "Who's ready for a hat trick?" he grinned, giving Cam a high-five. When Sully saw me, his grin quickly faded.

My stomach instantly turned into a knotted wreck, worse than my tongue had when reading *Fox in Socks* last night. Why did Micah have to invite Sully to come, too? Did he purposefully try to make this more difficult for me? And what about our "private" good-bye?

Forget it. It didn't matter anymore. I'd go to the game, and then get out of here. Who cared about that silly little promise I made to Micah?

Not me, I thought, watching Micah repeatedly check his phone throughout the first half of Cam's game, his face looking more and more disappointed each time. I finally snatched Celia's camera from him. Not only did he mess up the footage by digging in his pocket for his phone, it gave me a reason to avoid talking to both of them.

"Something wrong?" Sully wagered after Micah checked his phone for perhaps the twentieth time.

"I thought she said she'd be here," Micah mumbled.

"Who?"

"Tessa. At least she told me she would."

"So?" Sully muttered. "She's probably just busy. Maybe she forgot she had to work or something."

Micah frowned. "Yeah. Or something."

Suddenly, I felt bad for both of them.

I turned my attention to the game instead, noting that kindergarten soccer appeared more like Swarm Ball. Repeatedly, one kid pelted the ball while the rest of the players on both teams charged after it. In the first half, the weather held and Cam got an assist, adding to the bunch of goals his team scored. But in the second half, the leaden sky dribbled. Tiny droplets fell first, then fat plunks of rain. I handed Celia's camera back to Micah to slip inside his jacket pocket.

The intermittent drops grew in size and frequency, making it difficult to concentrate on the game or Micah or Sully. Though I doubted either one wanted to speak to me, especially when they both looked a little annoyed by my actions.

I shouldn't be here. It sounded like the second hand of a clock ticked loudly inside my skull to mark the passage of time until my imminent demise.

My eyes darted through the crowd huddled along the sidelines beneath the protection of their multicolored umbrellas. I almost expected to spot Hydros, Gaia, or Skye nestled in amongst the spectators. Bent on recognizing one of their evil faces, I failed to notice Cameron dribble the ball down the field on a breakaway until Micah elbowed me in the ribs.

"Check it out," he remarked. Cam kicked the ball past the last defender, and then charged after it. Suddenly, only the goalie remained between him and the net. "Go, little bro!" Micah shouted across the field.

"Go, Cam!" Sully cheered.

Momentarily forgetting my concerns, I watched Cam regain control of the ball. "Shoot!" I cried, crossing my fingers.

Cam planted his left foot next to the ball. With a swift kick, he launched the ball toward the goal. The goalie swooped down to grab it but the wet leather slipped through his fingers and rolled across the painted white goal line.

"Yeah! Good one, Cam!" I screamed, jumping in the air with jubilation. Cam looked thrilled as he sprinted back to his starting position, giving high-fives to everyone on his team, including his coach. Pride swelled inside me. I turned to Micah, my face beaming. "He did it!"

Excited, Micah wrapped his arms around me in a spontaneous hug that swept me off the ground. When he finally set me back down, I turned toward Sully. Caught in the moment, I reached out to embrace him, too.

Only his body stood cold and rigid, his face frozen in a very un-Sully-like scowl. I stepped back with a soft, "Sorry," too afraid to look him in the eyes.

Talk about killing the moment.

For the rest of the game, I silently waited in the rain, squashing my hands deep into my pockets, reflecting on my recent mistakes. I realized that everything came down to the same reason—I let myself get too close. Why else would I feel so conflicted? Proud of Cam and all our practices in the backyard, ecstatic when Micah swept me into a strong hug, and absolutely disgusted with myself for how I hurt Sully. I vowed I'd never let this happen to me again…if I could make it that long.

I heaved a huge sigh of relief when the ref gave three sharp blows on her whistle to end the game.

But not when Micah suggested, "Why don't we take Cameron out for lunch to celebrate his first goal?"

I shot him a I-thought-it-was-time-for-me-to-go look.

Micah hurled one back like, *And what about that good-bye?*

Then I realized Sully noted our whole exchange, wearing a wounded expression upon his face.

"Okay," I succumbed, trying my best not to look at Sully again. "To celebrate." I tousled Cam's mop of wet hair. After Sully climbed in the driver's seat, I caught Micah's eye and flashed him a determined look, *But that's it. Then I'm outta here.*

Sully started the car, and I slid in the back next to Cam. "I have to go on a trip," I began, the words getting caught in my throat. I needed to tell him. He had a right to the truth and he deserved to hear it straight from me.

I sensed Sully lean across the center console to listen. With a heavy sigh, I continued, knowing he also deserved to hear my explanation, especially after all I'd put him through.

"Oh." Cam's face fell. "Will you be back tomorrow?"

"Tomorrow?" I sighed again. "No, not tomorrow."

"Then will you be at my game next weekend?" His big brown eyes studied me expectantly.

I frowned. I wanted to tell him everything but couldn't. With Celia called in to the office this morning, the truth might upset him more. So I settled for, "I hope so."

Micah fired me a pointed look, like I gave his brother false hopes. I spoke from my heart. I would like to make it, even though I knew it'd never happen. In fact, I'd consider myself lucky to make it through the end of the day.

A few minutes later, Sully pulled into the Taco Bell situated on the beach. We hustled indoors to get out of the driving rain and selected a table by the window where we could safely watch the ferocity of the storm that brewed outside. The same dismal shade of gray cloaked the sky, water, and clouds. The incessant rain blended one into the next, making the distinction between each layer practically imperceptible. The storm surge pummeled the shore. I hoped this little celebration wouldn't take long.

"So what would you like?" I asked Cam.

"You know." He grinned back. His curls sagged against his head and his soaked cotton jersey clung to his small frame.

"Okay. Be right back." I told him and walked up to the counter, stepping into line behind Sully and Micah.

Aside from the employees, no other guests visited this Taco Bell on such a miserable day. I should be out of here in no time.

After they finished, I placed my order. "I'll have two soft-shelled tacos with only cheese."

The cashier asked, "No meat?"

"Nope."

"Heated?"

I shook my head. "Nope. Just plain."

"That's it?" The cashier's eyebrows perched high on her brow.

"That's it," I replied with certainty.

Sure, it seemed a strange request for a six-year-old, but Cameron knew exactly what he liked. You had to respect a kid like that.

While she explained to the kitchen staff in Spanish the specifics of Cam's unusual request, I peeked over my shoulder at our table. Then a huge sheet of rain pelted the window, making me jump. I glanced back outside where the ferocious waves ravaged the shore. All of a sudden, I realized it no longer mattered. My heart could take a backseat to everything else. I'd get Cam his food and then leave.

Really.

I carried the tray back to the table, ordering nothing for myself. Between the surge outdoors and Sully's stormy mood indoors, food wouldn't sit well inside my distraught stomach.

Celebration or not, I decided it was time for me to go. Setting the food down in front of Cam, I whispered to Micah, "That's it. I've gotta—"

But Micah held up his index finger for me to wait as Cam asked him, "Can I have a strawberry milk, too?"

I rolled my eyes. Normally, Micah would flat out ignore me. I sank into a chair next to Cam.

"Don't think they've got it. How about a Mountain Dew?" Micah suggested.

Cam's face soured as he scrunched his nose.

"Fruit Punch?" Sully asked.

Cam shook his head resolutely.

"What about a Pepsi?" said Micah.

Cam stuck out his tongue with disgust.

But before Sully could recommend another soft drink from the menu, I offered to get him his milk, knowing this exchange could go on for quite some time. Plus, the empty Taco Bell suddenly seemed cramped.

Heading across the street, I tucked my head further beneath my hood. The wild wind whisked the raindrops like miniature blades against my face. Completely drenched by the time I reached Safeway, I mopped my face and headed toward the dairy section in the back of the supermarket to make my selection.

When I returned to the front of the store to wait in line and pay for Cam's strawberry milk, I spotted someone with unusually bright green eyes. Wearing tight Capri jeans, a surfing Hoodie, and sandals, she pulled her russet hair back in a bun and wedged most of it under a black San Francisco Giants ball cap. Her eyes lit up and she gave me a small smile. Something about her looked vaguely familiar. She appeared happy to recognize me, too, so I guessed I knew her from school. I shook off the feeling of déjà vu as I paid for Cam's drink and returned to Taco Bell, eager to get out of here.

Because I certainly hadn't done a great job of it so far.

When I returned to the beach, something seemed weird, almost like the tide had pulled away, taking the sea with it.

For a brief moment, I stared at the expanse of sandy beach in confusion, noticing how much larger it appeared now than when we had arrived. Then I swallowed hard, realizing why those bright green eyes in Safeway looked so familiar...

I just saw Gaia.

I struggled for a breath. *They're here.*

CHAPTER TWENTY-SEVEN

I couldn't believe I hadn't made the connection at the store. In an instant, panic gripped my throat and I gasped for air.

"What's wrong?" Micah asked when I rushed into the restaurant at breakneck speed.

I pointed out the window of the Taco Bell. "We've gotta leave."

"Seriously?" he said, taking a bite of his Taco Grande. "We're not done with our food."

A chill ran up my spine when I noticed the waves breaking further and further from the beach, making the shoreline appear to recede. I'd seen this before. And it could only mean one thing.

"Leave it. It doesn't matter," I told him sharply. *How foolish of me to think I could hide in one spot this long!* Grabbing Cam by the wrist, I tugged him behind me and sprinted for the door with Sully and Micah in close pursuit.

"Get outta here now!" I yelled to the cashier and kitchen staff. I gestured out the window with fear. Trying to remember some Spanish I picked up from living here in California, I added, "*¡Rápido!*"

Confused, they stared back at me, unmoving. I assumed they'd run soon enough once that wave returned. At least I warned them in advance.

Leaving our uneaten food at the table, we raced to the car. Micah picked up Cam who kicked in protest because he wanted to finish his cheese taco and strawberry milk.

"Give me your keys," I told Sully.

"What?"

"Your keys." I held out my hand.

He frowned. "But you don't have your driver's license. And it's my sister's car."

I understood why he didn't trust me, especially after I'd let him down. Hard.

All our issues would have to wait. "See all that water pulling away? Well, it'll be back. And then some. Unless I get us out of here *now*."

"It's always about you," he grumbled and tossed me the keys.

Hopping in the driver's seat, I slammed the door shut and cranked the keys in the ignition, peeling out of the parking lot so fast that Micah barely had a chance to close his door before the first wave crest broke over the sea wall and spilled onto the asphalt. I bit my lip, knowing the subsequent waves would be much worse.

Sully moaned from the backseat when I squealed the tires, leaving black streaks of rubber. I turned left and accelerated up the hill. Cam continued to cry when we reached the first dip in the road and the water closed in, surging up the touristy side street with incredible speed.

I felt bad to have him stuck here with me. I doubted Celia ever drove this fast with him in the car. For a fraction of a second, I wondered how she'd feel about me going this speed right now. I knew she'd prefer this pace over letting her sons die.

Pressing the pedal to the floor, I dodged past the traffic of alarmed motorists and blew through a red light to climb the next hill. Seconds later, the sea covered the intersection, washing the stranded cars into one another.

"What are you doin'?" Sully shrieked.

"Didn't you see that? This wall of water isn't any normal storm. Hydros made a tsunami."

Just for me, I thought grimly.

"A tsunami?" Micah gasped.

Cam stopped crying long enough to ask, "What's a tsunami?"

"A tsunami's a huge wave that rushes inland, then drags everything back out to—"

Micah interrupted my explanation. "But the tsunami evacuation route is south of here. You're going the wrong way!"

I shook my head. "It's not safe. We have to leave the coast. It's the only way to save you now that they know I'm here."

I stepped harder on the gas, pushing the needle toward ninety on the straights and sped out of Pacifica toward San Francisco. In the backseat, Cam wailed. I supposed my description of the tsunami sounded a bit too graphic.

"Dude, why am I taking care of your little brother?" Sully

grumbled, trying to pacify Cam. "I should've called shotgun."

The rain pelted the windshield, coating it in a viscous haze. The wipers zipped across the glass in a blur but did little to aid my vision. I squinted into the storm, hearing Mr. Mendoza's disapproving voice in my ear, reminding me that I drove much faster than I should under these conditions. I zoomed past three cars traveling half our speed.

Micah gripped the dashboard. "Enough of this, Jordan. Seriously. What's going on?"

"I saw one of them. In Safeway when I got Cam's strawberry milk."

"Which I didn't get to finish!" Cam bellowed.

"Them who?" Micah asked. His voice barely carried over his brother's staggered sobs.

I rolled my eyes. "*Them*. The Elementals. The ones I told you about before. It was Gaia. Only I didn't recognize her at first."

"Gaia?"

"The Earth Elemental," I snipped, wishing he'd paid more attention that morning I first saw the super storm developing. "She caught me off guard...I didn't expect them to be here already. And if I don't get away from the coast, Hydros will wash everything out to sea."

Another wave crest hit the coastline like a barreling freight train. To our left, the rumble resonated over the driving rain and the Corolla's humming engine. Trees, homes, and vehicles crunched and crumbled in the destructive rising surge of water.

"Now don't spaz out on me," Micah said, his eyes widening. We climbed another peak in the road. Behind us, the water pushed inland toward the highway. "Like I told you before, no one's chasing you — it's just the storm. Really."

I looked into hazel eyes and I wanted to believe him. But I couldn't. When I peeked into the rearview mirror, I noticed the sea had flooded the road behind us.

Though Micah and Sully dismissed this storm as some natural phenomena that scientists had predicted for years, I knew the truth. Their powers had grown and they'd stop at nothing to capture me.

I needed to prove my point to Micah and Sully. "Did you ever hear of the Great Chicago Fire?" I asked.

"What does that have to do with anything?" Sully objected from the backseat.

Micah shot him a sharp look.

I said, "Well, that started because of me."

"Don't be ridiculous," Sully grumbled.

"That wasn't you," Micah retorted. "I heard a cow kicked over a lantern. It's in a song, isn't it, Sully?"

"I dunno," Sully said coolly.

I explained, "It did start in a barn, but it was all me."

Before I could continue, I threw a quick glance over my shoulder, hoping to change lanes. Most of the cars traveled faster than normal after that last wave crest hit the road, but it figured I'd gotten stuck behind a slowpoke. "Of course I didn't mean to," I said and flipped on my turn signal. "Skye helped me along with that, using her intense winds to make my flames leap from rooftop to rooftop."

We rounded the bend of the highway, and I looked out across the sprawling city of San Francisco that unfolded before me. How many more people would the Elementals leave homeless if I failed this time? I peeked at Micah next to me and Cam and Sully in the backseat. How many more of my friends would I watch die?

Suddenly the car swerved uncontrollably to one side. I braced the wheel, struggling to keep it steady, the road swaying beneath our tires. I knew Gaia caused this mayhem. I imagined her stomping her foot with greater power upon the ground until she sent out surface waves, rippling in all directions. With her mounting fury, these tremors would increase in intensity, like an earthquake producing multiple aftershocks until I caved to their demands.

My fingers gripped the steering wheel tighter, making my knuckles turn white. I refused to let this cycle repeat itself. The time had come to settle this for good. Not only must I stop The Three, but I needed to take one or more of them out so this threat could never exist again. Not in this magnitude, at least.

"Still don't believe me? Let's try something different." I glanced back at Sully, my body shivering when a spasm of pain shot outward from my chest. A terrified look passed over his face. He stared into my ebony eyes, now glowing like hot embers.

"Stop the car." He paled. "That is freaky. Seriously, Jordan, let me out."

"Just wait." Since I'd gone this far in revealing my identity, why not finish it? I took one hand off the wheel, poising it in midair for them to watch.

I winced, jolts of pain radiating down my arm and into my hand. Then I snapped my fingers together to form a ball of fire resting in my palm. While Micah and Sully gasped in shock, Cam shouted from the backseat, "That's awesome!"

"Now do you believe me?" I challenged them, balancing the fire with my free hand.

Micah stared from the flaming ball to me, speechless.

"I told you my real name wasn't Jordan. They call me *Pyr*, the Greek word for fire."

"But, I, uh—" Micah stammered.

Before he had a chance to complete his thought, our car unexpectedly swerved into the other lane. The fireball lurched off my palm.

"What are you doing?" Sully cried. The flames caught the Corolla's ceiling upholstery and set it on fire.

"It wasn't me!" I barked, knowing that Gaia must be behind all this. How else would the solid road shift beneath our tires? "Gaia's making the ground quake."

While I steadied the car back in our lane, Micah slipped off one of his shoes to stomp out the flames. "All right, all right! We believe you!" he screamed. "Just make it stop before you set Sully's whole freakin' car on fire!" From the backseat, Sully ripped off his shoe to help Micah squelch the flames.

I didn't need to look at them to feel the weight of Sully and Micah's eyes burning into me with disbelief and fear. I heard Cam chuckle. "Do it again!" he exclaimed.

Sully and Micah both wheeled on him. "*No!*" they shouted through heavy breaths.

I stepped harder on the gas pedal and we flew through the turns that led into the city. "You can see why I have to stop them," I said, my eyes filled with sincerity. They simmered to their normal black color. "I can't let this continue any longer. They'll stop at nothing to—" My voice trailed off as the sentence finished in my mind, *To rule the planet.*

"Wow," Sully said with a low whistle. "And I thought I had it bad with Mom making me take the SAT *and* the ACT this year."

A small smile made its way across my face. Only Sully would find a way to turn this moment into a corny joke. Nearing the city, I quickly read the signs, choosing to merge with the lane headed for the Golden Gate Bridge.

"No," Micah suggested. "Take the Bay Bridge. It'll lead you away from the ocean."

"Good plan," I thought. Hydros would pose less of a threat without the power of the vast Pacific to fuel her.

Despite our speed in getting out of Pacifica, the traffic now slowed to a crawl. We slipped into line to enter the Bay Bridge. *This is taking too long*, I fretted, knowing the congestion provided The Three with a better opportunity to catch me. I scanned the faces of nearby drivers, fortunately not recognizing a single one. My leg started to bounce with nervous energy. There had to be a faster way.

Luckily, once we passed the bottleneck of eastbound traffic that entered the lower level of the bridge, our speed increased. Though I knew we'd near safety once we spanned this section of the San Francisco Bay, I couldn't help but feel a little claustrophobic, surrounded by steel with the weight of five lanes of westbound traffic passing overhead.

With the city skyline shrinking as we entered Yerba Buena and Treasure Islands, some of my anxiety faded. We had made it almost halfway across the bay. Almost halfway to freedom. I knew I could get us there safely.

The Bay Bridge sloped downward when we neared the far shore. I couldn't help but feel a monumental weight lift from my shoulders. Somehow, I'd managed to elude The Three Elementals without destroying the entire city. Once we reached the other side, they wouldn't be able to catch up. I'd leave Micah, Cam, and Sully safely behind and flee across the continent. North, toward some desolate reaches of the Arctic, essentially suppressing their potential to wreak havoc upon any urban areas.

A broad grin filled my face, certain I finally had control of the situation and no longer lived in fear. I'd deal with them accordingly on my terms when I felt ready.

Then the bridge swayed, swinging wildly upon its supports. A single, scary thought entered my mind. *Gaia refused to let me go this easy.*

Cameron screamed. Cars swerved around us, slamming on their brakes and filling the air with the smell of burnt rubber. Behind us, a loud crash resonated through the confined space, a trio of cars colliding in a tangled mass of steel and shattered glass. My eyes darted from one side to the next, looking for a clear path to steer us away from the mess. I wove in and out of half a dozen cars before I heard an enormous crack overhead. I pressed on the gas, grazing the side of another car and squeezed the Corolla through a narrow gap in the road in an attempt to get out before the entire bridge collapsed.

"Sorry," I said to Sully. I gritted my teeth. Paint scraped off the driver's side door. Frozen with fear, Sully didn't respond. I guessed his sister's paint job ranked low on his list of concerns at the moment.

"Step on it," Micah advised, his eyes trained on the steel beams above. He gripped the dashboard intensely and we barged through another set of stalled cars.

I couldn't make it through fast enough. The trusses gave way, collapsing one section of the upper deck. I screamed louder than I thought humanly possible when the roadway above fell and pinned the tail of Sully's car, mostly on Cam's side. Gaia had succeeded in preventing our escape.

My pulse pounded in my ears. I peered over my shoulder, grateful the entire roof of the car hadn't caved in on top of us. "Are you okay?" I asked Sully and Cam. Micah and I ripped off our seat belts. Sully rubbed his forehead, like he must've ducked at the last second and slammed it against the back of Micah's seat.

But Cam didn't answer. All I detected was a painful moan coming from his side of the car.

"Oh, God," I breathed. "Not Cam." I glanced over at Micah, my eyes filled with dread.

"Let's get him outta here," he agreed. I moved to open my door. The crash had bent the doorframe, sealing it shut.

"Here, let me." He pushed me aside to get a better angle and aimed his foot at the glass. With one swift kick, he popped out the pane so we could squeeze through the window.

"I'll pass Cam to you," I told him.

Crawling into the backseat, I helped a dazed Sully unbuckle Cam. He appeared hurt but I couldn't determine how badly. "Are you okay, Cam?" I asked, receiving another groan for a response. The roof of the car slanted at a precarious angle over Cam's side. He definitely took the worst of the blow.

"It'll be all right, Cam." I tried to hide the fear in my voice and tenderly kissed his forehead. He didn't need anything else to upset him now.

After Sully wrangled his way through the window, I carefully passed Cam to them and crawled out. "We'll have to hurry. I doubt the bridge will hold for long, especially if Gaia suspects we're still here."

Micah nodded, cradling Cam in his arms. I took Sully's hand to lead him out of harm's way and this time, he didn't protest. We raced through the jammed cars, praying we'd make it off the bridge before Gaia unleashed another shock.

Dodging between cars, I chastised myself for staying this long. Now I'd jeopardized everything—the city, my friends,

Cam. All because I grew too attached.

Finally, we reached the end of the bridge. We only needed to find someone to give us a ride to the hospital. Suddenly, a yellow Volkswagen Beetle approached. I flagged it down, desperate for assistance.

The car stopped about twenty feet in front of us. But when the driver stepped out, I knew in an instant I'd made a huge mistake.

There stood Skye — her sinister silver eyes boring into my skull. "It's good to see you again, Pyr." Her light blond hair fell down her back, rustling in the breeze off the bay.

I swallowed hard when Gaia opened the passenger side door. She whipped off her San Francisco Giants hat and tossed it onto the road. Her sparkling emerald eyes narrowed, eager for a confrontation.

Last, Hydros crawled from the backseat. Standing tall, her wickedly blue eyes held mine. I glanced nervously over my shoulder at the bay, too close for my liking.

"Go get Cam some help. I'll handle it from here," I told Micah, sounding far more confident than I felt.

CHAPTER TWENTY-EIGHT

Gaia eyed my friends maliciously, her tongue licking her lips. She taunted, "So what will it take this time, Pyr? Watching all three of your friends die?"

"I hate you," I spat and ripped the Ace bandage off my arm. My eyes grew excruciatingly dry, like an intense fire burned inside each pupil, fueled by my animosity for her.

"We can change that," Gaia gloated, her vibrant emerald eyes gleaming. "Look what we accomplished with our dear Skye." Skye didn't even blink, like she possessed zero recollection of her former self.

I couldn't let that happen to me.

"You know the drill, Pyr. You either join us..." Gaia raised one foot over the ground, letting it hover a few seconds for effect.

Sneaking a quick glance over my shoulder, I spotted Micah, Cam, and Sully only a couple of blocks away. Why hadn't they made it further by now? Consumed with dread, I realized Micah would need some help in order to escape with Cam and Sully in their injured states. Hoping to guarantee their safety, I narrowed my eyes at Gaia, channeling my hatred toward her into a sudden burst of power infused with blistering pain.

"...or *die*," Gaia finished. The toxic words hung on her lips. "Perhaps your replacement will be more receptive to our request," she said, reminding me of the gravity of her intent.

Before she had a chance to stomp her foot upon the road, I whipped my hands from my sides. A pulse of agonizing energy shot down my arms when I sent a six-foot tall raging wall of flames in their direction to surround The Three. My eyes bulged from their sockets. I'd never managed to produce something so intense before. Then again, I'd never been quite this irate before, either. How many times must I watch the Elementals strip me of everyone I hold dear to my heart?

Never again, I promised myself. The fear would end today.

I kept my hands poised in their direction, though my recently healed arm quickly grew weak from strain. *Just a little longer*. I ventured a peek over my shoulder again. Micah must've turned a corner since I lost him from view.

"Good," I whispered, letting my arms relax for a fraction of a second. I knew he'd make it now. For the first time in my life, I'd spare my friends from their untimely fates.

But Gaia took advantage of my lapse in concentration. "Now!" she commanded in a wicked, low voice.

Then everything happened so fast.

Gaia dropped her foot upon the earth, making the road crack and buckle. The jolt knocked me off my feet and effectively extinguished my restraining firewall. A great fissure opened behind me, swallowing their yellow VW Bug with a twisted crunch of metal.

At the same time, Skye looked up, her silvery eyes reflecting the low-lying gray clouds. She raised one hand heavenward. A swirling vortex of pea-green mist descended from the sky, picking up dirt and debris as it neared the ground.

Meanwhile, Hydros extended one hand toward the bay. Off in the distance, a deep blue wave formed. I swallowed hard, watching it approach the land, knowing she would use her powers to swell the wave to enormous proportions once that massive power neared shore.

I didn't have much time. Adrenaline flowed like molten magma through my veins. I stretched both hands forward and gritted my teeth to block the pain. Then I rocketed a fiery blast that knocked all three clear off their feet.

I stared down at my arm, stretching it after the exertion. Don't get me wrong—it hurt a ton, but still felt much better than I imagined it would. Hopefully I had the endurance to keep this up long enough to eliminate one of them, though I still hadn't decided who posed the greatest threat.

They staggered back to their feet and I realized that decision held little importance. It'd be best if I could take out all three in a single swoop.

When Hydros lost her balance, her wave fell for a moment. Now, she commanded it to an even greater strength. Skye whipped the clouds into an angry, violent shade of olive green. Her vortex increased in speed, spiraling down the street toward me, picking up splintered pieces of fence and mailboxes that lay in its path.

Suddenly, I had an idea. A wickedly cunning idea. My eyes burned like hot embers from William Mills' hearth back in

Salem Village. And like the fiery lava bomb that took Lucius's life when Mt. Vesuvius erupted and destroyed Pompeii.

It stops here, I reminded myself, strengthening my resolve.

Excruciating heat traversed the length of my arms. I aimed my hands at the tornado to blast it with a steady stream of fire. The strong wind gusts caught hold of my flames, enveloping them and lifting them skyward in a spinning ball of fire that ignited the tornado against the dark gray clouds.

"Whoa," I breathed and stepped backward, awestruck by the beauty of this awesome, deadly firestorm. Gaia's eyes grew wide. The fire rose high into the sky in a whirling mass.

Hydros's monster wave neared shore. It had already tripled in height without even reaching the shallows.

Swallowing hard, I jetted a stronger flame toward the fire tornado, using my power to wrestle the blazing spiral from Skye and shift it toward The Three. From amidst the flames, flickers of trapped debris surfaced. *Just a little closer.* I exhausted my energy reserves to hurl the storm at The Three in time to silence Hydros's destructive wave.

In a sudden burst of speed, the fire tornado unleashed its fury upon them. I heard Hydros scream before she lost control of the water.

"Yes!" I exclaimed. Out of the corner of my eye, I saw the surface of the bay flatten as the rising swell quickly subsided. "I did it!"

Now for Gaia.

I directed the fiery twister toward Gaia when I noticed Skye studying Hydros's fallen form. I glanced over at Hydros, shaken to see a wooden spike impaling her thin abdomen. Blood pooled around her. Gaia bent down to comfort her ally. She cradled Hydros's head in her lap and soothingly stroked her flowing brown hair.

I didn't destroy Gaia and I didn't win Skye back, but I managed to get Hydros. Wasn't that enough? After all, she'd killed William Mills and I vowed to pay her back for his life. Surprisingly, a lump formed in my throat, reminding me of all the times I'd watched my friends and family die before me. I dropped my hands a few inches, grief filling my heart, remembering the pangs of loss.

Skye took advantage of my momentary lapse of judgment to regain control of her tornado.

Around me, the winds increased in ferocity, lashing my hair against my cheeks and threatening to knock me from my feet with each gust. Fighting to stand upright, I tried to form another blaze, but each time her gusts and updrafts extinguished it in an instant.

Skye's winds intensified, uprooting saplings and barreling over a telephone pole that toppled in slow motion, caught up in its lines. The transformer sent out a shower of sparks when it hit the ground nearby. I realized with dismay, that even with Hydros fading fast, I still might lose this fight.

I glanced around me, struggling to fight back. The winds battered my body and shook me back and forth.

Regain control. I lifted my hands to drive the winds back.

Closing my eyes in concentration, I sensed the familiar surge of throbbing energy fuel through my veins, funneling down my arms and out through my palms, until something struck me. A sudden burning pain choked my every breath. Opening my eyes, I glanced at my belly where one half of a metal rod protruded a few inches from my skin. The other half lay embedded in my gut.

My eyes grew wide with horror. I glanced back at Hydros

lying still in Gaia's arms, knowing I would soon suffer that same fate, with no one to comfort me.

Afraid that removing it would increase my bleeding, I tore off my jacket and wrapped the fabric over the wound. I slipped the sleeves around my waist and held it in place with a knot. I wobbled on my feet, knowing I didn't have much time.

In the midst of this chaos, a vehicle screeched to a halt, right by my side. "Get in," Micah said, opening the back door from inside.

"Shouldn't you be at the hospital by now?" I snapped.

"*Get in,*" he shouted, reaching for my wrist.

"No way." I shook my head adamantly and pulled away from his grip. "I mean it. Get outta here! I can't hold them off much longer."

"I was afraid you'd say that. We've gotta get Cam and Sully to the hospital," he said pointing to the backseat. "Pronto."

Speechless, I frowned, knowing I caused their injuries. In an instant, my own problems seemed trivial.

"Listen. I'm not leaving you here," Micah declared. "So can't you do something to hold them off?"

Renewed determination flared in my eyes, returning the fiery glow. "Right."

It's now or never, Jordan. I dug deep within my soul, mustering the last reserves of energy in a powerful, stinging blast. A huge gust of fire unleashed from one hand, connecting with Skye's tornado once more and rocketing upward. Swirling chunks of fiery debris encased the remaining Elementals. Inside, I heard two sets of panicked screams. Around us, the earth grew still and the wind lessened, like the lull of the storm in the eye of the hurricane.

Secretly, I hoped that would suffice. Not just to squelch their powers momentarily but to finish them altogether.

Micah's eyes popped. "Is that a fire tornado? Now *that* is cool!" he congratulated me, then pulled me into the passenger's seat and sped off.

I agreed with Micah. It did seem cool, but it had totally drained me. I glanced down at my belly, noticing a patch of blood stained the jacket despite my efforts to keep the rod in place. I bit my lip, pain replacing the rush of adrenaline from battling The Three.

"You're hurt," Micah said, following my gaze. His face clouded.

"I'll be fine," I managed. "It's Cam and Sully I'm worried about." I glanced at the backseat where Cam moaned in pain. Sully kept his eyes closed and pressed one hand to the back of his head.

While Micah drove to the nearest hospital, I carefully lifted up the jacket to peek at the wound. It looked bad. I doubted the doctors could help me this time.

CHAPTER TWENTY-NINE

Micah slipped into my hospital room, his face grave.

"Did you get ahold of Celia?" I asked, masking my own pain.

With a nod he said, "She's on her way, but it'll take her awhile with the bridge out. She's got to make a long detour now."

"And Cam? How's he?"

Micah shuddered, sadly shaking his head. "Not good. The doctors say his kidneys were crushed in the accident. He needs a transplant or he's terminal. Only there's a waiting list for a kidney donor."

"Meaning?"

"Even if they could find a match, it's unlikely he'll get one in time," he concluded with a deep frown.

"I'll do it," I offered. "Ask them to check if I'm a match."

"It doesn't really work like that," Micah said as he looked

away. "It's not that easy."

"Just ask, will you?" I begged. "There's no harm in asking, right?"

"They won't let you. Besides, you're so weak. I'm afraid you'll die." His eyes misted over.

He made it sound so final when I knew my biggest sacrifice in leaving this world would be losing Micah. But that shouldn't really matter. There couldn't be—wouldn't be—a future for us.

"I don't have much time left anyway," I told him.

Micah shook his head, refusing to meet my gaze.

"Just ask," I prodded. "Remember it's for *Cameron*. He has so much life yet to live."

"But—"

"And I've already lived more lives than I can recall."

"Still—"

"Please, Micah," I implored. "Do this. *For me*."

Micah sniffled, his eyes filled with sorrow. "Fine," he conceded with a heavy sigh and walked out the door muttering something about how it would never happen.

For a few minutes, I lay in silence, hoping Micah had it all wrong and my selfless action might indeed spare Cam's life. In the pit of my stomach, I knew my time drew short. And this time, I would not return. I might never see them again, but at least I spared their lives and eliminated Hydros for good, I hoped. So what if I died? I'd saved a lot of innocent people today and accomplished more than I ever dreamed possible.

Before I had a chance to ponder my bleak future, my door swung open. "Hey, Sully," I smiled softly, feeling genuinely glad to see him on his feet. "How's your head?"

"A little bruised. The doctor says I probably have a

concussion but I'll survive. How about you?" he asked in an apologetic tone.

I shrugged, and then kicked myself for doing so when another wave of pain shot through my gut. "I've been better."

"I'm sorry."

"Why are you apologizing? If it hadn't been for you, I'd be dead by now. I couldn't keep them off much longer."

He pulled a chair up to the side of my bed. His eyes held mine in earnest. "I'm sorry I didn't believe you. You tried to tell me, so many times. And yet—"

"No worries," I interrupted, gritting my teeth to battle the pain. "Besides, I should be the one apologizing to you. I didn't want to blow you off. I was only afraid they'd get to you."

"Plus there's Micah," he said in a low voice.

My eyebrows pinched together. "What's that supposed to mean?"

Nervously, he readjusted the baseball cap on his head. "Let's just say it's not the first time a girl's chosen him over me."

My jaw dropped. *He knew?*

"Sully, I—" I stammered, feeling worse than before. "I...I didn't mean—"

"Don't worry. I won't tell Tessa. Your secret's safe with me."

Under different circumstances, I doubted Sully would have let me go so easily. But he couldn't stay mad at someone who had so little time left in this world.

Giving my hand a squeeze, he added, "Anyway, I'm still glad I got to know you...if only for a short time."

Guilt weighed heavy on my soul. All this time I thought I'd lessen Sully's hurt by distancing myself from him. Instead, it turned out I pained him more. Why was love so cruel? So unfair? A sharp pain stabbed my heart, contorting my face with grief and shame.

Sully noticed. His expression turned grim. With a frown, he rose off the chair. "I'll tell Micah that you're..." He swallowed hard, unable to finish.

"Thanks," I whispered, my eyes filled with apology.

He leaned over the side of my bed to kiss me good-bye. His lips hovered over mine for a second before he changed his mind and planted them on my forehead instead.

"See ya, Jordan," he said, giving my hand a final squeeze.

My eyes brimmed with tears. My voice too choked to respond, I lifted my hand in a meager wave. Once again, I knew it didn't suffice. Unintentionally, I'd managed to hurt him even more.

Another bolt of pain shot through my body, threatening to cleave my abdomen in two. I clenched my jaw to contain the misery when Micah entered. His face looked bleak, worse than before.

"How's Cam?" I said before the tears ruled my emotions.

"He's sleeping now."

"So? What did they say? Am I a match?"

"The doctors are working to find a donor," Micah explained.

I frowned. "You didn't answer my question."

Micah heaved a heavy sigh. "I couldn't ask. I just couldn't."

"Micah," I scolded him, "you promised."

His eyes searched mine in earnest. "You don't understand. I'm still worried you won't..."

"Make it," I finished for him, every word a challenge to utter. Irritated that he wouldn't even check to see if I could help Cam, I grumbled, "Don't worry. I won't."

Micah wiped away a stray tear, puzzled by my nonchalance. Then his eyes lit with an idea. "How'd you do it before?"

I couldn't reply. Everything around me began to fade, like I only had a matter of minutes left in this world. If I couldn't donate my organs to save Cam, why cling to the trace of life that remained?

"Jordan," he said, his voice urgent, "Tell me again. How'd you do it before?

Willing my eyelids open, I focused on Micah's anxious face. "Do what?"

"Jump across time. Can't you do it again?"

Slowly and with extreme effort, I whispered, "I need fire."

"Then make some."

"Too weak. Hurts too much," I said, suddenly lacking the energy to form full sentences. "Never been this bad before. Can't handle the pain. Plus—" my voice trailed off. My eyes grew too heavy to keep open.

"Plus?"

"In hospital. Hurt others." Hadn't I intended to save mankind by sacrificing myself?

Micah grabbed the fire extinguisher off the wall and said, "It's okay. I'll be your backup."

"Can't." It took all my reserves just to answer his questions. I doubted I could produce a tiny spark, even if I wanted.

Micah frowned. "So there's nothing I can do?"

I closed my eyes and whispered a sad, "No. Even if I could jump..."

Perching on the edge of my bed, Micah leaned closer, waiting for me to finish.

"I'd never see you again," I grimaced, another wave of pain shooting through my belly. I wanted to tell him I never traveled to the same place twice but felt too drained to elaborate.

"Never?"

"*Never.*" But it didn't matter anymore. With Hydros and me gone, Gaia and Skye could never gain total control. So I guessed that meant I'd achieved my goal and spared humanity after all. It seemed such a small sacrifice when I thought of it that way. There must be something I could say to make him understand.

With the last of my strength, I continued, "I can't live like this. They find my friends...my family...and hurt them. Just to get to me. It's better...better if I'm gone."

"Better for who?" Micah looked up, his eyes finding mine. "You? And what about us?"

"Us?"

"Okay...*me*. What about me?" he clarified.

Tears built in the corners of my eyes. For such a long time, I'd thought he hated me. Gradually his hate grew into tolerance and then tolerance into friendship. Until yesterday, I never realized he felt anything else. To hear him verbalize this now was more than my heart could bear.

"Maybe a small part of me will always be with you," I said, assuming that once I died, they couldn't deny my request to help Cam, if it would work.

Micah's eyes shimmered. "You're not making this any easier on me, you know."

"Sorry," I mumbled. My heavy eyelids drooped lower with each passing second. "Tell Cam I said good-bye."

"I will."

"And thank Celia for me, will you."

Micah sniffled. "Absolutely."

Managing a faint smile, I forced my eyes open to look at him once more. My voice came out in the softest of whispers when I finished. "And you...thanks for putting up with me."

Micah looked torn, like he wanted to laugh and apologize at the same time. He set his hand upon my forehead and brushed my hair from my face. His eyes told me everything I needed to know — that deep down, he loved me, too.

The comfort I derived from that knowledge would carry me into the next world, until reunited with those I'd already lost. A warm smile crept across my face, my eyes closing. My strength faded, ready for the end.

"Come on, Jordan. Don't leave me yet." Micah laced his fingers through mine and squeezed hard to keep me alert. "You promised you'd say good-bye."

But I couldn't move. My body felt sluggish, the slightest effort exhausting all my remaining strength. My head tilted to one side, like a heavy load against the pillow.

I heard Micah sniffle again and felt his weight shift forward on my bed. Before I could muster the energy to shoot him a confused look, I felt his lips touch mine in parting — soft and sweet, like drops of dew caressing springtime blossoms. When I didn't immediately respond, he pressed his lips to mine with greater urgency, willing me to return to this world — and to him.

A sudden rush rejuvenated my soul, infusing it with unexpected bliss. My hands found his head and pulled him closer to mine, my lips moving with his. I sensed Micah's face light up in a wide grin as he kissed me longer and deeper than before. And it didn't feel like an it's-okay-'cause-Tessa-will-never-find-out kind of a kiss but a thank-you-for-everything kind of one. I should have believed Lucius, so very long ago in Pompeii. This was a real good-bye.

Filled with warmth from his touch, my pain slowly receded, replaced with a familiar calming sensation, like a glow radiating from my core. I forgot all our differences, long in the past. For now, it was just him and me — together — even though this moment proved fleeting.

Eventually Micah pulled away. His fingers brushed the side of my cheek. He surveyed my face, uncertain of what to say.

I looked up at him with a genuine smile. For once in my life, I stopped living in fear. I was tired of running. Tired of not feeling normal. I wanted the safety and stability of a family. This time I got all that and more.

As much as I'd miss Micah, I took comfort in the slight chance that a part of me might live with him forever…in Cam.

"Good-bye," I murmured, my voice fading fast.

Micah blinked back the tears. He leaned over, softly kissing my lips once more. When he pulled away to whisper a good-bye, his fingers traced my cheekbone. Though his face weighed heavy with sorrow, he managed a smile.

The pain in my abdomen receded, leaving me tired. So very tired. I sank deeper into my bed, my heartbeat fading. A team of nurses burst into my room and I glanced up at Micah one last time, his face blurring in my tears. Only this time, my tears carried joy.

I closed my eyes, ready to find peace at last.

EPILOGUE

"It's time."

A striking, yet unfamiliar voice pierced the darkness. Sweet like honey while determined and frighteningly powerful at the same time. I fluttered my eyelids, expecting to meet the bright lights of the hospital room filled with a bustling medical staff that fervently struggled to keep my weakened body alive.

Instead, I found a tall, dark woman illuminated by the soft glow of the thin crescent moon. Long black locks stretched all the way to the ground, framing her stunningly beautiful round face. My gaze rested for a moment on her warm brown eyes, full lips, and high cheekbones before tracing the length of her hair. Surprisingly, the ends of her long tresses glowed red-hot, apparently fusing with the molten lava that surrounded the soles of her bare feet, leaving her trapped on a tiny island of black rock in the middle of a superheated sea. I leapt to my feet, ignoring the throbs of pain that remained from my battle against The Three. Oddly, I no longer lay in my sterile bed, but sat perched on a rocky outcrop of my own, a warm breeze rustling my hair and hospital gown. My location made little difference. My soul filled with a sudden desire to rescue this woman from her precarious situation.

"Are you okay?" I called, uncertain of how to help. Yet she showed no signs of pain, her face perfectly at ease. Her waves of hair flowed into the ropy lava that encircled her spot. She took a step toward me, the surface of lava instantly cooling to solid black rock when it contacted her sole.

"Who are you?" I dared to ask. My jaw crept toward the ground. I marveled at her astonishing ability to congeal a material as hot as lava.

Without a verbal reply, she took another step closer, the ground once again solidifying beneath her feet. Then she looked upward, extending one arm in a graceful sweep across the heavens, every movement of her body aligning with perfect choreography to a silent song. I followed the arc of her hand, stunned by the remarkable brilliance of the velvety night dotted in pinpricks of light. The sky outside Micah's house never looked so clear, forever obscured in the polluted golden glow of nearby city lights.

The woman clapped once to command me to her attention, I assumed. Only her face showed little sign of irritation. Her clap playing an integral role in the dance, she fanned her arms away from her body. Her long, fluid fingers presented the land that hardened beneath her feet with every step she took closer to my perch.

I don't get it. Why am I here? And where am I, for that matter? I spun my head, looking for some sort of visual clue, but met only an enveloping darkness, dimly lit by the sliver of a moon and punctuated by starlight and the molten lava that surrounded this mysterious woman. Off in the distance, I detected the crash of breaking ocean waves against a rocky shore. The warm breeze carried no recognizable scents beyond the briny smell of the sea, making me believe no plant or animal life currently existed in her newly created land.

Suddenly, I felt very confused. How did I leave the hospital without the help of fire? Surely this pervasive blackness couldn't be all that remained for my soul after I passed from the earthly world. It seemed drastically different from the stories I'd heard of a promising afterlife. What about the fields of wildflowers that extended toward the horizon? The familiar faces of loved ones who departed before me? Or the choirs of angels that broke forth in jubilant song?

Unless I ended up below, doomed to everlasting punishment. I swallowed hard, terrified that my action of destroying Hydros had now condemned me to eternal damnation in the fiery recesses of Hell. An unsettling fear consumed me and I stared into the darkness, seeking answers.

The woman clapped again, snapping me from my dread. Her body swayed rhythmically, repeating her sweep of the heavens before presenting the ground by her feet. I watched blankly, as clueless as the first time. "Why the guessing game?" I asked. "Can't you just tell me straight out? You said something before. I know that was your voice."

The magnificent woman stood tall until she towered above me, her face flushed red. Directing her hand toward a section of rock behind her, she split the ground and sent a pillar of lava shooting high into the night sky. Globs of orange molten rock hurled through the air, momentarily suspended aloft before plummeting back to earth. I stumbled backward upon the refuge of my rocky outcrop, startled by her unpredicted fury.

With a pathetic glance at my cowering form, she turned on her heels, prepared to leave me alone in this chaotic world.

"No. Wait. You can't go yet," I begged. "I don't understand what you're trying to tell me!" Mustering new resolve, I reached out to her, frantically grabbing at her wrist to halt her retreat. As she wheeled her head around, her dark eyes flashed like glowing coals against the black of night. In an instant, her skin beneath my palm grew painfully hot, like molten magma flowed just below its surface. I released my grip with an alarmed yelp, blowing on my hand in a futile effort to soothe the burn.

Was this how I looked when I revealed my powers to Sully in his sister's car? No wonder he seemed so frightened as we fled Pacifica. I dropped my head, my eyes brimming with tears. I chastised myself for slighting someone who had once cared for me, regardless of the cost.

By the time I composed myself enough to look up again, her form had grown faint in the distance, leaving nothing in her wake but a dwindling spire of lava and a trail of cooled rock that parted the molten sea.

With a sigh of frustration, I sat alone in the blackness when her sharp voice rang clear in my ear — *You're still needed.*

"For what?" I hollered, squinting into the dark night, searching for any trace of her presence. Aside from the distant roll of waves against the rocky shore and the dying eruption, I received no further reply. Not that it mattered. Deep inside, I knew she spoke the truth.

The blackness faded and I heard a different voice declare, "She's coming to." I flitted my eyelids, confused by the brilliance and the flurry of activity that surrounded my bedside. A cluster of nurses clad in white medical scrubs hastily monitored my vitals and injected fluids through a tube into the sunken vein of my arm. Surprisingly, I spotted Sully waiting just beyond the bustling nursing staff, the previous hurt and grief now missing from his face. He stuffed his hands deep into his pockets, a crooked smile spreading across his lips. I looked for Micah, but realized at that precise moment the reason for his absence—Cam must be okay. Better yet, I could tell in the way Sully looked at me that he forgave me for everything I put him through. He seemed genuinely glad to see me...alive.

"Welcome back," Sully said over the clamor of nurses. His pale blue eyes warmed while his infectious grin widened.

Despite the uncertainty of the hellish realm within my dreamworld, suddenly I couldn't keep myself from smiling in return.

END OF BOOK ONE OF *THE ELEMENTALS* TRILOGY

Before You Go...

HELP AN AUTHOR

write a review

THANK YOU!

Share your voice and help guide other readers to these wonderful books. Even if it's only a line or two your reviews help readers discover the author's books so they can continue creating stories that you'll love. Login to your favorite retailer and leave a review. Thank you.

ABOUT THE AUTHOR

After graduating from Cornell University with degrees in Biology and Education, Debbie Kump taught middle and high school science in Maui, Seattle, and the Twin Cities and worked as a marine naturalist aboard a whale watch and snorkel cruise. Debbie lives in Minnesota with her husband, two sons, and three Siberian huskies. She especially enjoys writing early each morning; teaching; coaching youth soccer, hockey, lacrosse, and baseball; and dogsledding her kids to school.

For more information, please visit her website: http://sites. google.com/site/debbiekumpbooks/

www.ingramcontent.com/pod-product-compliance
Lightning Source LLC
Chambersburg PA
CBHW030241200626
46816CB00002BA/461